Secrets at
Maple Syrup
Farm

Available from
REBECCA RAISIN

A Gingerbread Café Christmas

The Bookshop on the Corner

Secrets at Maple Syrup Farm

The Little Paris Collection

The Little Bookshop on the Seine
The Little Antique Shop under the Eiffel Tower
The Little Perfume Shop off the Champs-Élysées

Secrets at Maple Syrup Farm

REBECCA RAISIN

CARINA™

This edition is published by arrangement with Harlequin Books S.A. CARINA is a trademark of Harlequin Enterprises Limited, used under licence.

First Published in Great Britain 2016
By Carina, an imprint of HarperCollins*Publishers*
1 London Bridge Street, London, SE1 9GF

© 2015 Rebecca Raisin

ISBN 978-0-263-92246-2

98-0516

Our policy is to use papers that are natural, renewable and recyclable products and made from wood grown in sustainable forests. The logging and manufacturing processes conform to the legal environmental regulations of the country of origin.

Printed and bound by
CPI Group (UK) Ltd, Croydon, CR0 4YY

REBECCA RAISIN

is a true bibliophile. This love of books morphed into the desire to write them. She's been widely published in various short-story anthologies, and in fiction magazines, and is now focusing on writing romance. The only downfall about writing about gorgeous men who have brains as well as brawn is falling in love with them — just as well they're fictional. Rebecca aims to write characters you can see yourself being friends with. People with big hearts who care about relationships, and, most importantly, believe in true, once-in-a-lifetime love.

Follow her on Twitter @jaxandwillsmum or visit her website to keep up to date with every 'once in a lifetime' romance, www.rebeccaraisin.com

To the girls I met in the UK and the ones who couldn't make it, thanks for your unwavering support and friendship, always.

For Graham Basden

CHAPTER ONE

With the beeps, drips, and drones, it was hard to hear Mom, as she waxed lyrical about my painting. Her voice was weaker today, and her breathing labored, but none of that took away from the incandescence in her deep-blue eyes.

Wistfully she said, "Lucy, you have a real gift, do you know that?" She patted the white knitted hospital blanket. "Look at that sunset, it's like I'm right there, stepping into the world you've created."

I sat gently on the edge of the bed, doing my best to avoid the wires that connected my mom to the machine. These days her hair hung lank—the wild riot of her strawberry-blonde curls tamed by so many days indoors, head resting on a pillow. I tucked an escaped tendril back, and made a mental note to help her wash it later.

"You're biased. You have to say that," I said, keeping my voice light. Beside her, I cast a critical eye over the piece. All I could find was fault. The sun was too big, the sky not quite the right hue, and the birds with their wings spread wide seemed comical, like something a kindergartner would do. When it came to my art, I still had a way to go before I felt confident. Mom was the only person I showed my work to these days.

"Hush," she said. "I could stare at this all day. If I close my eyes I feel the heat from the sun, the wind in my hair…"

That's why I'd painted the picture. She'd been suffering quietly for so many years, in and out of hospitals, unable these days to pack her oversized backpack and follow her heart around the globe. She'd been a wanderer, always looking to the next city, a new host of people, a brand-new adventure… but her diagnosis had changed all of that. Even though she never complained, I could read it in her eyes— she still yearned for that freedom.

My mom, a free spirit, looked out of place in the gray-white room. She needed sunshine, laughter, the frisson of excitement as she met other like-minded souls, nomads with big hearts and simple lifestyles. The painting, I hoped, would remind her of what we'd do when she was home again. A short road trip to the beach, where I'd sketch, and she'd gaze at the ocean, watching waves roll in.

"Honey, are you working a double tonight?" she said softly, her gaze still resting on the golden rays of sun.

I had to work as many shifts as I could. Our rent was due, and the bills were mounting up, just like always. There were times I had to call in sick, to help Mom. We lived paycheck to paycheck, and I was on thin ice with my boss as it was. He didn't understand what my private life was like, and I wasn't about to tell him! It was no one's business but my own. I kept our struggles hidden, a tightly guarded secret, because I didn't want pity. That kind of thing made me want to lash out so I avoided it. When I had the odd day off, I tried to make up for it by covering any shift I could. We needed the money anyhow. "No," I lied. "Not a double. I'll be back early tomorrow and I'll take you out to the rose garden."

She gazed at me, searching my face. "No, Lucy. One of the nurses can take me outside. You stay home and rest."

I scoffed. "You know the nurses won't take you all that way. You'll go crazy cooped up in here."

She tilted her head. "You think you can fool me? Not a double, huh?" She stared me down, and I squirmed under her scrutiny. "Don't worry about me. I've got plenty to do here." She waved at the table. "Sudoku, knitting, and…" Laughter burst out of us. The Sudoku and knitting needles were a gift from the lady in the bed over, who'd been discharged earlier that morning. When I'd walked in, Mom's face had been twisted in concentration as she tried to solve the puzzle of numbers. The yarn lay on her lap, knotted, forgotten. She didn't have the patience for that kind of thing, not these days, with her hands, her grip, unreliable at the best of times.

With a wheeze, she said, "There are not enough hours in the day to waste boggling my brain with knit two, pearl one, or whatever it is."

I laughed. "I could use another scarf or two. Who cares if you drop a few stitches?" A million years ago Mom had taken up knitting for a month or so, producing with a flourish a bright-pink sweater for me to wear to school. She'd been so damn proud of it, I hadn't had the heart to point out all the holes from dropped stitches. She knew though, and looped a pink ribbon through them, and said, "Look, it's all fixed with a belt." I wore that sweater until it fell apart, knowing how much love she had poured into every stitch. It was one of her foibles, taking up a new hobby with gusto, and then dropping it when something else caught her eye. It was a sort of restlessness that plagued her, and she'd skip from one thing to another without a backward glance.

She gave me a playful shove. "I'm not the crafty one of the family, that's for sure. That's reserved especially for you. Would you put the painting by the window? I'm going to pretend we're at that beach, drinking fruity cocktails, and squinting at the sunshine."

"We'll be there in no time," I said, knowing we wouldn't. It was January, rain lashed hard at the window. Detroit in this kind of weather had a gloominess about it; it cast a pall over the city, almost like a cloud of despair. It was different than other places in winter. Sadder.

I leaned the painting against the rain-drizzled glass, its colors too bright for the dreary room, but maybe that's what she needed—a bit of vibrancy to counter the gray. The bleak city was not our first choice, but rent was cheap enough for us to afford on one wage. It pained me to think of the places we'd lived when we'd both worked. I'd loved the sun-bleached streets of Florida, and being blown sideways in the woolly weather of Chicago. Those were happier times, when we disappeared for weekend escapades. Home for me had always been where Mom was, as we squished our too-full suitcases closed, and moved from place to place.

Stepping back to the bed, I pulled the blanket up, and settled beside her, checking my watch.

"Before you head to work, I want to talk to you about something." Her tone grew serious, and her face pinched.

"What, Mom?" I inched closer to her.

She cleared her throat, and gave me a hard stare. "I want you to make me a promise." She held up her pinkie finger.

"OK," I said warily. I'd promise my mom anything, she was the light in my life, but I sensed somehow this was going to be different. I could tell by her expression, the way she pursed her mouth, and set her shoulders. The air grew heavy.

"I mean it. You have to promise me you'll do as I ask, and not question me." Her lip wobbled ever so slightly.

I took a shaky breath as my mind whirled with worry. "What, Mom? You're scaring me." It was bad news. I was sure of it.

She shook her head, and smiled. "I know you, Lucy, and I know you're going to struggle with this, but it's important to me, and you have to do it, no matter what your heart tells you."

"I don't like the sound of this." I stood up, folding my arms, almost to protect myself from what she might say. I stared deeply into her eyes, looking for a sign, hoping against hope it wasn't something that would hurt.

"Trust me." Her face split into a grin. "I want you to take *one year* for yourself. To travel…" She held up a hand when I went to interrupt. "Hush, hear me out. Tell your boss tonight—you won't be coming back. Then go home and pack a bag, go to the station, and get on the first bus you see. The *very first*, you hear me? Let fate decide. Find a job, any job, save as much money as you can. I thought you might apply for that scholarship you've dreamed about at the Van Gogh Institute. You can stay with Adele in Montmartre. She's excited by the prospect."

Shock made me gasp. *Take a year for myself?* The Van Gogh Institute? I couldn't think. I couldn't catch my breath.

There was no way. But all I could manage to say was: "You spoke to Adele about this?" Adele was my art teacher back in high school. We'd kept in touch all these years. She was a mentor to me, and the best painter I knew. I'd left school at just fifteen, and only Adele knew the reasons behind my hasty exit. I hadn't been there long enough to make real friendships. She continued to teach me art on Saturday mornings, cooped up in our tiny apartment. I don't know if she saw something in my work or felt just plain sorry for me.

For years she arrived punctually every weekend, until a friend offered her a spot in her gallery in Paris. Saying goodbye to her had been heart-wrenching, but we kept in contact. She badgered me to share my work, and I sidestepped her gentle nudging by asking her about Paris.

"Adele's all for it," Mom said. "And before you go saying no, she agrees you should apply for the scholarship. It's time, Lucy. Your work is good enough. *You* just have to believe in yourself."

The Van Gogh Institute was a prestigious art school, notorious for being selective about their students, and far too expensive for me to ever have considered. Each year the school was inundated with scholarship requests, and I'd never felt confident enough to try for a place. Besides, I couldn't leave Mom. She needed me more, and whatever ambition I had with my art would have to wait.

"The deadline for entries this year is the last day of April," Mom continued to urge me. "So you've got a few months to decide. Maybe you'll paint something even more wonderful on your jaunts. You'll be spoilt for choice about which ones to send for the submission process." The room grew warm, as so many emotions flashed through me. The thought of sharing my work filled me with fear. I'd tried hard to be confident, but people staring at it, and judging me, made my heart plummet. I shook the idea firmly out of my mind before it took hold. Me leaving for a year? There were about a thousand reasons why it just couldn't happen.

I narrowed my eyes. What Mom was suggesting was just plain crazy.

"Mom, seriously, what are you thinking? I can't leave! I don't understand why you'd even suggest it." I tried to mask the hurt in my voice, but it spilled out regardless. We were a team. Each day, we fought the good fight. It was us against the world, scrambling to pay bills, get medical treatment, live for the moment, those days where she felt good, and we pretended life was perfect.

She took a deep breath, trying to fill her lungs with the air she so desperately needed. "Honey, you're twenty-eight years old, and all you've seen these last few years is the inside of a hospital room, or the long faces of the patrons in that god-awful diner. That isn't right. You should be out with friends, or traipsing around the world painting as you go—not working yourself to the bone looking after me. I won't have it. Take one year, that's all I ask." She gave me such a beseeching look, I'm sure I heard the twang as my heart tore in two.

"It's impossible." I summoned a small smile. "Mom, I get what you're saying, but I'm happy, truly I am. Any talk of leaving is silly." She must see? Without my work at the diner there'd be no money coming in. Rent, bills, medical treatment, who'd pay for all of it? And worse still, there'd be no one to care for her. How could she survive without me? She couldn't. And I doubted I could survive without her either.

"Your Aunt Margot is coming to stay. She's going to help me out, so you don't need to worry about a thing."

My eyebrows shot up. "Aunt Margot? When's the last time you two spoke?" Aunt Margot, Mom's older sister, hadn't struggled like my little family of two had. She'd married a rich banker type, and wiped us like we were dusty all those years ago after she tried unsuccessfully to curb Mom's travel bug. Aunt Margot's view was Mom should've put down roots, and settled down, the whole white picket fence, live in the 'burbs lifestyle.

According to her, Mom traipsing around America with a child in tow, working wherever she could, was irresponsible. There were times we moved so often that Mom homeschooled me, and Aunt Margot couldn't come to terms with it. If only Aunt Margot could see how much life on the road had broadened me. I'd learned so much and grown as a person, despite being reserved when it came to my art. We didn't need the nine-to-five job, and the fancy car. We only needed each other.

A few years ago, Mom tried to reconnect with Aunt Margot, their fight festering too long, but she didn't want anything to do with us nomads. Mom still didn't know I overheard them arguing that frosty winter night. Aunt Margot screeched about Mom breaking a promise, and said she couldn't forgive her. Mom countered with it was her promise to break—I still have no idea what they were talking about, and didn't want to ask, or Mom would know I'd been eavesdropping. But it had always made me wonder what it could have been to make two sisters distance themselves from one another for so many years.

For Mom to reconnect with Aunt Margot now meant she was deadly serious. Somehow, I couldn't imagine Aunt Margot living in our tiny one-bedroom apartment. She wouldn't lower herself. I'd sort of cooled toward my once-doting aunt, after hearing her spat with Mom. She'd been judgmental, and narrow-minded, for no good reason.

"We've been talking for a while now. We've really mended the bridges." Mom tried to rearrange her expression, but it was farcical, her smile too bright to be believable.

I squinted at her. "Really? Now who's messing with who?"

She threw her head back and laughed. "Well, we're on speaking terms at least. And she offered to help so you could go away for a bit. So I don't want to hear any more excuses. Got it?"

Stepping back to the bed, I hugged her small frame, resting my head on her shoulder so she wouldn't see the tears pool in my eyes. How could I tell her I didn't want to go? Leaving her would be like leaving my heart behind. Plus, accepting favors from Aunt Margot… We'd never hear the end of it.

Mom pushed me back and cupped my face. "I know you're scared. I know you think it's the worst idea ever. But, honey, I'll be OK. Seeing you miss out on living, it's too much. The young nurses here gossip about their weekends and all the fun things they manage to cram into each day, and then there's you, the same age, wasting your life running round after me. Promise me, *one year*, that's all. Can you just imagine what you'll learn there with all those great teachers? Just the thought... just the thought..." Her eyes grew hazy as she rewrote my life in her dreams.

I knew to grow as an artist I needed proper training, but that was for people who had lives much more level than mine. My day-to-day life was like a rollercoaster, and we just held on tight for the downs, and celebrated the ups when they came. But Mom's expression was fervent, her eyes ablaze with the thought. I didn't know how to deny her. "Fine, Mom. I'll start saving." Maybe she'd forget all this crazy talk after a while.

"I've got some money for you, enough for a bus fare, and a few weeks' accommodation, until you land a job. It's not much, but it will start you off. You can go now, honey. Tomorrow."

"Where'd you get the money, Mom?"

She rested her head deeper into the pillow, closing her eyes as fatigue got the better of her. "Never you mind."

My stomach clenched. She'd really thought of everything. Aunt Margot must have loaned it to her. And I knew that would come at a price for Mom. There'd be so many strings attached to that money, she'd be almost a marionette. There was no one else she could have asked.

When I was in middle school my father had waltzed right out of our lives as soon as things got tough, and since then not a word, not a card, or phone call. Nothing. That coupled with our lack of communication with Aunt Margot, a woman who cared zero about anything other than matching her drapes to her lampshades, made life tough. But we'd survived fine on our own. We didn't take handouts; we had pride. So for Mom to do this, borrow money, albeit a small amount, and have Aunt Margot come and rule her life, I knew it was important to her—more important than anything.

"I just… How can this work, Mom?" I folded my arms, and tried to halt the erratic beat of my heart.

Just then a nurse wandered in, grabbed the chart from the basket at the end of the bed, and penned something on it. "Everything OK?" she asked Mom, putting the chart back and tucking the blanket back in.

"Fine, everything's fine, Katie. My baby is setting off for an adventure and we're excited."

Katie was one of our regular nurses—she knew us well. "That's the best news I've heard in a long time, Crystal!" She turned to me. "And, Lucy, you make sure you write us, and make us jealous, you hear?"

I forced myself to smile, and nodded, not trusting my voice to speak without breaking.

Katie checked Mom's drip, fussing with the half-empty fluid bag. "We'll take good care of your mom, don't you worry about a thing."

"Thanks, Katie. I appreciate that," I finally said. She gave us a backward wave, and said over her shoulder, "Buzz me if you need anything." Mom nodded in thanks.

We waited for the door to click closed.

"What you're asking me to do is pretty huge, Mom." My chest tightened even as I considering leaving. What if Aunt Margot didn't care for Mom right? What if she upped and left after a squabble? How was Mom going to afford all of this? Did Aunt Margot understand what she was committing to? So many questions tumbled around my mind, each making my posture that little bit more rigid.

"It has to be now, Lucy. You have to do it now; there's no more time."

My heart seized. "What? There's no more time!" I said. "What does that mean? Have the doctors said something?" I wouldn't put it past Mom to keep secrets about her health. She'd try anything to spare me. Maybe the pain was worse than she let on? My hands clammed up. Had the doctors given her some bad news?

"No, no! Nothing like that." She tried valiantly to relax her features. "But there'll come a time when I'll be moved into a facility. And I won't have you waste your life sitting in some dreary room with me."

My face fell. We'd both known that was the eventual prognosis. Mom would need round-the-clock care. But the lucky ones lasted decades before that eventuated, and Mom was going to be one of them. I just knew she was. With enough love and support from me, we'd beat it for as long as we could. Her talk, as though it was sooner rather than later, chilled me to the core. There was no way, while I still had air in my lungs, that I would allow my mother to be moved to a home. I'd die before I ever allowed that to happen. When the time came, and she needed extra help, I'd give up sleep if I had to, to keep her safe with me. In *our* home, under *my* care. Going away would halt any plans of saving for the future, even though most weeks, I was lucky to have a buck spare once all the bills were paid, and a paltry amount of food sat on the table.

"You stop that frowning or you'll get old before your time. I've got things covered," she said throwing me a winning smile. "I'll be just fine, and Margot's going to come as soon as I'm out of here. Don't you worry. Go and find the life you want. Paint that beauty you find and I'll be right here when you get back. Please… promise me you'll go?"

I gave her a tiny nod, gripped by the unknown. I always tried to hold myself together for Mom's sake, but the promise had me close to breaking. Dread coursed through me at the thought of leaving Mom, the overwhelming worry something would happen to her while I was gone.

But getting back on the open road, a new start, a new city, just like we used to do, did excite some small part of me. We used to flatten a map and hold it fast against a brick wall. I'd close my eyes and point, the pad of my finger deciding our fate, the place we'd visit next. That kind of buzz, a new beginning, had been addictive, but would it feel the same without my mom?

CHAPTER TWO

The bus careered with a squeal and skidded off the road, startling me from slumber. Instinctively, I clutched hands with the woman beside me. Before shock fully registered the driver hit the brakes hard and we pitched forward in our seats. A shriek caught in my throat as we slid sideways toward a metal fence. I dropped the woman's hand and braced myself as the bus leaned so far to the left dusty-colored ground screamed into view.

"Glory be!" the woman beside me said, her voice edged with worry.

The bus driver swerved and stopped dead just before we hit the shiny gleam of the fence. The commuters let out a collective sigh of relief. My heartbeat thrummed in my ears, as I surveyed the pitch-black night, wondering where we were, and if our journey would stop here, on some lonely forgotten road. I took a gulp of air deep into my lungs, trying to gather myself.

"Sorry, folks," the bus driver said sheepishly, making eye contact with me in the rearview mirror. "Damn deer trotted on past without a care in the world. Everyone OK?"

I turned in my seat to check. People sat, eyes wide, mouths in an O, but no one seemed hurt in any way, just stunned awake by fright.

Commuters nodded. I rubbed my neck, and mumbled, "Yes."

The plump, brown-skinned woman beside me gave my knee a reassuring pat. "You'll be OK," she said, gazing at me with kind eyes. "Jimmy here's the best driver round. Deer be bad on this patch of road come night-time." She spoke with a rich southern accent.

"Thanks," I said, speaking on autopilot as fear collected me. "He did well to keep it from rolling over." A seasick sensation sat heavy in my belly and I shook my head in a kind of astonishment—wouldn't that be the worst kind of irony, promising Mom I'd leave on this impromptu adventure and not making it there because of a bus crash? The thought alone was enough to make me stiffen. I'd never considered something bad happening to me—Mom was always at the forefront of my mind—but what if it did? Then who would look after her? Aunt Margot wouldn't stay forever. I'd have to be careful, and not take risks if I could avoid them.

"Sure as God made little green apples Jimmy'll have a few more gray hairs by the time we reach Ashford."

The woman brought a sense of peace with her no-nonsense attitude.

"He just might," I said, my mouth dry. "I think my first gray might sprout up of its own accord too."

She tutted, giving my hair a cursory glance. "Nothing gonna dim that blonde mane o' yours."

The young woman in front of me rested her head on her friend's shoulder. Across the aisle a spotty-faced teenage boy wiggled in his seat, balled up his sweater, pushed it hard up against the window as a pillow. Everyone was settling back down, but I was too keyed up to do anything other than sit there, mildly panicked at how close we'd come to crashing.

Was it a sign that I was choosing the wrong path? It felt like a warning somehow. Even though I'd promised Mom

I'd explore for twelve long months, a half-day into the journey, I was regretting the decision with every ounce of me. The excitement of not having to pull double shifts at the shabby diner had dimmed the further away from Mom I got. When I'd quit work, the manager had barely raised an eyebrow. The other waitresses gave me small smiles, some heavy with envy, some full of hope that maybe one day they'd get out of there too. Right this instant, I'd swap with them in a heartbeat, and pretend this journey never happened.

It was hard to forget Mom's dazzling smile when I went to say my goodbyes. She'd radiated happiness. It was almost palpable, like she'd been cured, or something miraculous, but it was all because of me. She was overjoyed my travels were beginning in earnest, though in actuality, I'd have to stay in one place half the year to save for the rest of the trip, if I found a decent job. When it was almost time to leave it took all my might not to clutch her and sob, telling her I didn't want to. Instead, I'd held myself tight like a coil, and said I'd do my very best to enjoy myself. In an effort to lighten up a somber situation we played the "Remember When" game.

Remember when we slept in the lighthouse that night? Remember when we swapped our homemade dream catchers for a crate of apples? Remember when...

After that the Van Gogh Institute Scholarship came up about a hundred times, but I shrugged her off. I needed time. At this stage I didn't know if I'd make it without her.

"Where you from?" the woman asked, bringing me back to the present. She crossed her arms over her midsection, as we bounced softly along.

With a smile, I said, "Detroit." I pivoted a fraction to face her. She looked like the type who would chatter on regardless.

"Ah," she said, "the birthplace of Motown? Ain't that something?"

"It is." I missed it already. It was home. Where my heart was.

She studied my face intently. "Why the long face?"

I shrugged. I wasn't about to share my story with a stranger. Besides, there was no way I could say Mom's name. I held on to the promise I made as though it was something tangible, my secret. "Just saying goodbye." I tried hard to make it sound breezy and bit the inside of my cheek, willing myself to stay focused and not well up. Honestly, I was like a child going off to camp the first time. I knew Mom wanted me to "find myself" but I didn't think I was lost. She did.

With a raise of her eyebrows she said, "Goodbyes... surely are difficult. But sometimes, you gotta take the plunge. Life is for living."

"Yeah," I mumbled. My mom had said something eerily similar when I'd visited the hospital to say my goodbyes.

Snatching her purse from under the seat, the woman rifled around in it, before brandishing a brown paper bag full of something spicy-scented. "Here, eat. You as skinny as a rake." She handed me a chocolate-dipped gingerbread man. "Ashford—where we goin'—is about the nicest place on earth. Problem is, once you visit it's kinda hard to leave."

"That so?" I took a bite of the cookie, ravenous now I'd awoken. "I'm not staying for good," I said. "Just stopping by for a while."

She hemmed and hawed. "That's what they all say."

I smiled at the woman in thanks, all the while thinking maybe the bus simply slipped off the road because of a deer, and not because I'd made a bad decision walking away from my mom, when she needed me so badly.

"Did you make this?" I asked, holding the remnants of the gingerbread man, just his little chocolate-dipped legs.

"Why I most certainly did. I work at the Gingerbread Café. I'm CeeCee." She held out her hand.

"It's delicious." I shook her hand. "Lucy. Nice to meet you." It wasn't like me to chitchat so easily. Mom was the extrovert, the babbler; I took a while to warm up. Instead I people-watched, always lost inside my mind with how I'd paint the planes of their faces, or whether I could catch the question in their eyes, their own unique gaze.

I guess it was a safety mechanism of sorts, my lack of involvement with people. We'd moved so often, it was easier not to make friends than risk losing them. But alone, maybe I'd have to change that.

"We be seeing a lot more of each other, mark my words." There was something comforting about the woman, the way she spoke, the warmth in her.

***

After snatching some nap time, I awoke, squinting. The sky had lightened. The bus burbled along, making its way to Ashford. My sketchy plan was to find a job, *anything*. The money Mom had borrowed from Aunt Margot, I stubbornly refused to take. I used it to pay her rent a paltry few more weeks, and restocked her fridge and freezer—a surprise, for when she got home. All I had was the wages from the last few shifts at the diner to see me through, but I knew how to be frugal, and how to work hard.

I had to find a job quickly, and hoped at the end of each week, there'd be enough left over that I could save and send some home. I'd sleep better knowing my mom had a back-up plan and some independence when it came to money.

Resting my head against the cool glass, I watched as meadows dotted with the odd home or two flashed past.

The driver hollered out, "Ashford's ten minutes away, folks."

I nodded to him as we made eye contact in the rearview mirror. His face was lined with fatigue. He was probably dreaming of bed, while commuters snoozed fitfully behind him.

In the distance a property appeared. It was flanked by lots of trees, bare of leaves, and stood out beside the rolling snow-drizzled meadows.

As the bus lumbered closer, I pushed my face up against the glass again. My breath fogged up the window; I hastily wiped it with my hand. As we neared, I could make out an old cottage, decayed with age. Twisted vines snaked around porch poles like skeletons.

I pulled at CeeCee's sleeve. "Would you look at that place!" It was mesmerizing.

She sat up straighter, popping specs on the bridge of her nose. "That there's the Maple Syrup Farm. It's gone and got itself a new owner too. A real handsome guy but he tend to keep to his self."

"Why's that?"

She raised an eyebrow. "Folk say he's just one o' them lonesome types." She clucked her tongue. "Whatever that's 'sposed to mean. He ain't been there long, a month or two maybe. Still trying to make sense o' the place. As you can see, it needs a lot o' work. The cottage itself is over a hundred years old."

The driver slowed for a bend in the road. "It's eerie, like something out of a ghost story." The property was bathed in a filmy light almost like that one patch of land was a different color to the rest of the world. Sepia, faded somehow. All I could imagine was trying to capture it on canvas, painting daubs of russet and taupe, lashings of cloud white. Hoping my brushstrokes would reflect its bygone charm.

"Town folk believe there's a ghost there, but it ain't true. Old Jessup passed on not long back, and he left the farm to his nephew, Clay. Don't stop people talkin' out o' turn saying they seen Jessup wandering around those trees. He used to love them, talk to them as if they was people."

"Sounds like there's a story there." When I painted a landscape like the one in front of me, it was easy to get lost in pondering what had gone on over so many decades—the history of the place, and not just the facts, but the heart and soul of it, the *real* story. Who slept under that cottage roof a century ago? Did they dream of other places, or were they happy there? Did kids frolic by the lake, swim, climb trees, tumble down hills? Was there a woman at the hearth, stoking up fires and baking? Imagining lives long forgotten piqued my curiosity and made my fingers itch to pick up a paintbrush.

She yawned, and stretched her arms above her head. "Sure is. And Clay's only addin' to it by being reclusive."

I tucked a stray curl behind my ear. "Ashford's own little mystery."

She guffawed. "Sometimes there ain't much more to do than speculate about folk."

I laughed. The town must be a hotbed of gossip because of its size. "I guess so. What's he doing with the place? Is he going to stay?"

"Word is, he wants to tap the trees for maple syrup, like his uncle used to do before the arthritis got the better of him. Can't seem to find anyone who wants to work there though. It'll be a tough job, getting it all done without any help."

My ears pricked up. "Really?"

How hard could farmwork be? Physical, sure, but I was fit and capable. It'd be something new, rather than pouring endless cups of coffee for weary truck drivers. Or serving plates of greasy bacon and eggs to night-shift workers. Each day bleeding into the next with the monotony of it all.

How was maple syrup made? All I pictured was their beautiful red, almost carmine, colored leaves, ones I used to take from parks when I was a child and press between the pages of my diary, until they dried, holding their shape, like an exotic fan.

Farmwork would surely be a damn sight better than being cooped up in an old diner.

"Do you think he'd consider me for the job?" I couldn't contain my eagerness. A job on day one would surely be a good sign.

"I don't rightly know," she said thoughtfully. "You see, I don't know him like I know most folk, but there ain't no harm in tryin'."

Knowing Ashford was a small town, I seized on the idea of working at the farm. I doubted there'd be many other opportunities, and if I didn't snag something quick I'd have to move on and try my luck elsewhere. "I really need a job, CeeCee. Keep your fingers crossed for me."

Her big brown eyes softened. "You go on and see if he'll hire you, and then if he does, get yourself some wet-weather clothes. Being outdoors all day, that cold will surely sink into your bones."

"Thanks, Cee." Out of all the buses in the world, all the ways I could have traveled, I ended up next to CeeCee, and I thanked my lucky stars. With her help, I might have found a job, and at least I'd know one friendly face in town.

As we neared Ashford, the houses bunched closer together. In a driveway a group of kids were riding bicycles side by side in a languid, just-woke-up kind of way. Siblings, or next-door neighbors? I thought back to my childhood, moving from place to place, making friends, and then having to leave them. Mom's itchy feet, her gypsy-like wandering, kept us on the road right up until my teenage years. I turned to look back at the kids. It must have been nice, settling in one place as a kid, knowing nothing would change except that their bandy little legs would fill out, and they'd eventually ditch their bikes for cars. A lifetime of friendship built right next door to one another.

Just as the driver promised, ten minutes later the small town came rolling into view. Snow drifted down, making the place look as pretty as a picture on a postcard. Neat store fronts lined the road, and for a small town, they had quite a variety. Jimmy pulled the bus into a park, and turned off the engine.

I gathered my belongings, and inched my way down the rubber-floored aisle to the front. "Sorry for the scare," he said, his face brighter now we'd stopped. "Enjoy your day."

"You too. Thanks, Jimmy." I gave him a wave as I stepped off the warm bus and onto the curb.

Behind me, CeeCee marched from the bus and gave me a great big launch hug that almost bowled me over. "Begonia Bed and Breakfast is thatta way," she said pointing to the far end of town. "The only accommodation Ashford has."

"It's like you can read my mind!" Though I suppose it was obvious, a girl heading into a small town would need a place to stay.

She tapped her nose. "I always know. You go on and get settled then come back here for some breakfast. On the house," she added as I went to protest. "You need a decent meal 'fore you head off to the farm, if you sure that's the kinda job you want."

***

Meeting the exuberant CeeCee put a smile on my face and took some of the ache away. I wasn't used to being alone. Mom was always on my mind in Detroit, whether I was working or not. But the invisible cord that bound us was still there. Being so far away, the cord seemed infinite, and tugged, making me think she needed me.

Soft winter sun warmed my back as I walked, my steps heavy. I was so far from home I was almost under a different sky. I took in the charming streetscape, mentally framing up every view as a potential sketch, one that I could post home, show Mom where I was.

Cheery store owners nodded hello to me. I gave them a shy smile and averted my eyes. I headed toward the bed and breakfast, hoping the owner would have a room, something affordable too. When I passed a hardware store, I turned left at a sign advertising the lodgings, and meandered along until I found the B and B. Flowers spilled from pots in a riot of red, their sweet perfume wafting up.

The door opened, catching me, hand balled ready to knock.

A squirrely voice greeted me: "You must be Lucy! Come in, come in. I'm Rose." Rose was rail thin, maybe in her seventies. She had a full shock of gray hair pulled back from her face in a bun. Her hands were liver-spotted and quivered slightly.

"Yes, I am, err, how…?"

"CeeCee called," she said briskly, opening the door wide. "Said she met you on the bus. And that you were a dear little thing and I'm to make you comfortable, quick sticks. She's never wrong about people, you know." She gazed at me over the brim of her spectacles. "I see you are as pretty as a picture, all that lovely long blonde hair of yours, and those blue eyes… You know my mother, God

rest her soul, used to call that shade of blue China blue…
Did you know that?"

"Umm, no I didn't… thank you." I followed Rose
inside, slightly overwhelmed by her scrutiny of me.

"Come on in. You'll get used to me. I tend to say the first
thing I think. Most of us do, being so used to one another, I
suppose. Jimmy had another deer incident, did he?"

The small-town grapevine sure would take some
getting used to. In Detroit, you could be invisible if you
wanted. There was no way of knowing who was new,
and who wasn't. It was a big, busy town, and easy to be
just a faceless member of the crowd. It might be nice to
have friends, people who didn't know me, or my past. "He
managed to avoid it, but it was pretty close," I said, sure
that CeeCee would have told Rose the story already with a
lot more oomph.

When I caught sight of the living room my head spun.
Everything was floral. The curtains dusty pink with
carnations, the carpet a ruby-red hibiscus, the wallpaper
dotted with lemon-yellow daisies. I blinked the spotty
vision away.

"Sit, dear. I brewed a pot of tea. Chamomile, OK?"

"Great," I said. For someone so frail Rose moved with
quick steps, fussing with her skirt as she went. I took a
high-back chair and stared out the window while I waited,
absently chewing a nail, wondering how I'd escape with any
shred of dignity if the room was beyond my budget. It was
my first day off in aeons, and it was nice to sit down, and
relax. I was so used to rushing around that I was perpetually
dizzy with it all. Time to sit and sip tea was a novelty.

Rose strode back into the room, carrying a tray with tea
things. She poured the steaming brew into two delicate
china cups, and balanced one on a saucer, before shakily
passing it to me.

"So," she said, her eyes brighter than her years suggested. "How long are you staying?"

I blew out a breath. "I'm not too sure, yet. Depends on finding a job. I hope that's OK?" Maybe she'd want the money upfront and a definite time frame?

"You just let me know whenever you're ready," she said, fluttering her hand. "January's one of the quietest months for folks in Ashford, so I'm happy to have a bit of company no matter how long you stay for. I'll make up the back bedroom for you. It has its own bathroom—you'll be comfortable there."

"Thank you... I..." My voice petered out as I squirmed in my chair. Money angst, as usual. Almost every decision, every choice I made, was linked to money or the lack thereof. It was like chasing my tail, and just once I would have liked to be free of the never-ending loop of it.

Rose gave me a once-over. "The room is a hundred dollars a week, is that OK?" Before I could respond with anything other than raised eyebrows she said, "That will include meals, if you're here at night, and also your breakfast things."

"Are you sure? That doesn't sound like enough!" While I was all for saving, I didn't want to take advantage of anyone.

"It's plenty. Let me show you your room." She stood and smoothed her hair back. Rose was poised and graceful as if she'd been taught to sit with the right posture and sip her tea daintily with her pinkie finger pointing out. I picked up my travel bag and my art portfolio.

"It's right this way." Her skirt swished around her ankles as she strode.

We went through the kitchen, its wooden benches orderly, and continued down a hallway with walls lined with family pictures.

"Is this you, Rose?" I pointed to a picture of a glamorous woman, soaking up sunshine in a striped bathing suit, and big Jackie-O style sunglasses.

"Yes, quite the starlet wasn't I?" she joked. "That was me back in my beach bunny days—I spent far too long tanning myself to leather beneath the Californian sun, until I moved here, and swapped the sunbaking for hiking."

"You look great." Despite her age, I could still see that twenty-something woman in Rose, the quick smile, the grace.

"These are my grandbabies." Rose pointed to a picture of three boys with cheeky smiles and dimples.

"Are they in Ashford?"

She shook her head sadly. "They're all the way in Australia. My son moved there for work, so I rarely see them these days. The distance is too much for me to travel. My old bones suffer from the flight. Just because we said our goodbyes, doesn't mean they're not in my heart. Never mind." She grabbed my hand. "I've got you to look after now."

I returned her hand squeeze. She had no idea how much her words meant to me. I was missing my mom fiercely, but maybe Rose would help curb that loss a fraction. Even though I was hesitant making friends, Rose had a grandmotherly way about her. "Thanks, Rose."

Girls my age probably had a much better hold on themselves at twenty-eight than I did. But I was all sorts of lost without the anchor of my old life. Regret sat heavy in my belly, as I rued making Mom the promise in the first place. It was a foolish idea to jet around the world like a carefree itinerant. The year was going to drag on, until I could finally go home where I belonged.

Rose pulled me down the hallway until we came to a door. With a flourish she pushed it open. The room smelt musty, like it had been closed up for a long time, but it was neat. There was a double bed, and a small dresser. We shared a room in Detroit—usually I flopped on the sofa when I crept in. A whole bed to myself would be a luxury.

"Here's the bathroom." She opened a door off to the side, and my breath caught. "Everyone always does that." She laughed. While the bedroom was small the bathroom was huge, spacious enough for a double vanity and an old-fashioned claw-foot tub. "I made some renovations a few years back, and they knocked a wall through from the other side so the bathroom would be bigger."

"Wow, you did a great job. No flowers?"

She chortled. "I thought maybe one room should be flower free." She scratched her chin. "But I regret that choice every day."

The bathroom was all white, with touches of cream in the tiling. Thick, fluffy towels were stacked next to the bath. It was like an oasis for my tired, overwrought mind. I knew I'd spend a lot of time soaking in the tub. We didn't have one at home, and just the thought made me want to buy bubble bath, and a book to while the hours away indulgently.

"I'll leave you to get settled," she said. "There's soap and a few toiletries under the sink, and you just yell out if you need a hand." With that she stepped from the room leaving only the scent of her perfume.

Casting another cursory glance around the room, I placed my art portfolio on top of the dresser drawers, and swung my backpack to the end of the bed. Time to unpack, and make the room my temporary home.

From the front pocket of my bag, I took out a picture frame. In the photo Mom had her arms looped around my shoulders. The wind whipped around us making her strawberry-blonde curls tangle into my flaxen hair. Behind us the sun shone, making it look as though we had haloes, but it was our faces, the sheer happiness that radiated that I loved. It was taken pre-diagnosis, where the world had been ours for the taking, and the only routine we had was waking up each morning. I gave the photo a quick kiss, and put it on the windowsill.

When we found out about Mom's condition, and how easily it could deteriorate, our world swung dangerously off its axis for a while, until we regrouped, and collected ourselves. We'd hit a fork in the road, and veered the wrong way for a time, but eventually we had to accept it. There was no choice. We couldn't change the diagnosis; we could only do our best to make Mom's future as bright as possible.

Responsibility was thrust on us. Medical appointments and money woes ruled our days, but that didn't stop us dreaming. It hurt to walk in and see Mom staring at the TV, a filmy light casting shadows over her face, her ready smile gone.

I tried a multitude of ways to cheer her up in those first dark months. One night I found a bunch of old magazines, and bought a sunny yellow scrapbook. I told her to find pictures that inspired her, that made her happy.

We cut and pasted tiny squares of shiny paper every night. It was our dream travel book—we visualized what *could* be. It didn't take long for us to fill the pages with cuttings of spicy tapas in Spain, or diving with dolphins in Australia. The ruins of Rome. Tulips in Amsterdam. Famous paintings I wanted to see. Museums we wanted to wander inside. That was the thing about dreams—they could be as big and bold as you liked. Mom took a shine to scrapbooking, and unlike her other hobbies, she stuck with it.

With a wobbly smile, I took our dream travel book from my backpack, and flopped onto the plush bed. I creaked it open, its pages fat with cheap glue. The very first picture: a cutout of the Eiffel Tower, standing tall and proud, its night lights twinkling *bonjour*.

Did she know, all that time ago, that I should end up there? Maybe she'd always hoped I'd try out for the Van Gogh Institute. I'd often talked in an awed hush about visiting the Musée d'Orsay to ogle Van Gogh's portraits. Or taking a day trip northwest of Paris to see the garden where Claude Monet painted the *Water Lilies*. Pipe dreams, or so I'd thought.

Pleasure bloomed in my heart at the thought I might get to do these things, despite not having my mom with me. Once-in-a-lifetime adventures were within reach, if only I could do it on my own. Carefully, I tucked the scrapbook into the bedside drawer. There'd be time enough to flip its full pages. I yawned, so tempted to sleep. Without the usual rush of my life, I was as drowsy as a cat in summertime.

But I had to find a job. I'd dillydallied enough this morning. I could easily end up stranded and penniless here. Mom didn't have the same fears as me, always believing the universe would provide, that a solution would appear. As much as I loved the universe, real fear of being broke sat heavy on my shoulders.

With a groan, I pulled myself up and went to wash my face. The cool water refreshed me. The thought of breakfast at the Gingerbread Café was enough to inspire me to get going.

CHAPTER THREE

I recognized a booming laugh before I'd even got to front door of the Gingerbread Café. It was quickly followed by a shriek. As I approached the window, CeeCee's round frame was bent double, hooting as amusement got the better of her.

Pushing the door open, a jangle of bells announced my arrival. The café was busy. Customers lolled on chairs by the window, or cupped their chins, bent over a table with friends. By the fire an elderly gentleman had fallen asleep, a newspaper crumpled in his lap, his snores punctuating the chatter in the café.

The scene was completely opposite to the old diner I'd worked in, where men hung their heads over weak cups of coffee, their eyes vacant, as though their lives had passed them by. Night-shift workers, truck drivers, and women dressed in flashy sequins, holes in their stockings, their heels scuffed; they all had that same pall, a kind of defensiveness in their faces, a clenched jaw, stiff posture.

But here, it was almost like walking into a storybook. There was a relaxed and cozy air about the place, but somehow it made me feel on edge, like I didn't belong. They'd see straight through me, and know I wasn't like them. I was a drifter in their midst. They had easy smiles, and ready laughs, and I was so used to being guarded, and careful, so that nothing would be taken from me. No one wanted a sob story where I'd come from. And I was loath to share mine anyway.

I hung my coat by a rack near the door as my senses were assaulted with the sweetest smells. Chocolate, coffee, and the spiciness of gingerbread baking. It was like I'd been lifted up and transported to a sugary-scented paradise. Music played chirpily overhead, while customers sipped coffee and gossiped.

I walked to a display cabinet full of chocolate truffles in every shape and size, some dusted with some type of red glitter, some with delicate gold leaf. My mouth watered while I tried to make up my mind about which I'd choose. Thoughts of saving money dogged me—even though I needed these chocolates like I needed air to breathe. As subtly as I could, I whipped out my cell phone and snapped some pictures to send to Mom. She'd get such a kick out of the artistry on each truffle. If I did land the job at the farm, I'd post Mom a box of the gourmet chocolates home, as a celebratory gift.

"Well lookie here, it's Lucy." CeeCee pulled me into a bear hug so tight she squashed the air from my lungs.

After she released me from the squishiness of her ample frame, I said, concerned, "You're working after no sleep?" We'd napped intermittently just before dawn, but not enough that I could make my brain fire on all cylinders if I needed to. CeeCee must've had the energy of a child, dashing about in the café like she was. I slipped off my gloves, and rubbed my hands together.

"I've had so much coffee I won't sleep for days. Now what can I get you?" She waved to people walking past, and then focused on me.

I gestured to the chocolates, nervous as suddenly all eyes in the café landed on me. "How can you choose?"

She guffawed. "Ain't no way you can, my sweet cherry blossom. That's part of our cunning plan to keep folks vistin' every day! How about you take a seat by the window, and I'll bring you a gingerbread coffee and a selection o' my favorites?" She spun me around and nudged me in the right direction.

"Umm," I protested feebly as CeeCee trundled off, whistling a song, drawing amused smirks from customers. She'd said breakfast on the house, but even that was too much. I couldn't take handouts. "Cee…" She was already talking to another customer, so I took refuge at a table, and looked studiously out the window, avoiding the curious glances that came my way.

A minute later, CeeCee said, "Mind, it's hot." She placed a coffee, a plate of bacon and eggs, and a golden box full of truffles on the table. My stomach rumbled in appreciation.

"This is too much, Cee. You have to tell me what I owe you." I blushed, wondering how much such a deluxe breakfast would cost, frantically calculating in my mind.

She waved me away. "It's your 'Welcome to Ashford' meal, so put it out o' your mind, cherry blossom. It's just our way round here."

I knew CeeCee could see straight through me, and she was only being nice so I could save face. I finally managed, "Thank you, Cee. I really appreciate it."

"Anytime, sugar plum. Lil," she said. "This here's Lucy, the one I was telling you 'bout. First time being a passenger with one o' Jimmy's near misses!" She shook her head and ruched her skirt up to sit before gesturing to a curvy, blonde-haired girl, who gave me a big wave. Lil was beautiful in that all-American, girl-next-door way. I returned her wave, and smiled.

"Sometimes I think ol' Jimmy thinks he's a race-car driver or some such!" A trio of elderly women at the next table nodded, as if they knew all about Jimmy.

Rebecca Raisin

I grinned at CeeCee, the accident not as scary in the light of day. "He handled it well, but I'm not too keen to repeat the journey, that's for sure."

Lil wandered over and sat with us. "CeeCee was mighty glad you were there when Jimmy lost control. She might pretend to be blasé, but really she was scared witless. Isn't that right, Cee?"

"Hush now," CeeCee said. "Don't you give away my secrets." They gave each other a look, like best friends do, one where words aren't needed to convey a message.

"What made you decide on sleepy old Ashford?" Lil asked, propping her face in her palms.

It was almost like a spotlight shone down on me. The girls asked so many questions and I could see people peering at me over the tops of their mugs, inclining their bodies closer to listen. It was nerve-racking but I pulled on a smile and said, "It was as simple as catching the only bus out of town, which happened to be stopping here." I shrugged.

What I didn't say was the crying jag I'd had upon leaving had zonked me so much that I missed most of the journey, lost inside my head, in a lonely haze.

"Wow, I like your style," Lil said. "That takes some courage, just getting on any old bus."

"I figured it was fate. I'm… escaping for a year and seeing where the wind takes me." There. I was sure I sounded convincing enough. Maybe they'd think I was just a young girl with no attachments. No sad past, just an amiable soul, crisscrossing the globe.

"Ain't that something?" CeeCee said. "Everyone's gotta have an adventure at least once in their lives. When you're as old as me, you'll know. Time flies, quicker than you ever imagine." She stared into the distance, as if she was thinking of someone else. I followed her gaze to an empty store across the road with an old sign advertising handcrafted furniture.

She shook her head as if dislodging a thought. "Anyways, you're going to love it here. I can always tell." Hefting herself from the table, she gave my shoulder a pat. "You go on an' eat now, and if you run out o' truffles you go on and let me know."

Lil groaned. "I was hoping for a five-minute sit-down, Cee." She made a show of pulling herself up from the chair. "She'd work me to the bone quick as look at me." She winked at me.

CeeCee narrowed her eyes. "Ain't that the truth? The cakes don't bake themselves, sugar plum." I hid a grin at the way they teased each other. I could imagine them confiding in each other, and always having someone on their side. It made me wish for a friendship like theirs. Could I ever be that open with someone other than Mom? I'd never had the chance to create a lasting bond with any of the girls I'd met on our travels, because we'd never stayed long enough. It would be nice to have someone to confide in, someone who'd keep your secrets.

Lil gave me a dazzling smile, and said, "CeeCee's excited because she's making apple tarte tatin—from a recipe given to her by a certain Frenchman who shall remain nameless."

CeeCee put her hands on her hips. "You gonna keep razzin' me about Guillaume, I'm gonna march over the road and tell Damon that *you* the one who ate the pie he ordered especially for a customer o' his." I wondered how all these people fit together: friends, lovers, customers?

Lil's eyes went wide. "OK, OK. Sheesh, how was I supposed to know it was for *his* customer? You can't just bake something that smells like heaven itself and leave it in front of me like some kind of invitation. Anyone would have done the same." She glanced at me, hoping for an ally. I grinned, and stared into my mug.

"But the whole pie?" CeeCee shook her head and faced me. "The amount that girl eats—must have hollow legs. Come now, Lil, let's bake and you forget all about my Frenchman." She blushed. "I'm too old for this kinda carry on," she said, her voice lilting.

Lil laughed and bent to whisper, "It's her new boyfriend but we're all supposed to pretend he isn't!"

The girls were like a breath of fresh air, their routine comical, as they badgered each other with good nature.

"Don't think I didn't hear that," CeeCee said mock sternly. "Eat, Lucy, 'fore you waste away on us."

With my head spinning from it all, I bit into the first chocolate truffle, and closed my eyes as I savored the flavor. The taste sensation exploded in my mouth— dark chocolate, and cherry with a hit of liqueur, encased in a tiny ball of goodness. All of life's problems could be forgotten when you ate chocolate as delectable as this. While I was still jittery about being here, the girls somewhat assuaged that with their antics.

A young woman dashed into the café, flicking her glossy brown curls over her shoulder. "I need coffee!" she yelled dramatically. "Preferably by an IV, if you can."

CeeCee cackled like a witch. "And let me guess, chocolates served up by the pound?"

The girl pretended to be surprised, clapping a hand over her mouth. "How did you *know*? You're like… the chocolate whisperer!"

"Probably because you say that every day, my sweet cherry blossom. Lucy, this here's Becca—works at the hair salon up the road." CeeCee turned back to Becca. "Why don't you go sit over there with Lucy. She's new here, looking for work." CeeCee gave her a pointed stare. "And we drove right on past the Maple Syrup Farm this mornin', if you get my drift."

Becca gasped. "You did? Let me go speak to this exotic creature."

I would have blushed like crazy if people back home spoke of me in such a way, but here it was done with such humor and warmth. So far the townspeople were lively and funny, and so open it was like watching a play being performed, and I was the audience.

With a sweep of her hand, Becca sat regally at the table. "Lucy, my lovely. Work, you say?" She arched an eyebrow in a theatrical way.

"Why?" I said, oddly out of step with the latest customer to spill through the doors. Was no one here quiet and unassuming? Each person I met one-upped the last with their antics. I'm sure it would make living in Ashford fun but it was so foreign to me. I played along, hoping I'd get the hang of their easy camaraderie. "Are you expecting me to dance on tables or something?" I said, safe in the knowledge that was probably not the case.

She whacked the table, her eyes twinkling with mirth. "No, no!" she said. "But are you really looking?" Her voice dropped to a more neutral tone.

"I really am."

"It's not a pretty job…" Her forehead furrowed, and she surveyed her nails, as if buying time. "Actually, it's rather, well… messy."

I surreptitiously glanced at my own nails. They were chipped, the light pink polish bitten to the quick as I'd made my way here. "That's OK. I'm in no position to be fussy right now."

"Great!" Her voice carried around the café. "My cousin needs a hand."

CeeCee piped up. "Becca is Clay's cousin. That ramshackle property we passed on the bus… the Maple Syrup Farm."

The very same job I was intent on applying for. The chance meeting with Becca was great timing—maybe she could give me some pointers on what to tell the so-dubbed reclusive Clay. "So what should I do, Becca?"

"Just mosey over there and say you're ready to work. He needs someone urgently so don't take no for an answer." She wrinkled her nose. "But it's not going to be easy."

I waved her away. Easy? How hard could farmwork be? Outside, surrounded by the beauty of nature, I'm sure it would be as easy as ABC. And something my hippy mom would enjoy hearing about.

More important was landing the job. My whole future hinged on it. "Any advice on how I can convince him that I'm the girl for the job?" My voice pitched, giving away the worry I felt. No doubt he'd prefer someone who knew exactly what farmwork required, but I was convinced I could do it. Maybe it was desperation speaking, but given a chance, I'd show him I was more than willing to work hard.

Becca cocked her head, grimacing slightly. "Stand your ground. Clay's… sort of used to being alone. But he really does need help, otherwise he won't get the trees tapped for syrup." The words spilled out quickly, like she was trying convince *me*.

Stand my ground? I imagined Clay—a man used to being alone—as some crinkle-faced, weathered farmer, set in his ways. "OK, any other tips?"

She waited a beat. "Don't take anything he says to heart."

I frowned. "I'll keep that in mind. So no need to spout on about my love of the outdoors, or my urge to… farm?"

Laughter spilled from Becca's bright-pink lips. "No, definitely no need for that. Just be confident, and don't give in when he says no on sight. He seems to think he can do it all alone sometimes, and then resents the fact he can't."

"OK. I thought maybe I should be the full bottle on farming equipment or something, so he knows I'm capable."

"Nope." She flashed a smile. "He can teach you the basics. You'll be fine."

"Right," I said, feeling strangely confident. "Thanks, Becca. It'll be a beautiful place to spend time. I'll head over and see what he says." I caught the wide-eyed look Lil and Becca exchanged and wondered just what kind of man Clay was.

Not an easy one, by the look of it.

CHAPTER FOUR

After leaving the café, I strolled along the main street of Ashford, peering into store windows, soaking up the atmosphere, when a travel agency caught my eye. I gazed at posters of exotic locations. One had Indian women dressed in vibrant-colored saris. Another had an orangutan with an almost human-like face, the text below suggesting a vacation to Sumatra. Gondoliers in Venice. The Eiffel Tower in Paris.

The wanderlust in my DNA pulsed a little quicker. Before Mom had me, she'd hotfooted it around the globe— these posters reminded me of her travels. I had albums of her twenty-something face, carefree and lit with wonder as she stood, wrapped in sky-blue cheesecloth, next to an elephant that dwarfed her. She'd been on safari in Africa, before heading to the UK to work in a pub, where there were photos of her holding a pint glass filled with black stout, saving for her next jaunt.

Nothing had held her back; she'd siphoned every ounce of joy from her life, before she was struck down. She'd squashed so much into her days, each hour counted. There was something timeless about it.

"Can I help you?" A man popped his head around the archway of the door, startling my reverie. My gaze darted to his sweater that read *Take the plunge*, *visit New Zealand*.

What would New Zealand be like? Another place to add to the one-day list.

"Have you got any brochures for Paris?" I stuttered, feeling put on the spot.

The slightly stooped man motioned me inside. I glanced at my watch—a few minutes wouldn't hurt. After all, for once, I didn't actually have to be anywhere. The sudden freedom gave me a sense of euphoria. The farm could wait another ten minutes. It wasn't like Clay was expecting me... unless the Ashford grapevine had reached him already.

"I've got brochures for Paris, Pakistan, Peru. Whatever you want." He was jolly, and ruddy-faced.

He rifled through a stack of shiny brochures before finding one with a picture of a couple smooching under the Eiffel Tower.

"Anything else?" he asked handing me the brochure. "I'm Henry, by the way."

"No, that's perfect. Lucy," I said, and held out my hand to shake. I wanted to grab a fistful of brochures, to cut them and paste them into our scrapbook, but visiting these places might become a reality now, and without Mom, it didn't seem right to fill the book anymore. It had been *our* project. Our wish list.

"Have you been to Paris?" I stalled, wanting to stare at the exotic locations, dream of another life, a different me. The wonderful things I could capture on canvas. Chance snapshots, like an over-ripe coconut felled from a tree, the bandy brown legs of its lopper.

"Paris? Sure have. Let's see." He ran a hand over his head. "Must've been thirty-odd years ago now. All I had was a few French francs in my pocket, and a backpack hitched over my shoulder. The people there, they were something else, inspired, eccentric." There was glimmer in his eye as he recalled his vacation. "Always wanted to go back there."

"Why didn't you?" The eternal question. Why did people leave the places they loved?

He scratched the stubble on his chin. "There was always somewhere new to discover. Once you're hit with the travel bug, well, you just want to go ahead and see it all." His voice softened as he gazed over the top of my head, almost as if he were back in Paris, the young man he must have been thirty years ago. "I wanted to walk those back streets, and find joy in patches of the world that so many before me had been to, leaving only their footprints, and maybe a piece of their heart, their lives indelibly changed."

My mom would love Henry. She had that same faraway look in her eyes when she recalled her travels before she was housebound to a degree. It was hard not to feel glum. Mom should be here too, plotting her next trip, and following the summer. "Seems like there's two types of people: those who wander the earth, and those who don't," I said.

He gave me a wide smile. "If everyone had the means, I'm sure it'd be more prevalent. That's all they're missing, that first big trip… the weight of the world someone else's problem. What about you—where are you staying?"

He wanted to know which type I was. "At Rose's B and B." I shrugged. "Everything depends on a job."

"I hope you find what you're looking for," he said with a genuine smile.

"Me too. And I hope you get to visit more places soon, Henry."

His smile waned. "Sometimes, life gets in the way of our dreams. But I have the memories." He tapped his heart.

I don't know what his story was, but his wanderings had been cut short, just like Mom's. He couldn't know that I understood—it was almost like caging a bird. Instead,

I gave him a pat on the shoulder. "Memories last forever," I said, hoping it was true.

He nodded. "So, what about you, Lucy? Is Paris on the cards? Or are you still in the planning stage?"

I grappled with the same inner turmoil. Would I apply to the institute? Was I even good enough to try? But Adele was in Paris, so either way, if I continued to travel, Paris would be my first port of call. It wouldn't hurt, to keep an eye on flight prices, while I saved up the money.

"I don't know for sure yet," I said, "but if any cheap flights become available will you let me know?" I knew, deep down, if I went to Paris, I would regret not applying for the institute if I had to walk past it every day. Even though I still felt like a novice.

"Sure! And if I can be of any assistance just let me know. I've got a bunch of maps, and well-thumbed travel guides, feel free to stop in and peruse whenever you like."

"Thank you," I said with a smile. I folded the Paris brochure and tucked it into my backpack. "I'd love to. I'll get myself sorted with a job and I'll be back."

We said our goodbyes, and I walked outside. Across the road a second-hand bookstore had a display window of travel books. It was like the universe was showing me the way. Instead of stepping inside, I kept on, heading to the Maple Syrup Farm. There was no point dreaming of foreign locales until I'd secured a job. And in a town as small as Ashford, there was likely to be minimal work available. I'd have to prove to Clay I was more than capable of farming, whatever the heck that entailed.

And heeding Becca's advice, I wouldn't take no for an answer.

Glancing down at my outfit, I grimaced. Really, I should have worn something more practical. It was icy cold, and I was layered in a pink knit sweater, with bling-y beading across the bust, topped with a faux fur coat. I was a little on the bohemian side for Ashford, with my feather earrings, and bangles, which clinked together as I strode. If Clay said yes, I'd have to spend some money on more suitable work clothes.

Alone with my thoughts for the long walk to the farm, I couldn't stop thinking of all the things Aunt Margot needed to know. Mom needed help with even the simplest tasks like showering, and I wanted to make sure Aunt Margot did it in such a way that Mom's dignity was protected. I decided to call her myself, even though Mom had expressly asked me not to. Reaching into my bag I pulled out my phone and dialed the number. It had been years since we talked, and I wondered how she'd act.

"Lucy, how lovely to hear from you after all this time." Her words were soft, measured.

"Yeah… it's been a while." I was a touch frosty, remembering the way she erased us from her life. I knew she would be footing the bill now, for Mom's medical needs, but that didn't make me any less wary.

"Your mother says you're off gallivanting, just like she used to," she said with an air of distaste.

I rolled my eyes, safe she couldn't see me. "Yeah, something like that. Only for a year."

"You should think of college. It's not too late you know."

"Yeah." *No*, college wasn't for people like me. "So, I wanted to touch base about Mom, and a few things—"

A guttural laugh came down the line. "There's no need," she said. "Everything is organized."

I frowned. "That may be, but there's a plastic chair in the bathroom you just need to—"

She cut me off again. "As I said, your mother will be fine, Lucy. Don't worry about chairs or bathrooms for goodness' sake. Do think about what I said about college. We can probably help you too. It's becoming a pattern."

I stiffened. We didn't want her help, and if I was home we wouldn't need it now. She was infuriating. "I can get by just fine, Aunt Margot. But with Mom, I want to make sure she's looked after right." It was all I could do to keep my tone even.

"Darling, don't be mad. I can hear it in your voice. You're so much like her, you know. Stubborn, and silly, at times. She threw her life away; you don't need to as well."

I'd always felt Aunt Margot was jealous that Mom was so carefree, and that the American dream—a house, two point five kids, and a nine-to-five job—didn't appeal to Mom at all. Did it really matter how you chose to live your life as long as you were a good person?

I breathed in deeply, letting her toxic words float away before responding. "She hasn't thrown her life away, in fact she's lived more than most people double her age have!"

She clucked her tongue. "Living out of a suitcase is *not* living. And you're on the same path. I worry about you, Lucy. With a role model like that what can you expect?"

I held in a scream. "Aunt Margot, don't talk about Mom that way," I managed through clenched teeth. "Did you get the list I left there?" I'd left detailed instructions, but still, I wanted to clarify things.

"Yes, yes. You know your mother, Lucy. It would be easier if she was more upfront sometimes."

"What does that mean?" My mother was as transparent as water.

She sighed. "I *can* keep a promise," she said. "Unlike her. So I'll leave it at that."

"What? Is she OK?" What was she talking about?

"She's fine, Lucy. Jesus, I'm not a monster. If anything happened I'd let you know. I'm just saying, as *usual*, your mother does things her own way, and as *usual* I don't agree with her. But let's not rehash the past—it's already colliding with the future."

She was referring to the promise Mom apparently broke all those years ago. "Put Mom on," I said.

"Sorry, darling, she's asleep. You'll have to try again later."

"Fine, I will," I said, and hung up as anger coursed through me. This was why we didn't need help. Someone like Aunt Margot holding it over us. She had the power, and poor Mom was probably stuck there every day having to listen to her bring up her issues every five minutes.

I stomped toward the farm, even more determined to get the job, and send money home to Mom.

***

I'd eventually calmed down, as my feet found a rhythm while I walked. Thirty minutes later, the farm appeared. With my head inclined, I stopped, shoved my hands deep in my pockets and surveyed the place.

The Maple Syrup Farm was, at best, a ramshackle mess. The front gate hung off its latch, creaking in the wind, pitching backward and forward like an invitation to enter. In the distance you could make out the cottage. Gnarly old vines twisted around porch posts as though they were slowly strangling them. Cottage windows were smashed, leaving only dirty shards of glass clinging to their perches. Mountains of junk had been abandoned across the land for so long that grass had grown over them. Odd sticks of wood protruded like arms in supplication. The decaying façade of the place was somehow compelling rather than confronting.

Behind the gate, the property spanned for miles. Long snow-dotted grass swayed like green ribbons and grew into everything, wild and free. Even down the graveled driveway the grass had crept over like it was intent on taking over, burying the vestiges of ground.

I pushed the creaky gate open and walked purposefully, convincingly, like I'd been on a million farms before and knew what to do. As I neared the cottage music blared from inside. I stepped onto the porch. It was rotted in places, worm-wooded. I covered my ears against the noise as I dodged holes and hoped to God I made it inside without tumbling into trouble in my boots.

Whoever was inside the small cottage was belting out lyrics to "Pony" by Ginuwine like he was the only person in the world. Clay? I couldn't really see an old farmer type listening to such provocative music, but it took all kinds to make a world, as my mom was keen on saying.

With a quick rap on the door, I set my shoulders, pulled my coat tighter and waited. No answer. There was no way he'd hear me with the volume up so high. With a shrug, I opened the front door, and stuck my head inside.

My mouth hung open at the sight before me. Clay was not old. Not weathered. Not wearing overalls.

He stood all six foot something of him, on the top rung of a stepladder, wearing only tight denim jeans, holding a drill. His broad shoulders moved to the beat of the music, his biceps flexing in time. As he turned and leaned I caught sight of his sculpted abs, the grooves and valleys of them, the color of his skin, tanned somehow in wintertime. He was the epitome of the perfect male model. I imagined him nude, and wanted to paint him in explicit detail because it would make such a stunning portrait.

The tight denim jeans accented his butt, and he thrust his hips to the rhythm of the song. That kind of taut, strong body would be a joy to paint. Just watching him made me uncomfortably warm. I had been wanting to capture a man on canvas, their intense lines and lengths, especially one as chiseled as this.

He flicked his dark-blond hair back, and turned suddenly, one hand grasping the top rung of the ladder. When he caught sight of me the singing and, sadly, the thrusting stopped abruptly.

I walked to the stereo to turn the music down, before saying, "Hi, nice drill you have there." *Nice drill you have there?* I promptly closed my mouth, and hoped my brain would catch up with my voice. In my effort to come across convincing, like I knew what a drill was, I sounded like I was flirting. Or just plain stupid. "What I meant was—"

His expression darkened and he spoke over the top of me. "You lost?"

I tilted my head, confused at the hostility in his voice. "No." I appraised him—a hot guy with a bad attitude. I'd been expecting to see a middle-aged guy wearing overalls, *not* someone half-dressed, and mesmerizing from a painting point of view. The fierceness in his eyes—would I capture it?

He jumped down from the ladder, a fine sheen of sweat glistening on his abs. From a sofa covered with plastic, he snatched up a crumpled tank top and pulled it over his head.

"No need to get dressed on my account." I resisted the urge to clap a hand over my mouth. "What I mean is, just be as you were…" The words were coming out wrong, in my effort to be someone I was not.

I blushed.

He scowled.

"Can I help you?" He let the drill drop, the cord slipping slowly through his fingers—he didn't take his eyes off me, before it hit the ground with a clunk. For some reason the gesture seemed highly erotic. But the steely glint in his eyes told a different story.

Thoughts of traipsing back down the driveway, jobless, flashed through my mind. "I'm here about the job." I raised my chin.

His face cracked into a cynical smile. He snatched a rag from the coffee table and wiped his brow, all the while chuckling to himself. I held his stare, while he gave me a once-over. His eyes were a mesmerizing, deep, dark brown, almost fathomless. I should have changed my outfit before I set off. He couldn't take me seriously for the job, looking like some kind of bohemian.

"A job?" His mouth twisted. "I don't think so." His gaze traveled the length of my body once more and I tried hard not to squirm.

"And why not?" I asked, remembering Becca's word of warning. *Do not take no for an answer.*

He sneered. "Do you even know what the job is?"

"Farming, or a farmer, or a farmer's assistant. Who cares about the title? All you need to know is, I am more than capable of… farming." Way to go, Lucy, I silently berated myself. Say farmer one more time. He had me on edge with his cool stare. I hoped the desperation wasn't evident in my voice.

"Who sent you here?"

I tried to hide my smile at his phrasing—it was almost like a line out of a mafia movie. Was this guy for real? "Your cousin Becca. She said you can't find anyone else." *And now I see why.* If I wasn't so desperate for a job I would have told him exactly what I thought of him and breezed out. But there was also a stubborn side of me that wanted to show him he was wrong about me. I could… farm, as well as anyone else.

He raised an eyebrow. "You think I can't find anyone?"

"I don't see people lining up to work for you." He blanched. If it was a tug of war, I'd just retrieved a bit of the rope. "But I am perfectly able to do the work."

"Is that so?"

"Sure is." I pursed my lips.

He took two steps toward me and stood so close I could feel his breath on my face. My pulse quickened—for one second I thought he was going to kiss me. He said, "You think you can handle it?"

Shivers coursed through me. "I can handle anything," I managed, gulping at his proximity. I didn't know if he was referring to the job? Or himself? I was in two minds whether I could handle either, but the thought of getting back on a bus and being in the same predicament elsewhere firmed my resolve. There was no chance I'd let a guy like him peg me for a fool. I hadn't worked my butt off my whole life to be judged on the spot by the likes of him.

"I bet." He looked so deeply into my eyes I was sure my heart stopped.

I blinked rapidly and said, "I need a job. *This* job, and I'm not leaving until you say yes."

A rivulet of sweat ran down his forehead. "Your threats usually work with other people?"

"Yes." Well, technically, no. I was never in the position to threaten anyone, always relying on the mercy of managers, or landlords. I wasn't desperate enough to let anyone hold anything over me, though. My pride wouldn't allow that.

"Look, I don't know who you are…"

"I'm Lucy," I said levelly. If I didn't find work, I wouldn't have much more than the bus fare home. The universe wouldn't provide, and I'd scurry back, tail between my legs, having failed and broken my promise.

That would upset Mom. She'd think I did it on purpose because I wanted to be with her. "So what do you say?" I flashed him a smile, hoping it would lighten the tension that hung between us like fog.

"I need someone who can haul logs, and drive a tractor, help tap the maples. Somehow I can't see you doing that, in your finery." He flicked a hand toward me. Why the heck didn't I change clothes? And finery? He was only wearing a pair of jeans when I walked in, in the middle of winter!

"I have other clothes, obviously."

"Goodbye, Lucy." He went back to the stereo and turned the music up to an ear-piercing level.

I wanted to shriek at him. Just once, I'd love for one person to give me a break, a chance. Instead, I stomped to the stereo and switched it off.

He spun to me, his eyes blazing. "What's your problem?" He pressed his lips together.

How dare he! I pushed myself up close and poked a finger into his chest. "*You're* my problem. Is this because I'm a girl? What, you don't think women can work as hard as men?" If there was one thing I'd learned from my mom it was that I could do anything I set my mind to, and I wouldn't allow a man to tell me otherwise.

The muscle along his jawline pulsed. "Well can you?" he hissed.

"Give me two weeks," I said. "And if you don't think I can handle it, I'll leave."

"Four weeks," he muttered and turned the music up, but I could still make out his words. "Don't think I'm gonna take it easy on you." He grabbed his drill, and climbed back up the ladder.

My shoulders relaxed. With his back to me, I caught my breath, relieved that in the heat of our exchange I'd come out victorious. I knew he was desperate for help, and that's the only reason he gave in. But I'd show him. I'd be the best goddamn farmer's assistant there was.

I cupped my hands around my mouth and yelled over the music, "I'll see you at nine tomorrow."

"Six," he yelled without turning.

Did people really wake up that early? My shifts at the diner were always at night, until the early hours of the morning. I'd fall into bed at dawn for a few hours' sleep before waking later to help Mom. If there was time I'd steal an afternoon nap before my shift started again. The body clock was going to get a shock, that's for sure.

I left quickly, shutting the door with a click, just in case he changed his mind.

CeeCee said Clay was a loner. She forgot to mention he had a chip on his shoulder so big its missing piece could sink the *Titanic*. I walked back to town, my footsteps lighter.

I'd done it.

Secured a job in a tiny town and that would take the pressure off for a while at least. I felt like dancing down the street, the weight of the world forgotten for one brief moment.

I had to find a store that sold clothes for farmers. What exactly did farmers wear? First I had to ring Mom and tell her everything.

***

"A Maple Syrup Farm?" Her voice was groggy, as though I'd just woken her. "I bet it's tranquil too. I knew you'd do great, honey."

"Thanks, Mom. How's it going with Aunt Margot?" From the background noise, I could tell she was still in hospital. Had Aunt Margot been with Mom when I called earlier, and somehow forgotten to mention the fact that Mom still hadn't been taken home yet? I couldn't ask, because I'd told Mom I wouldn't call and bombard Aunt Margot with advice.

"Yeah, yeah. Everything's rosy here. Never mind all that."

"I can hear the machines beeping."

She coughed, the racking echo making my heart hurt. Eventually she continued: "Tomorrow, I'll leave. Just waiting for some more test results. Aunt Margot is flying in soon and will drive me home. You're supposed to be forgetting about this place," she chided. "Tell me all about the job."

"I was going to go over the list—"

"She knows all about that. Don't you worry."

I debated whether to argue the point. Mom's care plan was convoluted at the best of times, without an emergency cropping up.

"Which tests are you waiting on? Did they take more bloods?"

Offhandedly, she said, "Same ones, the results were held up." It'd happened a handful of times before and always resulted in her staying a day or two longer. Being so far away, and not able to consult the doctor like usual had me on edge. Mom was the type of person to go with the flow, not make waves, but sometimes, especially when it came to hospitals, you had to be that pushy person, the one who demanded explanations, otherwise you'd sink into the background, faded, forgotten because they were so busy, so understaffed.

"Usually when you speak to someone on the phone, you actually *speak*," she said. "I can hear those cogs in your brain ticking over."

Her voice was bright, despite the coughing fit. Maybe I was reading too much into it because I wasn't with her. "OK. OK," I said with a small laugh.

"Well, talk, honey! What's the job entail?"

I smiled, thinking of what she'd make of the farm. "We'll be tapping the maples for syrup, and driving tractors." What else had Clay said? "The place needs an overhaul, but it's beautiful, in its own ruined way."

"And that's fate, taking you somewhere like that, and with the click of your fingers, you land yourself a job."

"Mm," I mumbled. "But what if I'm not cut out for that kind of thing?"

"How hard can it be? Wake up when the birds do and get to work. All that fresh air will be a balm for your soul. You're a tree-hugging hippy, just like me. You just haven't found the right trees, yet. Maybe this is your chance?"

Laughter barreled out of me. "Yeah, maybe all I need is a good ol' hug from a maple tree."

She clucked her tongue. "Trees have feelings too, Lucy. I think you're on a winner."

I shook my head. This was her way, sensing an energy in things: trees, grass, flowers, and teaching me to really *see* them, look at them like they meant something. And while it probably sounded cuckoo to most people, it had given me a greater appreciation when it came to painting or sketching. But I jibed her anyway, "You're one step away from pulling the tarot cards out, Mom."

"Oh, please, I've been doing your cards since you left. And I see a bright future for you, full of all the things you should've had already." Mom's voice cracked. She paused, pulling herself together before changing the subject. "Tell me the owner of the farm is some hot, buff, love god."

I spluttered into my hands. "Mom!"

"What?" I pictured her face, the expression she pulled when she was trying to appear innocent, when she was far from it. "A vacation romance is a must! So tell me about this mysterious man."

I stifled a giggle. "Well he's certainly buff, and I *did* see him shirtless—"

"SHIRTLESS!" She said the word so loudly it was in capitals.

"Shirtless, *and* sweaty. It was as good as you imagine it to be." We'd always talked more like best friends than mother and daughter, and when it came to men it was no different. Back home, my relationships had been sporadic, life was too busy, but on the rare occasions I dated Mom knew all the details. Well… almost all. A girl has to keep a few secrets.

"You've been in town all of five minutes and you've seen a half-naked guy?"

"What can I say? Just lucky, I guess. And while he is nice to look at, he's so far from my type he's not even on the *maybe* list. Besides, I'm not looking for love, I'm looking for…" What was I looking for? Just a way to fulfill my mom's wish.

She interrupted. "Oh yes you are!" Her cackle rang out. "Go on, what's he like?"

I weighed up how to answer without causing undue worry. "He's recently inherited the Maple Syrup Farm, which is really run down, and he's kind of… angsty."

"A moody jerk in other words?"

I bit my lip to stem the giggles that threatened to pour out. "A major moody jerk."

Mom harrumphed. "Oh, sweet baby Jesus, you've found yourself a bad boy. He won't know what hit him, meeting the likes you of you. He's one fortunate guy. I want to be kept informed. Promise me?"

Mom knew I could be fiery at the best of times. Life was far too complicated as it was without anyone trying to bring me down a peg. My ex-manager at the diner had tried his damnedest to break me—I don't know why, but he had it in for me. He'd steal my tips, which I relied on, and say customers had complained about me. Or he'd roster me on when I'd specifically asked not to fill that shift because of one of Mom's appointments. A weasel of a man who knew he had me over a barrel because I needed the money. He was swiftly sorted out with a glass of ice-cold water over the head, and a phone call to the owner of the diner about the deficit in the takings. No one had the right to treat me that way, especially not someone who did it just for kicks.

"I'll let you know every single thing I do on the farm, tree hugging, raking, hoeing, erm…"

"No," she interrupted. "Keep your hoes to yourself. I mean about the love god!"

"Clay?" I feigned surprise.

"Oh Lord, his name's Clay?"

"Right." I knew she'd understand.

She sighed. "It couldn't be more perfect. I bet he's a hulking muscle man with an intense scowl. Gosh, ring me tomorrow and tell me everything."

Mom's enthusiasm for my news brought a smile to my face and I said, "I will, I'll be energized from the outdoors and ready for anything life throws at me." With daily phone calls to her, maybe I could enjoy this adventure. Mom sounded brighter just hearing about Ashford. Would that invigorate her, living vicariously through my travels?

"The tarot did throw up the lovers' card each and every time I shuffled."

I scoffed. "Yeah, you're right, I'm going to love those maple trees something bad." If only she'd seen Clay in the flesh, then she'd know he was a no-go zone. Someone that frosty wasn't in my dreamboat book, no matter how gorgeous he was. But it was nice to make Mom happy even if it was all hot air.

The chat had fatigued her. Her voice came back barely audible. "And paint what you see. I know you'll find beauty there."

We rang off, and I fell back against the bed, my heart tugging. Mom spoke about beauty as though it were a person, a real tangible thing. She saw it everywhere: in the reflection of a raindrop on a leaf, or the way a cloud moved across the sky as though it were searching for a mate. So far, without her my world was tinged with gray. Though the edges colored a little as I thought of my new job, and the girls at the Gingerbread Café.

I moved the bedside table away from the wall to use as a makeshift desk, and took my watercolor paints from the drawer. Taking some water from the bathroom, I leaned over my new space, tapping the brush against my chin. Of course, I'd paint him. I couldn't think of anything other than the lines of his body, the way he held himself taut, like he was afraid to let go, to show too much of himself. The psychology of art helped me to see through a person's actions, right to the core of them. And somehow I knew Clay wasn't what he made himself out to be. As the painting took shape, the fluid brushstrokes softened the fire in him. I'd have to use oils; he was too intense for dreamy watercolors.

***

After washing my paintbrushes up I joined Rose in the front room. We sat drinking tea out of dainty cups. "Where would I find a clothes store?" I asked, taking in the way she did everything elegantly, from sipping, to crossing her ankles.

"There's only the grocery store, my dear," she said with a shrug.

"The grocery store? For clothing?" I tried to mimic her, by sipping the tea, and not slurping.

"Yes," Rose smiled. "They sell everything, from groceries, to clothes, even kayaks. It's a one-stop shop."

Small-town living would take some getting used to. What was I expecting, a mall full of boutiques? "Right. Handy then. Do you need anything while I'm out?" I placed my teacup on the saucer and stood.

"No, dear, you just tell Bonnie I sent you. She'll look after you."

The grocery store had the most eclectic range. Thin aisles were jam-packed with toys, bedding, even a range of beside lamps. From what I could garner there was no particular order. I was yet to see any foodstuffs, but I'm sure they were crammed in there somewhere.

I went in search of Bonnie, who helped me find the clothing section.

"Now what exactly are you after?" she asked, with a Texan twang. Ashford was full of a multitude of rich accents. Maybe what CeeCee said was true—people came here, and never left. I could see the appeal, the way most of the locals were warm and welcoming, though I'm sure just like any other place, there were less perfect people.

I folded my arms. "Clothing to suit farm life. So I'm guessing some kind of slicker, and maybe some rubber boots?"

"Great! We supply all the farm folks round here, so I'm sure we have just the thing."

Bonnie shuttled around the store, yabbering to herself, as though the thought of helping me excited her. She unearthed everything she thought I'd need and led me to a change room.

"I'll wait here." She shooed me in, and pulled the curtain closed. "You holler out if you need another size. These clothes are the *very latest* in farmer's attire so I think you're going to be super excited." Her high-pitched twang had a tinge of hopefulness to it.

"OK," I said, not convinced. The clothing looked like something the Ghostbusters would wear. The slicker was fluoro yellow, and plastic, and made a crunching sound as I pulled it on. The pants were so big at the thigh I felt like Ronald McDonald. Lastly, I donned the hat, which was as wide as it was tall. My reflection looked like some kind of backwater hillbilly. Surely not? Was it so cold outside farmers dressed braced for an apocalypse?

"How do they fit?" she asked chirpily.

"Erm…" Laughter threatened to burble out of me at the sheer ridiculousness of it all. I was a ghostbusting, burger-selling, cowboy-hat-wearing farmer.

Bonnie drew the curtain back with a flourish. "Oh, now, don't they just fit you real great?" She smiled so genuinely I didn't have the heart to tell her otherwise.

Clay hadn't been dressed like this. I wasn't sure farmers actually wore such clothing, but maybe I was wrong. Maybe Clay had been barely clothed because he was working indoors, and once outside we'd need to be protected from the elements. Because if there was one thing I was sure of, nothing was getting through the layers of plastic that now crinkled noisily over my body. I held on to the curtain. "I'll take them." Bonnie had the puppy-dog eyes down pat, and rewarded me with a happy squeal.

"You've gone and made my day," she said, closing the curtain, so I could change back. Her smile threatened to swallow her up, and it dawned on me that maybe Bonnie didn't get many customers, just like the travel agent Henry, who appeared hopeful seeing a new face in town. "I'll go and ring them up for you. And I'll throw in a pair of socks, since you've been real nice. They're a new brand. Meant to help with the circulation, you know, for the diabetes?"

I didn't know. But I played along, anyway. "That sure will come in handy. Thank you, Bonnie."

CHAPTER FIVE

My alarm shrieked, waking me from a deep sleep. Groggy, I rubbed my eyes, and yawned, taking an age to remember where I was. The shadows were unfamiliar. When I flicked on the bedside lamp, and the flowered wallpaper stared happily at my crumpled frame, it all came back. Begonia Bed and Breakfast. And day one of working with the half-naked, intensely arrogant Clay.

With a groan, I wrenched the covers back and dressed quietly in the shoebox-sized room. The last time I'd seen five a.m. was coming off a double shift at the diner. Maybe once I acclimatized this would be better, watching dawn break, fresh, after a good night's sleep.

I tried to creep quietly but the garb I wore had other ideas, and crinkled like someone scrunching cellophane. Once outside, I breathed fresh air deep into my lungs. The sky was awash with gray, not even a bird chirp for company.

I crinkled along, wishing I'd made a cup of coffee for the journey. Rose had given me a travel mug for that very purpose but I didn't want the shrieking of the kettle to rouse her. I turned the corner and headed down the main road of Ashford. It was gloomy, the store fronts somber without the light of day and their cheery owners.

A beam of light coming from the Gingerbread Café caught my attention. I resisted the urge to fist pump as thoughts of strong coffee danced through my mind. I jogged up the road, and spilled through the door in a flurry.

Lil jumped, her eyes wide. "You scared the bejeezus out of me!" She clutched her chest. "Coffee?"

"I will love you forever." As much as I loved drinking cups of tea with Rose, a strong dose of caffeine would fire up the old brain synapses and enable to me to make sense at such an early hour.

She grinned and went to the percolator, poured two mugs, and motioned to a stool. "I bet you haven't eaten." She stared me down the way my mother would, even though Lil and I were probably around the same age, give or take a few years.

"No, I was going to but…"

"Say no more." Lil expertly moved around the kitchen, gathering bowls and utensils before cracking a couple of eggs, adding some spices and whisking. "French toast, OK?"

"Do you always make people's dreams come true?" I said faux seriously.

She threw her head back and laughed. "I try."

There was something about Lil, something indistinct that made me act differently with her. She had a unique energy. I sensed her life hadn't been smooth sailing, but she'd come out the other side. Studying people in the background for so many years had made me read people on a deep level, somehow seeing past the cosmetics of a situation and finding the heart of them. For that reason, I connected with her more easily than I usually would have.

While Lil worked, I walked around the café sipping my coffee and taking in every tiny detail. It was cozy and warm, not just from the fire, but also from the little touches they'd added to make it kitschy and cute. The walls were painted the color of dark chocolate, gingerbread-man bunting hung in garlands, twisted with rows of fairy lights, which pulsed like stars.

Hand-knitted throw rugs were tossed lazily on sofas. Fat fluffy mismatched cushions perched on chair seats. By the bookshelves was a veritable mountain of European pillows adorned with cartoonish dinosaurs or pink-swathed princesses. I imagined toddlers falling into them face first, shrieking with joy, the stack taller than their little bodies. In a corner a green plastic table sat tucked away, full of jars of brightly colored pencils, and craft supplies so kids could create while their parents took a break from their day over a cup of tea and a plate of something delicious.

Lil and CeeCee's passion for their business and customers shone through from the way they greeted their customers, to the way they joked with one another, and the love they poured into baking. It was so far from the diner I worked in it was hard to reconcile the two. The diner had needed a damn good scrub, and some life poured into it, but it was always busy because of its location, and the customers who frequented didn't seem to mind the seventies décor.

On the bench by Lil, knobbly loaves of bread cooled on a wire rack. The scent of fresh bread reminded me of my mother, and how once upon a time she loved baking, humming while she kneaded dough, flour dusting her forearms. These days, even baking was too much for her. Sometimes, it was hard not to let the bitterness creep in. She was such a vital person, and her condition snatched that away from her.

"What's on your mind?" Lil asked, taking two slices of freshly baked bread and dipping them into the egg mix. "You're away with the fairies."

"Oh, it's nothing." I walked back to the stool, cupping my face in my hands, and watching her work.

"Nothing? Doesn't look like nothing." She raised her eyebrows and gave me a look that meant share my woes.

People were so perceptive in Ashford. Maybe it was because they all knew each other, and could read moods like some people read the ocean tides. When they asked you a question they stared you full in the face, giving you their undivided attention. Like you mattered. That the words that fell from your lips were important.

"Every now and then sadness catches up with me, that's all." I ran a hand over the bench, wiping down bread crumbs. "I wonder if I'm making the right choice by leaving my old life."

Lil clucked her tongue. "Leaving is always hard. But I suppose, you won't know until you try, right?"

I toyed with the coffee mug, avoiding Lil's sincere-eyed expression. Sensing my mood, she went to the stove and lit the element, then groveled under the bench for a frypan. She dropped a dollop of butter into it, which slipped and slid around the black pan, melting into a sunny yellow liquid.

"Waking up at five a.m. brings out the maudlin in me. I just need to get used it." I tried to make a joke of it, lightening my tone, and forcing a wide smile. I hadn't devoured the first coffee of the day; I was still half asleep at such a crazy hour of the morning—that's all it was. In the still of the dawn, reality always seemed that much more frightening, and sometimes harsh and cold. Who was I pretending to be? I wasn't an artist. I wasn't anything, except my mother's daughter, and running off to change that didn't feel right. Shouldn't I put her first always?

"You'll get used to it, Lucy. Things will get easier over time." Lil flipped the buttery brown French toast, and glanced back over her shoulder at me. "*Viola.*" She pushed the dish in front of me, and gave my shoulder a squeeze.

"You're some kind of miracle worker," I said, gazing at the plate, glad for the interruption of breakfast so my somber thoughts didn't fall out in a sad jumble.

"Wait!" she held up a hand and then dashed to the fridge, pulling a bottle out. "Maple syrup!"

"Of course!"

She drizzled a helping of syrup over the French toast and took the stool beside me. "As soon as you've made the first batch of syrup, you tell Clay we want some. Nothing better than locally made produce."

I nodded. "Can you imagine making it? I can't wait to see how it's done."

"It'll be wonderful." Lil picked up a fork. "Eat," she said. "And remember to stop by tomorrow on your way. I love a bit of company in the lonely dawns. I'm not as good as Cee with dispensing advice, but if you need a shoulder to lean on, I'm here."

"Thanks, Lil," I said, truly grateful. CeeCee and Lil had a way about them, a genuine kindness that took the edge off my homesickness.

***

After refusing a lift from Lil, I trekked down the long, dark road out of Ashford. By the time I arrived at the farm I had my hands shoved deep in my pockets. I walked down the driveway, my eyes wide at the view ahead. Before the winter sun had risen, the snow-covered maple trees looked . hauntingly beautiful in the dark of the morning.

It was a touch before six, so I sat on the back porch, not wanting to wake Clay. There was no sound from inside the cottage. Time marched on; the sky slowly shifted from a moody gray to a diaphanous blue. It was like being inside a dream.

I imagined setting up a canvas here, capturing the sky before it changed hue. But I couldn't. I would hate Clay peering over my shoulder at my work.

For me, painting was deeply personal, and private. It was like my heart was right there on the canvas, along with the brushstrokes, leaving my soul exposed. My mom said I was all sorts of kooky to think such a way, but she understood.

I wasn't ready for judgment—I wasn't good enough yet and what I painted sometimes was murky and hazy with grief, a way for me to get all those feelings out, not let them simmer too long inside me. That's why I'd never applied for the Van Gogh Institute in case they replied with a negative. I imagined these geniuses of the art world, shaking their heads, confused by my clumsy attempts, like I was a fake, a phony, pretending to be as good as them.

My pictures, whether sketched or painted, reminded me of how I felt, what I did, even though the subject might be something as innocuous as a piece of fruit, like the bruised bananas on a lunch tray, served to Mom in hospital. Like a metaphor, the damaged skin of the fruit, a once-perfect thing, marred by all those who had touched it, leaving it indelibly changed. The paint—bleeding, soaking into the canvas—took some of the angst away. Whatever I was feeling, I purged part of it when I painted. Life made sense when I could recreate it in color.

But now the world in front of me was different. The farm would be another chapter. Could I catch the light here? Would my art evolve?

Sitting on the porch, the cold settled in my bones. I jiggled to warm up, wondering if I should just go inside but slightly hesitant in case Clay was undressed. He'd be the type who wouldn't appreciate a girl wandering into his sanctuary. From what I'd gathered he was a private sort.

I knocked, and pressed my ear against the door. The cottage was silent, bar a few soft creaks: the wind, wrapping itself around the old place. Nerves fluttered, but I settled them with one of Mom's wacky affirmations. Today will be a good day. *Today will be a good day.*

After another two quick raps, I pushed the front door open. The fire crackled in the living room, so I wandered over. With my back to it, I called, "I'm here!" feeling like an intruder. Where was he? Wrenching myself away from the warmth I walked through the cottage calling his name. About to give up, I spun on my heel only to come face to face with him. "Oh. My. God." My hand flew to my mouth. He was so close I could see the amber flecks in his eyes. "Are you some kind of serial killer? Who creeps up like that?"

He was like Dexter, standing there mute, clutching some ginormous piece of metal. He was so silent, I couldn't even hear him breathing.

"And who lets themselves into a stranger's house?" He gave me that same maddening look, like he wanted to eat me for breakfast.

"You said six; it's past six." I tapped the face of my watch. "I was waiting outside for ages." I didn't say how much of a culture shock the early wake-up was for me.

His face softened, and I breathed a sigh of relief, until he said, "What the hell are you wearing?"

I blushed. And creaked. Goddamn it! "Erm, farmer's clothing. I asked an expert and this is what she recommended. Why, is it not suitable?" Lil hadn't mentioned my outfit at the cafe, so I'd taken that as a sign it was the norm. Clay's unnerving stare had the ability to make me second-guess myself.

"You look like an astronaut."

I scoffed, but knew it was true. "Well you look like a... a..."

"A… what?" I took in his clothing, tight jeans, and a barely-there tank top same as the day before.

My brain unscrambled. "Like some kind of stripper wannabe. Who are you channeling? Magic Mike?" He brought out the worst in me riling me up for no good reason. "I mean, aren't you cold?" All the while I was silently cursing Bonnie for hooking me up with clothes that were obviously *not* the latest in farming wear.

"Cold?" He dropped his voice to a low growl. "I'm a warm-blooded male, Lucy. Can't you tell?" He tilted his head. It was like a tennis match, volleying insults back and forth.

I scrunched up my face, like I'd sucked a lemon. "Is that so?" I get he was all sorts of hot, but really? A warm-blooded male—what was he insinuating? I'd had boyfriends in the past who'd tried to take the lead as if I didn't have a brain in my head. The alpha-male affliction. I was sure Clay was a carbon copy of that kind of guy. And a narcissist to boot. "You don't look all that warm to me, Clay. In fact you look downright chilly."

I gave him a slow, dismissive, once-over, dragging my gaze from his face, down his body, and ending at his feet, which were not as ugly as most feet are. Goddamn it. He would make a great subject, those fiery eyes of his, and that clenched jaw, the way he held himself, tightly coiled, ready to pounce.

"I'm not on the market for a girlfriend, that's all."

"*Excuse me?*" I held in a harrumph, wary of going too far and losing the job before it began. "Well, I'm just here to work, so that's one less thing to worry yourself over." Clay seriously needed to lighten up. In the past maybe women had thrown themselves at him, but I certainly wouldn't be one of them. Only one thing kept me from walking out that door: money. Money for a future that would be hundreds of miles from the likes of him.

He gave me the *oh yeah* face like he didn't believe me. "Can't say I'm not relieved. So that's settled then. Now, let's do some work, *if* you can handle it."

"That's what I'm here for, besides the thought-provoking conversation, that is." My words poured out, honeyed with sarcasm. If I'd been sleepwalking through the morning, I was certainly awake now. He brought out a different side of me, one I didn't know, but liked nonetheless. There was no way I'd stand there and let him try and mock me.

He reached out, his hand near my breast. My mouth went wide to protest. "*Excuse...*" He pulled a sweater from the hook behind me. I swallowed back the sentence.

"Better cover up, hey? I need you to focus today." He winked. He *actually* winked as though I'd get a kick out of staring at his muscles, like some kind of lust-struck fool.

"Unless you're a fan of frostbite, it would be wise to wear something warm, your *warm blood* can only do so much in winter..." I sneered as he pulled the sweater over his head. It killed me that my turncoat eyes darted a glance at his body before it was sheathed in fabric, and not crinkly farmer fabric either. He had muscles, and lots of them. Really such a body was wasted on a guy with an ego the size of Texas.

"Follow me," he ordered, walking blithely past.

Today will be a good day.

We went outside, the cold shocking the air from my lungs.

With a grunt he pulled the barn door wide open. Inside was neat, benches were free of clutter, and tools were hung methodically on a board in order of size. Definitely Dexter traits.

With his back to me he said, "We have a lot to do today." He threw a tool belt at me, which I caught one-handed as it whizzed past my ear. "You can start outside, head to the fence line, and pull the ivy off the posts. If you manage—" he gave me a pointed stare "—to get it all done, then you can sand them back, ready to paint come springtime."

He strapped on his tool belt, and went to the wall. He selected a few tools and pushed them into the loops of his belt. I waited for him to tell me to choose which ones I'd like.

"Grab what you need," he barked.

"OK…" I stared at the wall of shiny silver tools. None looking remotely like gardening implements.

"Let's go." He'd already turned and walked away. Hastily I snatched some shears, and a pronged fork that might be good to remove ivy.

He stomped off, and I scrambled to catch up with him. "Head west, and start by the lake, and work your way backward."

My mouth hung open, as he pivoted and walked in the opposite direction than he'd pointed to. I was working alone? I'd expected we'd tap the trees, or do something together, until I'd learned more. Maybe this was my chance to prove I could work steadily, alone. With gusto, I walked west, marveling at the beauty of the snow-covered farm. I shivered slightly, until my quick steps warmed my body. I would get all the posts done and surprise him, walk confidently back and ask what next.

When I got to the fence and looked down the line, the posts growing smaller as my eyes tracked the distance, my heart sank. There were hundreds of them, as far as the eye could see. Surely, there was no way I could wrench ivy from every single post in one day. I knelt down, and twisted the tendrils of ivy loose, wincing as they tore into the soft flesh of my hands.

While the fences did need mending, by exposing the old posts, and taking the green-leafed shield away, I was also taking a little of the beauty away, and I wondered if Clay would think so too. The farm, overgrown and derelict, told its own unique story, and while we were restoring it, we were also erasing chapters of its past.

A few hours later the snowfall had increased, and Clay came searching for me. I was shivering, and still wrenching away ivy. With a grunt, he motioned for me to come inside. When I stood, my back cricked into place. A stretch had never felt so good. I furtively checked the palms of my hands, blanching when I saw the damage I'd done.

Back inside I warmed myself by the fire, waiting for instruction from Clay.

"There's lunch in the kitchen for you. After you eat, you can help rip the old drywall off in here until the snowfall slows." He went back to work, ripping down walls, and carrying the detritus away. It was like he was racing against time. He went fast, and had a determined look in his eye. Everything was invisible to him except the job he was focusing on.

***

The sky darkened, the sun retreating behind dense skies. With a soft sigh I used the crowbar to pry off a piece of broken drywall, my pace slower than Clay's. Thick dust particles floated up, catching in the light, before swirling down over me, making my nose itch. It was a dirty job, and my fingers ached from tearing away the vestiges of the wall. Blisters popped up, making it difficult to hold the crowbar without letting a sob escape. There was no way in hell I was going to admit to Clay I was struggling. I'm sure at the first sign of weakness he'd say I wasn't cut out for the job. My pride and my bank balance wouldn't have that.

"Last wall," he said, standing and stretching. His sweater rode high, exposing a deep V, like an arrow, a direction. I'd never imagined it could be so visually appealing, like the human body was designed with a symbol showing you the way to pleasure…. I gasped, dropping the crowbar, which clanged to the wooden floor.

I made a show of searching the floor for it, so Clay wouldn't see the blush creeping up my skin. What the hell? I blew out my cheeks. It wasn't him… it was simply his body. Why couldn't he be the clichéd lumberjack, a heavily bearded, middle-aged, overall-wearing farmer? Instead, he was—I flicked my gaze back to him—he was… still stretching, his jeans slung low, he was tanned *all* the way down. I was asphyxiating, I was sure of it.

"Turn the fire off," I groaned, pulling the crinkling, suffocating, plastic-wrap-like clothing from my neck.

Clay lifted a brow. "Turn the fire off? It doesn't actually work that way. Maybe in your world…"

He was having a dig at me over my clothing yesterday. He'd pegged me for someone other than I was.

"Yeah, where I'm from you click your fingers, and fires go out." I gave him a pointed stare. "And we use little hovercrafts too." Suddenly the heat was gone from my body, as I stared at his cold-eyed expression. As hard as it was to bite my tongue, his one-liners irked me, and I found myself responding.

"Are you running from something, Lucy? Bad debts? A bad marriage?"

I scowled. I hated the fact he could see I was out of my comfort zone. And in a way, I *was* on the run, running toward some indistinct future.

"Far from it. I'm merely working my way around the world," I said, huffiness getting the better of me. If Clay knew what my life entailed, he'd quit his yapping quick sticks, but my past was private. I wouldn't have him feel sorry for me—when people knew my story and stared at me with that pitiful look in their eyes, my blood boiled. As though what I had to do to survive, and to make Mom's life as easy as possible, was seen as a penance, and it evoked sympathy I didn't want, or like. It wasn't a burden caring for my mother, it was a privilege. And again I was hit with a bout of worry that Aunt Margot wouldn't do it right.

Glowering, I flopped on the plastic-covered sofa, not caring that Clay would probably make some kind of snappy comment about stopping.

"So what's *your* story, Clay? Word is you're a little on the reclusive side? Got something to hide? A dead body or two buried around here?"

He lifted an eyebrow. "You part of the Chinese whispers gang?"

I shrugged. "It's a small town, there's bound to be talk."

"Well…" the fire was back in his eyes "… there's nothing *to* know. The sooner they learn that the better."

"Maybe. But you ever think you're fueling the fire by hiding out?" Was he just a broody hothead? I sensed there was a lot more to Clay than met the eye.

"Who said I'm hiding out? I'm not going to fall over myself trying to fit in."

I held up two fingers. "Peace. I really don't care what you do or don't do, I'm only pointing out that usually in small towns everyone knows everyone's business and you might do well to get to know them if you plan on making a decent living here."

"I don't need anyone," was his curt reply.

Everyone needed someone, surely? But I bit my tongue. I was here to save money, *not* save Clay.

"You should…"

"Yeah, work, I know." I took the crowbar and bent down, prizing parts off the remaining wall, flinching slightly when I gripped the metal pole, sure one of my blisters popped. Gloves—why didn't Bonnie supply me with gloves? My farmer's assistant outfit was terribly flawed.

"The snow's slowed down," he said. "Head back outside to the fence line."

***

A week later, I still wasn't used to the manual labor. Each night my legs were heavy with fatigue, and walking back into town took double the amount of time when I wasn't buzzing off a steaming hot gingerbread coffee, and a cinnamon-sugar pastry. Even though my hands were blistered and my feet sore, there was no chance of me accepting a lift from Clay out of principle. He said he wasn't going to go easy on me and he hadn't. Every day was a fresh challenge and I did my best to rise to it.

After another interminable day, I trudged down the icy road back to town, so tired I was almost sleepwalking.

When the main street came into view, I almost wept with relief. So. Close. To. Bed.

Storekeepers were rolling shutters down and packing chairs away. Some leaned against the brick of their buildings, and chatted to neighbors. Inside the Gingerbread Café, CeeCee was dashing about, wiping tables down, and restacking magazines into neat piles. I stumbled through the door to say hello, and hopefully buy something, anything, for dinner if I stayed awake long enough to eat.

She turned to the jangle of the doorbell as I walked ape-like—arms dragging beside my legs—to a table.

"Glory be, what's gone and happened to you?" She scurried over, her face lined with concern.

I dropped my head onto the table. "I thought farmwork was easy. Turns out, it's not."

CeeCee let out a roar of laugher. "Oh, sweet child, are you just getting back now? It's gone seven already."

It hurt to talk so I just nodded, one step away from falling into a deep, possibly dribble-mouthed sleep. I hurt right down to the marrow of my bones.

"That sure is too long a day. Why'd he make you stay so long?" She frowned.

I managed a half shrug. "Probably because we spent half the day arguing. So between that, and a few accidents, the day lagged on."

She folded her arms and looked down the bridge of her nose at me, worried. "What kinda accidents?"

"Rookie farmer's assistant mistakes. I've been trying so hard, but sometimes, I have no idea what he's ordering me to do. And I don't want to ask. He races around doing tasks so quickly you'd think he was on a deadline. So I bumble along, hoping I'm doing the right thing. Apologizing when I'm not. He's not exactly approachable. It's easier to try and do it myself. He hollers out orders, and I follow."

CeeCee's face relaxed. "Sounds as though you're doing a great job. I know he's not easy to work for. There's been a gaggle of people come and go from that place."

"I have no idea if he likes my work or not—he doesn't say. Just yells out the next missive and stalks away, back to hammering, and drilling and making lots of noise."

The streetlights flicked on outside. I was probably keeping CeeCee from her nice warm home.

"You might be just the thing he needs, slap some sense into that handsome head o' his. Folk tried to make friends but he ain't interested. Don't see how he's gonna sell maple syrup if he keep turning people away who just tryin' to make his acquaintance."

Cee bustled to the fridge and took out a casserole dish.

"I don't think he cares, Cee. He's one of those good-looking hot guys with zero personality."

"He just might be. I'm fixin' you some pumpkin soup," she said, ladling the liquid into a small saucepan, and heating it on the stove.

"If I could move, I'd hug you." The aroma of spiced soup filled the air, making my mouth water in anticipation.

"Never mind that. It'll get easier," she said with her back to me, stirring.

I must have fallen asleep, because next minute CeeCee was shaking me gently on the shoulder. She placed a steaming bowl of soup down, and a thick piece of buttered bread.

"Again, the Gingerbread Café makes all my dreams come true."

She laughed and came back to the table with a second bowl, sat across from me, and smiled. "That's our job. Get that soup in. You so skinny I can't even see your shadow."

***

"You sound like you're drunk!" Mom said, worried.

I was only half awake, my mind slipping between conversation, and sleep. "I'm so tired. Golly."

"Go to bed, honey. You don't need to call me every day. Just get yourself used to the work first…"

I managed, "I love you," before cradling the phone like it was a teddy bear, and falling into a deep sleep.

CHAPTER SIX

I'm sure my snoring must have woken Rose up most nights. It had woken me on a number of occasions. As the days bled into each other, my body still ached whenever I stopped what I was doing.

I'd never slept so deeply in my life. A hurricane could have torn past and I would have been none the wiser. But the mornings were another story. After being prostrate for hours, I awoke stiff, and all folded in on myself. Limping to the bathroom, I hunched over, unable yet to stand up straight as my muscles protested every movement.

It was my second week at the farm, and as usual I wondered how in the heck was I going to walk all that way with my body stiff and sore. But I knew, once I started the long trek, my blood would pump through my tender muscles, making me limber. The body was a miraculous thing, the way it coped. It didn't stop me from having a ten-minute mind battle with myself about jumping back into bed, and looking for an easier job.

I remembered the aborted phone call with Mom, the night before. I should have just zombie-walked my way to bed and gone to sleep as soon as my head hit the pillow. My incoherent mumblings might have worried her. I debated whether I should call now but I didn't want to wake her.

Because Clay continued to make such a big deal about my work clothes, I put them on again, not worrying about the coat of dust that streaked them, and really having no choice. It wasn't like I had any other suitable farm wear. And my money couldn't stretch to another outfit. They were warm and waterproof and they'd do. Clay paid me a decent amount, but I had to save as much as I could, just in case I did apply to the Van Gogh Institute. If I did, and was somehow accepted, I would need enough money saved to live on for the entirety. The formidable tutors were well known for lengthy class times, and a barrage of tasks to complete at home. There wouldn't be enough time to hold down a job as well. I'd promised myself I'd try and send money back home for mom too, so I'd have to be frugal.

Brushing my teeth, I smiled when I thought about a quick stop by the café to catch up with Lil. Mornings with her perked me up for the rest of the walk to the farm.

Grabbing my scarf and looping it around my neck, I tiptoed from the house, and locked the door. The town, in its deserted state, looked almost like it was taking a deep breath, before dawn would break. As though the store fronts were stretching, and letting out big, long, sonorous yawns with the wind whipping past, before customers would trickle in for another day.

The yeasty smell of fresh bread baking swirled out from the doors of the café, invisible to the eye but so rich and thick, it was almost like I could see the scent dancing its way outside, trying its best to sail down to nearby houses and wake people from their dreams. I longed to sketch the fanciful idea… the sleepy town, under the cover of darkness, being woken by something as simple as bread baking. I imagined a little girl, with rosy-red cheeks warm from slumber, waking to the smell. I'd sketch her full, baby-like cheeks as seen through a window, the scent pirouetting inside her small room, as gentle as butterfly kisses.

With a smile, and a mental note to recreate the little girl through the window, I stepped into the warmth of the Gingerbread Café.

"Good morning," Lil said cheerfully. "You're just in time. Grab that apron over there and help me cut out the next batch of bobble-headed people."

I took a red apron off the hook and tied it around my waist. "I should warn you, I can probably mess up even the simplest task in the kitchen."

She guffawed. "Not under my tutelage." Lil's face was radiant with happiness at such an early hour. It must've been great to be a morning person. While I was awake, I wasn't quite ready for the world. Lil hummed as she rolled out the gingerbread mixture, and made room on the bench beside her for me to cut out the shapes.

"Don't you like cooking?" she asked, as she rolled out another layer.

"I only know the basics. I worked a lot before I came here, so my meals were more heat and eat, if you know what I mean." I tried to make balanced meals back home, but more often than not, being time poor, we'd eat microwaved meals, served with handfuls of cherry tomatoes, and a few stalks of celery.

"Well you have to learn then," she said, grinning. "You can start here. Meet me in the mornings and I'll teach you. Though they'll mostly be sweet foods, at least you'll know what real baking is all about. The secret is *love*."

"Love?" I raised an eyebrow.

She flashed me a toothy smile. "Yep, it's that simple. You have to bake like no one is watching. Just pour all your love into it, and it will never fail. Trust me." She tapped her nose. "That's all you have to do."

"OK, I'll take your word for it," I laughed.

"Everyone can cook, well, unless you're my mom, but she's an exception to the rule." She clucked her tongue.

"Why? What's she like?" I took the gingerbread-man-shaped cookie cutter and pressed it into the mix.

"In terms of cooking?"

I nodded. Lil's hands flew around the bench as she talked. She could roll out the mixture, stir pots, and maintain eye contact with me.

"Well the latest series of disasters got her banned from the café… except as a customer, and even then, I keep a beady eye on her."

I placed the bobble-headed people onto a baking sheet Lil had lined with parchment paper. "Oh, wow, what on earth did she do?"

With a look at the heavens Lil said, "She knocked over my wedding cake, completely destroying it the *day* before the wedding. Tripped over cords and cut the power to the fridges, ruining all the cakes. Set fire to a tea towel, which made the smoke detectors shriek, while I was still in the process of cleaning up cakes she'd dropped. All while I was trying to get things finished around here so I could walk down the aisle. It was woeful! I managed, by the grace of God, not to strangle her. Just." She held her thumb and forefinger close together.

"Oh, Lil! That must have been so stressful before the wedding." I tried to stem the giggles, as Lil managed to laugh, all the while shaking her head. "What did CeeCee have to say about it all?"

Lil's eyes clouded. "Cee was away. Her best friend, Janey, had come home from hospital…"

"Is she OK, now?" I stopped and turned to face her.

Lil bit her lip, and averted her eyes. "Sorry," she said and plucked a tissue from a box under the bench. "It's just

Janey passed. She had cancer so CeeCee went to look after her and to say her goodbyes."

"Oh I'm so sorry, Lil. That must have been truly awful for you all." I patted her shoulder, and could imagine just how horrible the final goodbye would be.

"It was. While there was so much to look forward to with the wedding, there was that sorrow too. But you know, the whole town rallied, just like they always do when someone needs a hand. I'll always remember that Christmas, and everything that happened. Janey's husband, Walt, needs our help now. We take meals to him, and try to coax him out of the house. But it'll take time."

"He doesn't want to leave yet?" I could empathize. I'd often thought of my own future, just me. It was enough to make me curl into a ball, and want to shut out the world, no matter what needed doing.

She shook her head. "Not yet. But a few days ago, Cee found him in the workshop out the back of his place. He wasn't back to making furniture as such, but was sitting there staring at the wood like he was waiting for inspiration, so maybe it'll happen soon."

It dawned on me, the first day I met with CeeCee in the café, she stared at the empty furniture store like her heart was broken in two. "So the furniture store's been closed for a while?"

She nodded. "We all took shifts in covering the business for him so they'd still have an income while Janey was receiving treatment. But in the end, we sold out of everything. Walt handcrafts that furniture himself. So there was no one here to make any more."

"How does he survive without the business?" I moved the full sheet of bobble-headed people to the opposite bench, and started filling a second one.

Lil took a deep steadying breath. "Well, that's what we're all worried about. We know he needs an income and we've got no way to help him without anything to sell. But how can he craft furniture when he's grieving so bad?"

My heart ached for a man I'd never met. "I wish I could help." The concern on Lil's face was enough to know the man needed a miracle. Imagine losing your wife, and then your business? It wasn't fair.

"We'll work out a way," she said. "We always do. My mom, while she's a danger in the kitchen, is really good when it comes to solving problems—maybe she'll find a solution. She's got a heart of gold, that woman."

"Must be nice having her so close." Lil's mom, despite her loveable faults, must have been a lot of fun to be around, and my heart ached for my own mother. To have her near, even if she upended a bunch of my oils, or knocked over a still-wet canvas, I would've taken that any day of the week.

Lil stilled her busy hands, and glanced at me. "I love her dearly. She's as batty as they come, but I wouldn't change her. Are you close with your mom?"

In the quiet of the café, and with Lil's openness, I felt I could trust her to talk about my mom, my old life, the one I missed so much.

Somehow I knew she wouldn't pound me with platitudes. "We're really close. Like best friends. I've been caring for her the last ten years or so… She's sweet, spiritual, and always ready to laugh, despite how tough her life is. I hate being away from her. Mom had been one of those people who bounced out of bed in the mornings— she'd spring into my room, her voice sing-songy, and demand I join her outside for a yoga session. To *soak up the vitamin D*, she said." It hurt, knowing her body wasn't capable of exercise anymore. She'd cared for herself, and done all the rights things, like eat organic food and drink eight glasses of water a day, yet she couldn't outrun this.

"Oh, Lucy." Deep concern reflected in Lil's big blue eyes. "Life is so hard sometimes. This explains the sad goodbyes you were talking about."

I finished my second sheet of bobble-headed people, and wiped my hands on the apron. "It sure is. Saying goodbye was *the* hardest thing I've ever done."

"So where's your mom, now?"

I averted my eyes. "Back in Detroit." It was hard to even say the word, let alone think about it. She was so far away. "My Aunt Margot has flown in to help out."

"I'm guessing by the look on your face this working vacation wasn't your idea?" Lil gave me a gentle smile.

"No, it wasn't. Mom asked me to make her a promise. Take a year for myself. She wants me to apply for the Van Gogh Institute in Paris, for the July intake." I lifted my eyebrows—my way of showing it was a lofty ambition. "Mom wants me to concentrate on art, and making a future for myself but what she doesn't understand is, it's not the same without her. Yeah, I have to work hard to keep our heads above water, but I'd do that forever if it meant we were together. She says I have to fly the coop, and put myself first." My words came out in a rush—once I'd opened up, they seemed to spill out of their own accord.

Lil clucked her tongue. "You know what they say, mothers always know best. Sure, you'll miss her every hour of every day, but maybe you do need to go out into the world and see what's out there? And being able to visit Paris, and live there as an art student, gosh, I'm no expert, but I bet there's probably a million people who'd trade places with you."

What would I find? Beautiful scenes to paint. But all that seemed hollow in comparison. "What if something happens to her while I'm gone?" There, I'd finally admitted to someone that was my fear. *What if* made living in the moment impossible.

"And what if it doesn't?" Lil said diplomatically.

I shrugged. "I'm scared, that's all." It took all my strength not to cry. I knew Mom's motives, but it didn't make it any easier. Deep down, I worried Mom knew something that I didn't. That maybe her condition was worse, and she was sending me away because something bad was going to happen—to spare me.

"Sounds to me, like your mom's got a big heart. And she must be confident in her health to ask you to take a year out for yourself. She wouldn't send you away, if she thought something would go wrong."

"But she can't really know—that's the thing, Lil. No one knows what will happen. The doctors can make assumptions based on the past, but any moment, her condition could deteriorate. And that's what concerns me. What if I'm a million miles away and I can't get back to her quickly enough?"

Lil touched my shoulder. "You're only ever a plane flight away. Your mom must have bucket loads of inner strength, and courage, and she's got your best interests at heart. I know how hard it is. But you have to trust her. Trust *yourself.* And think of it like you're making her wish come true."

Making her wish come true?

"I guess, I hadn't thought of it quite like that." Deep down, I think I expected a phone call by now saying, come home.

"So why not give it a shot? Travel, work, and have some fun. It's not like you can't call her every day. But wouldn't she prefer to hear you bubbly with all you've seen and done? Rather than treating it like some kind of forced exile?"

Mom wanted me to enjoy myself, I knew that, but it was harder to put it in practice. "She was the ultimate nomad so this trip, I suppose, is a way for her to reconnect with her travel memories too." It could have been the caffeine coursing through my veins, or more likely Lil's pep talk, but the future shone a little clearer.

Lil put the rolling pin down and dusted her hands on the apron. "I'm sure she'll love hearing all about the Maple Syrup Farm. And of course, Ashford, small as it is." She motioned for me to stop, and sit on the stool. She went to the counter and poured two cups of coffee.

"She'd love it here," I said. "Anyone would." And it was true. I hadn't stumbled upon a place like Ashford before. Or more likely, people like Lil and CeeCee.

We sipped our coffees in the still of the café. "While you're here we'll bake and *that* can fix almost anything."

I smiled. "It surely will."

"Don't you go leaving too soon." She smiled over the rim of her cup. "We're just getting to know you."

"If the job works out at the farm, I'll stay as long as I can. The more I can save, the better. And it's worked out really well so far, staying with Rose, and being able to wander into town easily."

"Handy—basically everything is walking distance here." She laughed. "Another small-town tick."

"Surely there's a bad side to Ashford?"

Lil grinned. "Of course! It's the home of tall tales, and century-old rivalries, but that's just on Mondays."

I threw my head back and laughed. All the while wondering if I'd become part of the place, including the gossip, whether good or bad.

CHAPTER SEVEN

The farm rolled into view and, while dilapidated, it was still breathtaking from the road, the way the trees spanned for miles, surrounding the property like sentinels, their solemn trunks snaking upward, as though they were reaching for heaven. Snow drifted lazily down, settling on the ground like a blanket of white. Rows of maple trees lined the outermost edges of the property. Majestic old trunks climbed into the deep-gray sky, their branches bare of leaves in the wintertime.

I trudged up the driveway, ready to face another day with Mr. Gruff. My hands ached from the damage, but the pain in my back and my legs was a touch better after the long walk from town. It would take some getting used to, the sheer amount of physical work, but I wasn't ready to give up yet.

I stumbled up the porch, and rapped on the front door loud enough to wake the dead so we didn't have any more misunderstandings. Clay appeared, dressed, and firmly in place was his granite-faced expression. That attitude. Honestly, he'd definitely never get crow's feet; he didn't smile enough to wrinkle.

"And good morning to you too," I said, sarcasm evident. "You do a nice imitation of resting bitch face, Clay. Takes some practice, so you've gone and managed to nail it. Well done."

With an eye roll, he moved to the side, so I pushed past him, and went into the living room to warm up by the fire. Problem was, being covered from head to toe in plastic did have its disadvantages at times like this. I wanted to be warm, but I didn't want to melt—it was a very fine line.

"Do you always insult people like that?" he finally managed.

I put a hand to my chest, and feigned surprise. "Me?"

"You."

"I was merely stating a fact." I smiled sweetly. "So what's the plan today?" I was all for following Clay's lead but I liked to be organized, and when you worked with someone who spoke in monosyllabic bursts, it was hard to know what the day would bring.

"The plan is work. That's all you need to know." He ran a hand through the dirty blonde of his hair. And managed to do the hot-guy scowl that he'd probably perfected since he was a teen. I could see girls falling for that damn bad attitude, wanting to get the cold steel of his heart, but not me. He was so gruff he was almost a billy goat.

My plastic garb was becoming uncomfortably warm, and shrinking against the back of my legs. I took a step forward just as Clay did and we bumped into each other with an *oomph*.

"That old trick, Lucy?" He cocked his cocky head. "How many times can one girl *accidentally*—" he made air quotes "—bump into me before it becomes obvious?"

I gasped. "I think you're the one with spatial issues, Clay." I glared at him. "I haven't forgotten the old creep up behind me like a serial killer thing! Are you *trying* to intimidate me? Because it isn't working." How did we get to this point so quickly? He had a way of making me speak up and say things I normally wouldn't. I'd given myself a stern talking-to about swallowing back retorts. I had to keep this job, but sometimes it seemed impossible. *He* was impossible.

He blew out a minty breath. "Can we actually work? Or are you going to spend the day crashing into me to get out of doing anything?" With his hands on his hips, he wrinkled his brow, as if I was the one holding up the day's progress, when it was in actual fact him.

"You're such a jerk," I said under my breath, though he was standing close enough to hear it.

"It's been said before." He turned and picked up some kind of ginormous hammer. "Time to rip up the floor in my bedroom."

I followed his muscled frame to the back of the cottage, wishing my heartbeat hadn't sped up on account of watching the way he strode, the denim of his jeans fighting against his body. If he wasn't so unlikeable I'd probably have appreciated the fine sight in front of me but I had a certain standard when it came to men, and bad-attitude, bad boys were not on the list. That kind of guy could only spell trouble, and I didn't need drama.

"What are you doing?" He turned, giving me a hard stare.

Bewildered, I said, "Umm, helping you?"

"Is the fence line finished?" The ivy. I'd been going back and forth between jobs, and still the ivy clung to the posts in places. The thought of heading outside in the icy winds was enough to make my stomach drop. But I'd said I'd work as hard as anyone else.

"Right," I said with forced cheer. "I'll be back."

I zipped up my jacket, and spun to leave. As I stepped from the porch, snow drifted down like confetti, and despite the cold, the vista ahead was truly breathtaking. I sized up squares of the view, committing each nuance to memory so I could paint it later. The way the maples in the distance stood earnestly, dappled with white flakes, the wind blowing through them, like a whisper. I'd never felt so attuned to any place before... almost like I'd been here in another life. My mom would have a field day with that line of thought.

When I reached the fence posts that were still ivy-covered, much to my surprise, there was a pair of thick gloves, and a thermos that was hot to the touch. Glancing over my shoulder, I half expected Clay to be watching me from the cottage. He wasn't. But a small part of me softened toward him a little. He must've seen the damage to my hands that I'd taken pains to hide. Perhaps that stone-cold heart of his had a little warmth to it after all?

Pulling on the gloves, I bent and set to work, determined to get the posts free of ivy as quickly as possible—though, the ivy was beautiful to me. The green foliage, with its white maze-like veins, each leaf a small miracle, a thing of beauty. Maybe Clay wanted to fireproof the edge of the property by removing anything that when dry was combustible come summertime, but to me, ripping out these leaves hurt. I was killing something of value, no matter whether he thought of it as a weed or not. My mother had ingrained into me the mantra to live and let live, so destroying something as pretty as ivy hurt a little.

***

After hours outside, the cold settled into my fingers, despite the gloves, and my stiff hands seized. With great difficulty, I twisted the thermos open and took a swig of sweet milky coffee. I teetered, wondering whether to go inside, or continue on. My nose was numb, and my ears were not faring much better.

Surely Clay wouldn't expect me to stay outdoors all day in a blizzard. I trudged back to the cottage, taking the handful of tools with me.

Clay was in a bedroom, which was clear of any furniture. He was swinging an oversized hammer, bringing it back to the floor with a momentous *thwoar*, the boards breaking and flying into the air, like a shriek.

I stood back and watched him heft the weight of the hammer, beads of perspiration edging his brow line.

After a few minutes, and a huge stack of broken floorboards, he stopped and noticed me hovering. "You get it done?"

He took his sweater off, and wiped his face with it, that body of his encased in a tight tank top again. "There's still more, it's just… I needed to warm up for a bit. Thanks for the gloves, and the coffee."

He ignored me, and held out the hammer. I looked at it, and then him.

"Well?" he said.

I blinked. "You want me to try?"

"Be careful. The sledgehammer might be too big for you."

I scoffed. "Why, because I'm a girl?"

He tutted and went to the window, wrenching it open. Dust from the floorboards swirled, making the room cloudy. "Because it's *heavy*."

I tried to heft it over my shoulder like Clay had done but I only got as far as my waist. I tried once more, determined to get it into the air and back to the floor with a force that would shake his insides, but it was impossible. "It's too heavy," I conceded. With the stiffness of my hands, and the blisters, I couldn't get a strong enough grip on it.

"Go grab the broom and start picking up the debris."

"Aye, aye, Captain." I gave him a mock salute, trying to get him to at least smile, and went to find the broom and a bag big enough for rubbish.

When I returned Clay was swinging the hammer like a man possessed. His hair flew up from his face with each heave, and every single muscle in his arms flexed and rippled. Muscles like that had never appealed to me before, but with Clay, it was all hard-working, well-earned brawn and if I forgot about his personality, I had admit to feeling a trifle electrified watching him.

"Clean by the window," he said. "And then I'll smash out the section by the door, and we're done."

I swept the broken shards of wood into a corner before bagging it all up. Once again, I was covered in a thick layer of dust that had probably been living under the floorboards for a century or so.

Clay balanced on wooden beams that had held the floorboards in place. Underneath you could see earth. The house was so old there'd been no slab, just thick floorboards to protect it from the elements. He gave me a lopsided grin as he wobbled and then regained his balance.

I picked up the rubbish bag, and stood in the hallway as Clay tackled the last bit of flooring by the doorway. A few more sexual-sounding moans escaped his mouth as he worked, so I forced myself to look at the patch he was smashing to oblivion rather than directly at him.

"Clay, wait!" I yelled, pointing. There was a metal chest just visible under the last of the flooring he was about to hit. "It looks like a treasure chest! What do you think's inside?"

Annoyance at my interruption flashed in his eyes. "No idea."

"Well pick it up."

"Who cares, let's keep going."

"What? You're not going to leave it there, are you?"

He shrugged. Not even an ounce of curiosity in him.

"I'll pick it up." I jumped down to the hard ground, and bent to inspect the chest.

Whoever had buried it had obviously done so for a very good reason. It could be Clay's uncle's, or someone from even further back. My fingers tingled to open it and see what secrets we'd find.

"It's light." With one quick movement I lifted it, and placed it by the door, the only space that still had enough flooring to rest it on. With as much grace as I could muster, I swung a knee up and groveled on the floor, until I was teetering. Clay grabbed my elbow, and helped me stand. "Thanks," I said.

I pulled my coat tighter, cold from the air melding through the open window and the chill from the exposed ground. "Well, are you going to open it?" The chest was tarnished with age, and I wondered what kind of mystery it contained.

"Why? It's probably just full of junk like everything that's scattered around the farm."

"What if it's not? I can't see someone hiding a chest here if it was only junk." Secreting a box under floorboards screamed desperation to me. Whoever hid it there didn't want anyone to find it. Clay turned his back to me and threw the hammer down on the rotted floorboards once more. I waited for him to swing it safely back up before I tapped him on the shoulder.

"Clay, aren't you intrigued?" What if it contained something pertaining to the farm? The inner child in me thought of myths from fairy tales: a magic lamp, rubies and emeralds, a map. But really, I thought it might be something sentimental, something secret.

He spun to face me, frowning. "Not really."

"Can you just open it? Then we'll know whether to keep it or put it outside with the other trash." I wondered if Clay was being obtuse just to rile me.

He huffed, "Fine, if it'll stop you harping on about it."

I rolled my eyes. "Just open it."

He made a show of dropping the sledgehammer on the floor with a thud, wiping his face, stepping around me exaggeratedly so we didn't touch, before finally bending down and creaking the box open.

I held my breath. Inside piled somberly were a stack of red leather-bound journals wrapped tightly with twine, as if it would stop their secrets from spilling out.

It was all I could do not to gather them up and flick through them. "Whose were they, do you think? Your uncle's?" The red leather had faded, but you could see they'd been loved, the way they were tied, each loop exact and bound together, like they mattered to someone.

Clay shrugged. "No idea, I never met the man."

"You never met him?" Surprise made my voice rise.

"No, why? Does that bother you for some reason?" Again, he pulled the hem of his tank top upward, and wiped his face with it. When he exposed his body like that, it was hard to focus.

Instead, I stared down at the journals, wondering why someone would choose to hide them there. "No, it doesn't bother me, but you inheriting the farm, I just presumed..."

"You presumed wrong."

I ignored his steely-eyed gaze. "Are you going to read them?" I asked. Honestly, it was like talking to a rock. A very subdued rock.

"What for?"

"You're not the least bit curious?" His eyes were bright, and even though he was feigning disinterest, his expression told a different story. I continued: "What if it's a brilliant manuscript? Or someone's memoir? Wouldn't you want to read it?"

"No." And just like that, his granite face returned. "Now can we work?" He motioned to the remaining piece of flooring.

"Can I borrow them? I'll read them and report back."

He waved me away. "You ever think they might be blank?"

"Doubt it. Don't see anyone hiding a box of old journals under the floor if they weren't full of secrets."

"Fine, take them. But bring them back, once you're done."

"Fine, I will."

"Work?" He motioned to the hammer.

"Right." I shifted the box so it was out of the way and continued picking up shards of wood, feeling a tad victorious.

***

Back at the bed and breakfast, half delirious with fatigue, I called Mom, eager to see how she was doing and fill her in on everything. First I tried the home phone, and was rewarded with a robotic voice telling me the phone was no longer connected. Shoot. Had I forgotten to pay the bill? Next, I tried Mom's cell phone.

She answered after the second ring. "Precious! How are you?" A TV sounded in the background, a news anchor's voice, deep and serious.

"Oh my goodness, Mom. I'm beat! How are you?"

She laughed, which came out like a croak. "Peachy, honey. So what's the love god like now? Has his attitude improved?"

It was so good to hear her voice. "The love god? He wishes. He's so frosty, he's almost a snowman. But it's still fun in some weird way, to tease him. He really doesn't understand humor. It's all work, work, work, and a few grunts, and moans about well, work. Suits me fine, I'm only there to make a buck anyway."

"Young love." She giggled. "Have you painted?"

"Oh Mom, yes! And it's almost like someone else is holding the brush... which is great because my hands are a mess. But it's like..." I struggled to sum up how it felt to paint scenes here, the magical world I'd stumbled on, the colors, the light so different from Detroit. "It's like, the darkness of my past paintings has been replaced with an epic kind of... translucence. Does that make sense?" I hadn't acknowledged it until that moment that my art had morphed into something deeper, more complex than before. And instead of using angry hues of scarlet, and charcoal, I daubed the canvas with bolder choices: limes, teals, dashes of cobalt, splashes of rose. Aside from the beach scenes I'd painted for Mom, my previous work was almost volatile, hostile, as I dealt with pain I couldn't outwardly show.

"It makes perfect sense, honey. I had an inkling it might be so." Her voice returned slightly slurred, a marker things weren't going as great as she made out. "You need to have a nice long bath, and throw in some Epsom salts. That will help your aching muscles, and those precious hands of yours."

Mom had an old-fashioned remedy for everything, from washing my hair in beer to make it shiny, to drinking apple cider vinegar for a boost of energy. "That's a good idea, Mom. I'll do that when I hang up. So how's it going with Aunt Margot? Is she coping OK?"

"Yeah, she's doing just great," Mom said, lowering her voice.

"Is she really?" For someone not used to the day-to-day tasks involved with Mom's care, it would take some adjustment.

"Well, of course she is. We're having a blast."

"You are?" Aunt Margot must realize her behavior toward Mom in the last decade or so had been callous. Maybe she was trying to atone for it now. It made me smile, to think perhaps they'd gone back to the way they were when they were younger, before Aunt Margot morphed into someone who only cared about money. But that kind of neat fix, the letting go of grudges, didn't ever come naturally to Aunt Margot. And on the phone, she certainly hadn't sounded like she'd chilled out.

"You stop worrying. I can hear it in your voice."

I held in an anxious sigh. "OK, I'll try. I just miss you like crazy."

Her voice softened. "I miss you too, honey. But things are fine here, same old same old, and nothing to report. Whereas you, I want to know *everything*!"

I absently plucked at the tassels on the bedspread. "I've made a couple of friends already. Lil and CeeCee from the Gingerbread Café. They're so sweet and welcoming, it kind of feels like I've known them forever. At first it was a bit of a culture shock, these people being so flamboyant, and comical, wanting to include me…"

"Oh, yeah? You're gonna meet a lot of people like that. It's the beauty of traveling. Tell me about them."

How could I sum them up in just a few words? "They're always laughing, and joking, wanting to fatten me up. Lil's teaching me to bake."

"Baking? I bet that's been such fun! So I take it the café's not like the diner then?"

They were worlds apart. The diner consisted mainly of frozen meals, zapped in the microwave, or hamburger patties grilled till they blackened, but at the Gingerbread Café everything was made from scratch. I laughed, and said, "Nope, nothing like the diner. The girls say the secret to their food is that it's all made with *love*."

Mom giggled. "I like the sound of your new friends."

"You'd love them. Hey," I said, "while I remember, I tried the home phone first. It says it's cut off? I thought I paid that bill a month or so ago?"

"Oh, darling, I gotta run. That's Aunt Margot back from shopping." A rash of voices came down the line; it sure sounded like a lot more than one person. "Let's speak tomorrow?"

"Sure, Mom. But you do need a home phone in case of emergency. Will you let me know? I can check the account online."

"I'll get Aunt Margot to check. Remember you're taking a break!" she said hurriedly.

I frowned.

"Goodbye, darling." And with that she clicked off. I stared at the phone for a minute. I hadn't had a chance to tell her about the journals we'd found that day.

Making a mental note to check the phone bill online, I went to run the bath, pushing the worry away as best I could. Otherwise, it'd build up into a giant ball of stress, and I'd end up with a migraine, which I couldn't afford to have, needing to lie down in a dark room until it passed.

But, Mom hung up far too quickly… Maybe she was just tired, or wanted to greet Aunt Margot properly. Shopping at this time of night though? I took a deep breath. It could have been for a quart of milk. Or filling a prescription? A light globe, even. They were both adults, and I was fussing over nothing. It was so hard to disengage from my role as Mom's carer.

I lolled in the old-fashioned tub, the steaming hot water like a tincture. My muscles had stretched and snapped to the point they throbbed in time with my pulse.

I'd thought farm life would be a cinch. A little garden work, some sweeping, maybe the odd hay baling, but not this. Heaving wood from one pile of junk to the next. Ripping down walls, pulling up floors, and carting it all away for hours on end so that my arms eventually numbed and I had to glance down and check they were still attached to my body.

With the bathwater lapping softly, I was tempted to close my eyes, and sleep, so I extricated my aching limbs as gently as I could from the bath, and threw on a robe.

I pulled the comforter back, and sank into the soft mattress with a sigh. Getting into bed after a hard day at the farm was bliss as my body became one with the squishiness of the underlay. The moon had only just risen, but it was almost lights out for me. I tossed and turned like a cat to get comfortable, and then grabbed the first journal from the pile.

The pages were yellowed with age, and musty. The first entry was dated almost thirty years before, the handwriting elegant with loops and swirls.

Time moves slow here. The winter winds squall outside in the pitch of black night. Almost as if she's here with me, talking to me the only way she can, through the elements. I miss her every second of every day, but more so in the dark of midnight.

I thought I saw her today, her reflection in the window as I wandered back from the copse of maples. I ran, ran like a man possessed, hoping to catch her. But the shadow faded as I neared. It's as though she's there, hovering on the edges of my life, in the mirror, the lake, the glint of sunshine on a piece of metal. I see her but I never quite catch her. Maybe I'm imagining it, but I like to think she's waiting for me. In this place or the next.

My chest tightened. *In this place or the next.* She died? The passage was poetic, haunting. Was the author Clay's uncle or a previous long-forgotten owner of the Maple

Syrup Farm? I flipped the page, careful not to rip the delicate parchment. I gasped. On the next page was the most exquisite drawing. It was a woman's face, close up, and even in faded lead pencil, her eyes were radiant; she was breathtakingly beautiful. My skin prickled. Was he an artist? The following page the writing continued.

I woke, like I always do, with the feeling that I'm being pressed from my head down to my feet. A heavy weight, it knocks the breath from my lungs, and makes me scrunch my eyes closed in pain. I lie there, unable to move, my heart sore with the knowledge I'll never touch her again. Never feel her heart beat next to mine.

Another sketch, of the same woman, this time with her lying in a bed, her hands under her head. The beauty of it took my breath away. I looked for the artist's name but there were no markings. I suppose he wouldn't sign his own journal. Imagine being able to draw like that... so detailed, and lifelike, I could almost feel her shallow breaths float from the page.

This place it will save me from myself. Nowhere else have I felt the vibration from the land, like a sign I belong.

He wrote so beautifully, but it was full of melancholy. Maybe as I continued reading there would be more clues as to who he was and I'd learn more about his art. Tomorrow, I'd sketch, hoping one day I'd be as good as he was.

My eyelids grew heavy, so I tucked the journal away, and fell into a dream-filled sleep. When I awoke, all I could remember were the colors, great swirls, and lashings of paint on a too-white canvas. Hazy visions, of her eyes, the girl from the sketch.

As though I knew her.

CHAPTER EIGHT

A few weeks later I was stepping into the Gingerbread Café to find Lil grinning and holding out an apron. My daily baking sessions had been a highlight, and I'd learned so much in those quiet mornings, while the town still slept, and it felt like Lil and I were the only people in the world. She was so patient, and explained each step carefully, waiting for me to jot down notes, or ask questions.

"In celebration of the Maple Syrup Farm running again I'm going to teach you how to make fudge. Specifically maple walnut fudge. It's easy, it's delicious, and you can go ahead and throw just about any flavor in and it'll work."

I pulled the apron over my head and tied the strings at the back. Lil had the bench laid out with ingredients, and mixing bowls. "Fudge sounds great! What should I do?"

"It's as simple as melting all the ingredients, and then pouring the mix into a baking dish and putting it in the fridge to set."

"OK." I opened a can of condensed milk, and broke up a block of white chocolate. Lil added them to a pot, and flicked on the flame. In Lil's kitchen I felt at home, she glided around me, fussing with things, and it was one of the times in my long day that I could just be me. My worry floated away—nothing mattered except the recipe in front of me. When Lil would show me a complicated technique, and produce a cake that was art on a plate, I was in awe. Her art and my art were vastly different, but our motivations were the same. She poured every ounce of herself into what she did, and you could see her passion reflected back in the dish. It was amazing watching her create something out of a few basic ingredients.

"What else?" I asked as she stirred the pot, the scent of the condensed milk sweetening the air.

"Add the butter, the maple syrup, and then the walnuts. You take over."

I added the ingredients to the pot and took the spoon.

"And remember, don't have the heat up too high or you'll scorch the chocolate."

I ducked my head to check how big the flames were. "Is that really it? It's so simple for something that tastes so amazing!"

Lil laughed. "It's that simple. Now pour that into the dish and we'll put it in the fridge to set."

With great care, I tipped the molten mix into a dish lined with parchment paper, and put the pot in the sink. "If there's not a piece of this left when I come back tomorrow I'll cry. I mean it, I'll throw myself to the ground and pummel the floor, like a toddler."

"I promise I'll save you some." She rubbed her belly. "It's not me who eats all the food, it's the baby, I swear it. It was that one time, I sat down to eat, and accidentally inhaled the whole pie and no one has let me forget it!" Her face was radiant with laughter.

"You're pregnant?" She nodded. "I didn't know! Congratulations." I hugged her.

She lifted her apron, and you could just make out a slight swell to her belly underneath her sweater. "Thank you. It's this little munchkin, you see. That's my story and I'm sticking with it."

I gave her a wide smile. "So if there's no fudge left, it's the jellybean's fault?" I pointed to her belly.

"Exactly."

We giggled as Lil put the dish of fudge into the fridge.

"Now that's done we can eat. All that talk about food has me hankering for something."

I wiped down the bench while Lil sliced bread and toasted it.

"So tell me all about the hunky Clay," she said, taking slices of bacon and sizzling them in a pan. "You always avoid my questions about him." She waggled her eyebrows. "What's he really like?"

"I do not avoid your questions about him!" I laughed. These last few weeks with Lil had taught me so much about friendship, and the way in which we bantered back and forth was natural now, rather than my first awkward attempts at fitting in. When the toast popped, I slathered it with butter. "For starters, he's the most argumentative guy I've ever met. You can't say anything to him without a rebuttal of some sort. But that might be because I find it hard not to disagree with him. He keeps the day's plans to himself… like some kind of power trip, and I tend to get uppity at him. I like knowing what's in store. But he prefers to bark out one-word orders, like Fence! Paint! Clean!" I did an impersonation of Clay pointing, eyes fierce.

Lil giggled as she tonged the bacon atop the toast, and added a slice of cheese, which flopped, melting quickly. She added a handful of peppery-scented rocket and a pinch of salt and pepper.

"So what's his secret? Why does he hide out there?" Lil's voice was light, and I knew she was more interested in what made Clay tick than idly gossiping. He was new, and didn't want to make friends, which made him stand out even more.

"I don't know, Lil. I think he's just one of those people who likes solitude. We found a bunch of journals hidden under the floorboards, and he didn't blink an eye. Wasn't the least bit interested in reading them. But I tend to think sometimes the whole broody guy thing is an act. I catch him smiling at me, or sizing me up when I lift piles of wood that weigh almost as much as I do, but then he catches himself, and turns away."

"He's a puzzle all right." Lil's eyes lit up. "What are the journals about?"

I wasn't sure if I was meant to keep the find to myself. Maybe Clay was intrinsically a private person, but the journals weren't his, so he probably wouldn't care. "They're mainly about a woman. I think she passed on. But they have the most intricate sketches accompanying the writing."

"Hmm," she said, absently. "Jessup was a lot like Clay. He kept mainly to himself."

"They must be his, then. The person who wrote them lived alone." I shrugged. "But whoever it was, their work is top notch. I dare say professional."

"Maybe you were meant to find them, being an artist yourself."

I blushed. I don't know why I was so shy when it came to even talking about my art. "Maybe. They're out-of-this-world good. I'm not even remotely close to that level."

She gave me a stern look. "I doubt that. I'd like to see your work. Maybe I could buy something from you to hang in the café. That way when you leave, we'll have something else to remember you by."

"Oh, no, no. I have a long way to go before my work can hang on anyone's wall." Just the thought was enough to make my toes curl.

"Why don't you let me be the judge of that?"

Some of my paintings were murky with grief, red with anger, or sunny yellow with love. They weren't good enough to share, and they told too much about me for me to feel comfortable.

"Soon," I said. There'd be nothing worse than Lil flicking through my portfolio and feeling compelled to choose a picture because she had to. I'd never be able to look her in the eye again.

"When you're ready," she said, giving me a dazzling smile.

***

When I stepped into the cottage my breath caught. The walls were painted, the floorboards polished to a shine, highlighting the whorls in the wood. Even the furniture had been re-covered and rearranged. If you looked from outside, the way the cottage leaned, its chipped and faded face, you'd never imagine inside was functional, and remodeled.

"Wow," I said, leaning against the door jamb. "This place looks amazing." The furniture had been his uncle's cast-offs, but Clay had re-covered the sofa in royal-blue velour and sanded back the coffee table, and lacquered it. I admired the fact he didn't simply replace it with new stuff. I had a thing about people ditching memories like that. I guess it had been ingrained in me to use whatever I had at hand, and not to waste even *if* we could have afforded it. By the front door there was a buffet I didn't recognize. "Where did you get that?" I knew Walt's furniture store was empty, and I couldn't imagine where he'd get something so well made around here.

"I'm a carpenter," he said. "Well, I was." His eyes shadowed.

"Was? What happened?" His mouth set into a tight line.

"I don't have that business anymore." He wasn't as closed off today. Usually he would have told me to forget it, and stalked off. I weighed up whether to push for more details. "Seems trust isn't always a two-way street."

"That doesn't sound good," I said lamely.

He let out a hollow laugh. "No, it wasn't. But I'm here now, thrown the proverbial lifeline."

So had the inheritance come at the right time?

"Will you concentrate on bottling and selling maple syrup?" We wandered back to the living room. The plastic cover was gone from the sofa, so I flopped into it, hoping to rest after the long walk to the farm.

He stood in front of the fire, and watched me, like he was deciding whether to respond. I waved a hand in the air to say go on.

"Yeah, maybe."

I sighed inwardly. To get Clay to participate in conversation was almost impossible. I hoped he was thinking ahead business wise, if he had no other options to fall back on. I changed tack. "I made some maple walnut fudge at the Gingerbread Café this morning. Lil's excited that she'll be able to buy syrup from you. She's a great cook, and I think she really tries to help people in business here—sounds as though it's tough to stay afloat." I knew I was babbling, but I wanted Clay to at least try to help himself.

"I wouldn't know. I don't go into town much." He tidied the living room, picking up strewn bits of newspaper, relics from when he'd painted the walls.

"Why?"

"Why does it matter?"

Here we go. He was so testy, all the time. "Well, I'm thinking of *you*, Clay. If your big old plan is to sell maple syrup, you're probably going to have to meet the locals, and tell them about the farm, since they'll be the ones buying it."

"They either will or they won't. I'm not one to get all pally with people."

"Geez, I hadn't noticed." I gave him an eye roll. "They're good people, they look out for one another."

"Look, Lucy, I didn't come to Ashford to make friends, I came here to fix up the farm. Shall we?" He stalked outside, so I followed behind, wondering what the hell had happened to him to make him so short with people.

I caught up with him at the entrance of the barn. "You think people will buy from you when you're so dismissive?"

He frowned. "Not all of us are like you, Lucy. Some of us prefer our own company."

What could I say to that? He was so moody, maybe it was best if he kept away from the people of Ashford, who seemed genuinely happy to band together and help each other out. "Well, I hope you find someone to work for you."

"You're not staying? Farm life not what you expected?" He strapped his tool belt on in the gloom of the barn.

"I'm staying." I pushed my chin out. "But not forever. Farm life suits me just fine, but I'm heading elsewhere eventually. Sure it's fun for you hiding out here, but after a while, won't you be bored?"

The tools clanged together on his belt as he walked outside. It was like playing catch-up, chasing after him as he moved on. "How *could* I be bored here? Look at this place."

It was breathtaking, the way the farm slowly came to life with soft dappled sunshine poking through clouds. The air fragrant with possibility.

"Yeah but what about night-time? What do you do?" From the amount of work that was done before I returned each morning, I knew Clay just kept on going. How he wasn't exhausted was beyond me, but didn't he want to relax? Have a beer with a friend? Head into town for dinner?

"I fix the cottage, or sort out the barn. I don't sleep much, so I work."

Obviously he was in much better shape than me, just hearing the word sleep provoked a yawn. "I fall into bed and sleep like a baby, a very loud, snoring baby. I'm amazed you don't as well with all the physical work."

We got to the fence line and Clay dropped to his knees near the posts of my nightmares. I'd spent so long on freeing them from ivy, they invaded my dreams. "Sleep tends to dodge no matter what I do."

"Doesn't it catch up though, and you eventually go to bed zonked for like a day?"

"No, never does. Anyway, now we're all caught up about our sleeping patterns, if you wouldn't mind, I'd like some help removing the broken posts so we can replace them. *If* you've finished your inquisition?"

I sighed. "Yeah, regular old chitchat can be tough if you're used to using a scowl to convey meaning. You'll hear no more from me."

***

We took a break for lunch. Clay made us sandwiches, which I wolfed down with an insatiable hunger. The hard work gave me an appetite I'd never had before.

"I only managed a few pages of the journals," I said to Clay, who was still chewing. Everything he did was measured, from the way he ate to the way he spoke. Often he stared at me for an age, like he was deciding if what he had to say sounded OK in his mind first, as opposed to me who blurted out any old thing to stop the conversation from stalling.

"What were they about? Farm life, and all its bedazzling glory?" he said, his face twisting sarcastically.

"*No.*" I stretched my arms behind me, turning my face to the winter sun. "Diary entries, eloquent and poetic. A man who'd lost his wife, or girlfriend. I don't know if she died, or just left. And beautiful drawings, you have to see them. Does that sound like your uncle?"

Clay shrugged. "No idea, all I know is he was a crazy old man. He didn't keep in touch with anyone except my mom."

I closed my eyes, the desire to sleep strong now I had a full belly, and time to sit down. "How did you know he was a crazy old man, if you didn't meet him?"

With a wave of his hand, he said, "Family gossip. I don't get into it much, not my problem."

He was infuriating. "But he gave you his farm? Aren't you curious at all?"

"Nope."

"Right." I bit into the sandwich, to stop myself from hollering at him.

"Let's get back to work."

I shook my head. What kind of mean-spirited person was he? A man, poetic and artistic, gives him his farm, his legacy, and Clay doesn't give a damn.

CHAPTER NINE

Back at the bed and breakfast, I was clattering around Rose's kitchen, a little more invigorated than I'd been for an age. After a month and a bit in Ashford everything still ached, but I was almost used to the heavy-legged sensation at night-time, knowing bed was close.

Mom had sent me a bunch of text messages saying she was having an early night, and not to forget to drink three liters of water each day, and chant some affirmations. She'd signed off with love-heart emojis, having just been shown them at the last hospital visit by a young nurse. I'd held off from responding in case the ping of the message woke her.

Rose sat at the table, sipping a glass of white wine. "Are you ready to be impressed?" I asked, carefully balancing two bowls of spiced pumpkin soup.

"I'm ready."

I placed the soup in front of her and grabbed a basket of sliced sourdough I'd picked up from the café on the way home. "CeeCee's recipe?" Rose asked.

"Yeah, how'd you know?"

"I've been a regular down that café for years now. You tend to get to know who cooks what. This soup's been a winter warmer favorite of mine for aeons."

"Oh no, so you can compare the two. Bad news for me!" I laughed. CeeCee had scrawled down the recipe for me when I'd stopped to buy some soup only to find they were all out. I'd wanted to make a nice meal for Rose, but something simple I couldn't mess up.

"It's delicious," Rose said, dipping her spoon. "All those long days, and you've managed to make a lovely dinner. Are you still enjoying the farm? I don't know how you manage all those hours."

I blew out a breath. "I actually am. While Clay's not the sunniest person in the world, he's fun to look at. And there's something inspiring about standing up, a crick in your back, at the end of the day and knowing you've achieved something."

Rose took a sip of wine. "We were all excited to hear the farm had a new owner. Poor Jessup hadn't been able to keep up the place for years. We were sorry to hear he passed on, but happy to know his farm would stay in his family and not be sold to some developer. We hoped maybe whoever took it over would continue to tap the trees, make the place new again."

"Clay says he was a crazy old man, but somehow I can't see that." I'd told Rose all about the journals, and she said they were definitely Jessup's.

A cuckoo clock in the living room chimed eight o'clock, so Rose waited before saying, "He wasn't crazy, far from it; he was a recluse. Didn't like to get out much, didn't accept any invites when people tried to befriend him. He was always polite about it, but that was just his way."

"Well, his nephew isn't much different, except he's not as polite about it."

Rose gave me a small smile. "The town, of course, was rife with gossip about what brought Jessup here, lots of conspiracy theories flew around town for the first few years, until his sister visited town, and brought with it his story—well a version of it anyway. Word was, he'd lost his wife in an accident, and retreated to the farm, which had been vacant for a long time—so long most locals weren't sure who'd owned it previously. Jessup was so mired in grief, we all just backed away, and hoped he'd come to town when he was ready. But he never did. That sister, the one who visited all that time ago, would be Clay's mom."

So many secrets for such a small town. "What did you make of it all?"

Rose put a hand to her heart. "He was a shadow of a man by the time I met him. Like the life had been zapped out of him... But he was nice, just lost, and broken by then. He sold maple syrup, so eventually he had to chat to locals, but he still held back, didn't make small talk for the sake of it."

"You think he would be proud his farm's getting fixed up?"

"I think so, dear. He had plans for that place—that was one of the only things he talked about that brought some color back to his face. But age got the better of him. And by himself, he just couldn't do it. He wouldn't accept help from anyone. Some people are just private like that."

I buttered a piece of bread and dipped it into my soup. "That explains all the half-done projects around the place. He must have struggled to do it all."

Rose placed her wineglass down, and said, "People say they see him there, at dusk, a silhouette by the maples. But it's just the memory of him they're seeing. That's where he always seemed to be, right near those trees, almost as if he was talking to them."

My skin broke out in goose bumps at the thought. He was still there in spirit. Wandering behind us, stepping lightly on our footprints. CeeCee had said something similar about Jessup when we met on the bus. It was a bittersweet notion, that the man loved that place so much he was loath to leave, even in death.

"Did you ever see him painting or sketching?" I asked.

She cocked her head, thinking. "No, but then, I only ever saw him by the applecart. That doesn't mean he didn't. Who knows what he did behind closed doors. Gives me comfort thinking he had something like that to pour his heart into."

"There's something about his work," I said. "I was flicking through it again, and it's almost like I recognize it, but how could I?" The style, the complexity, it was as though I'd seen it before. It was the way he accentuated the woman's eyes, so full of depth, so intricate that it was hard to focus on the rest of the drawing, almost as though the eyes told their very own story—the reflection in them, the density. But an old farmer? I didn't know any artists with the name Jessup. Still, that nagging feeling irked me.

"Do you think it's a sign you should be concentrating on your work more, dear?" She gave me a half smile. "There's no point wasting a gift like yours. You can't keep it secret forever, can you?"

I'd shown Rose a sketch I'd done the year before of some yellow daisies, because she was a flower fanatic. She had such a gentle way about her, I'd felt confident enough to see what she thought. "You think it's fate that I found the journals that just so happened to be full of sketches?"

She laughed, and dabbed at her mouth with a napkin. "I certainly do."

"My mom would totally agree with you, Rose." She believed nothing was coincidence, just invisible arrows from the universe, directing your life if you kept an eye out for them. "Lil said the same thing about my art."

"Time to be loud and proud about what you love."

The night before I had studied the sketches in the journals for so long my vision had blurred, trying to break down his technique, and see how he managed to make the girl's face so soft, yet so lucid, like she was real. Compared to him, I was an absolute rookie. I could learn a lot from his work. And I felt honored to be able to gawk at the sketches, uninterrupted. It was like a gift.

"It's so nice to have someone to sit down and eat dinner with," Rose said.

I gave her hand a pat. "Tomorrow I'll make something fancier."

"It's lovely having you here, Lucy. And don't you worry about cooking, let me make something for you. You can't work all day and then trudge home and do more."

I went to protest when Rose's gaze flicked to the bench that was covered with discarded pumpkin skin, open jars of spices, and an alarming number of dirty pots since I'd only made a so-called one-pot soup. "Oh, I was going to clean all that up," I laughed.

"You just walk home safe and sound, and I'll have something nice waiting."

***

After a quick shower, I dived into bed, eager to read the journal before the sandman found me. The comfort of the bed was a sure-fire eye closer.

Tapping for maple syrup has given me purpose. I feel an affinity for the ancient trees. The sugar season is short, only six weeks or so. These thick-trunked trees provide for me. It's like a kind of alchemy, making their water-like liquid into thick luscious syrup. It's a lot of work, there are so many of them. But I talk to them. They're like friends standing guard over me. I can't lose a drop of their precious nectar—it would be an insult to them—so each day I trek over and empty their overnight hauls. It's like a present from them to me.

It's a science getting the spiles in at the right angle, and then taking the fluid and boiling it slowly to the exact right temperature. One misstep and the batch is ruined. I take things slowly; I will not waste a drop of what my maples produce for me. My arthritic hands make everything laborious, and sometimes fear seizes me: I won't be able to tap them soon. My body slowly gives up on me. Each day there's a new concern, legs that don't bend right, a heart that misses a beat. But I have to try.

Their trunks are luminous at night when the moon shines. Stars glitter above showing me the way. When nightmares collar me, I wake sweating, my heartbeat erratic, I go to them. Talk, as though they're listening, my secret keepers, my friends who don't judge me.

In the sleepy mornings, with my journal in hand, and my back against a tree, I write in the hope that it heals me somehow. Some days, the darkness doesn't come, and I think it's because of them, the maples. I sit, soaking up their energy like a panacea. Being that close it's almost as though they understand my pain and absorb some of it. The crazy ramblings of an old man, in love with some trees.

When I can't see through the fog of the past, I work. Until sweat drips into my eyes, and my hands ache. When I'm stooped over like the old man I've become, then I call it a day. I can sleep then, dreamless and weightless.

It was as though I absorbed his words, felt the essence of his pain. The maples were like magic for the old man. I'd make Clay listen. I wondered if he knew the trees only produced for six weeks. Timing was everything, when it came to the syrup.

His next sketch was of the maple trees, with spiles embedded into their trunks, and a bucket hanging over it to catch the drips. Could it be that simple to tap them? My breath caught when I noticed a woman in the far left corner. He'd drawn her sitting by the lake, hands clasped around her ankles, a voluminous skirt draped around her. Again, the detailed eyes, almost like if you stared long enough she'd come to life. I *must* have seen his work somewhere before, I kept getting that shiver of recognition. Adele would know; I'd learned almost everything art-related from her.

I closed the journal and ran a hand over the cover, hoping the old man had found peace eventually at the farm, and dialed Adele, mentally calculating the time difference from America to Paris, and hoping it wasn't the early hours of the morning.

Adele answered, "*Oui?*" Her voice was hazy with sleep.

"Whoops," I said, realizing I'd counted the hours the wrong way, and it would be just after six a.m., instead of six p.m. "Sorry, Adele, I didn't mean to wake you."

Her voice came back brighter. "Lucy, is that you?"

"Yes," I laughed, she dropped the French and continued in English. "Oh my word, how are you? I've been expecting a phone call ever since your mom rang." Adele's words came out thick and fast, like machine-gun fire.

"I've been meaning to ring but things have been hectic."

I heard the rustle of bed linen. "You should have heard her, Lucy. She's excited that you might apply for the institute. She hasn't sounded that upbeat since your first day at high school." Adele had met Mom on the front steps of school. Back then her condition was still manageable, not as noticeable, without the wheelchair, and the rasping breathing. It was so good to hear Adele's voice, someone who knew us, and what life had been like.

"I know," I said softly. "It means so much to her. But I haven't decided yet. I'm not sure if I'm ready, and I don't want to blow my chances, submitting work that's not right."

Adele's voice softened to a honeyed tone, "You're ready, Lucy. Come on, I've seen your work; you know you are. One day she will be gone, we *all* will be, and the last thing she wants is you left with nothing but grief. You should apply, and see what happens."

I knew it was coming. I knew Adele well enough but the words still stung. "I'm thinking about it," I finally said.

"How's your work now you're out of Detroit?" Her voice was back to its brassy tone.

"It's evolved… like I see things clearer here. That murkiness has gone."

"Nothing like a new view for some perspective. So where exactly are you? All Crystal said was you were off on an adventure for the year, and perhaps winding your way to me, which I seriously hope you do." She spoke with emphasis.

"I'm in Connecticut, the little town of Ashford. Working on a farm if you can imagine!"

She laughed. "Like mother like daughter. That would suit you, all that fresh air."

It was so good to hear Adele's voice. She was almost like a second mother to me, and I'd missed our chats since I'd been in Ashford. "Yeah, Mom's already been at me to hug the trees, consider their feelings, you know the drill."

"I bet she's doing your tarot cards as we speak. I miss you girls." Her voice grew sad. "Maybe we can both travel back to see Crystal once your year is up?"

"She'd love that." Mom loved Adele's lively way of speaking, her forthright nature. "There's something else, though," I said. "We found some journals here, full of the most exquisite sketches. I think they belong to a man who owned the Maple Syrup Farm, but the thing is, he hid out there for years, didn't get to know anyone. But his work, it's familiar to me... like I've seen it before, but I can't place him. All I know is his name was Jessup."

"What makes you think you've seen it before?"

"The way he draws the subject's eyes. Wait until you see. It's breathtaking."

"OK, well take a pic with your phone and send it over. I'll see what I can find out. Until then, you keep on with your own work, you hear? And I want to know when you've submitted to the Van Gogh Institute. I'm well aware of the deadline..."

I laughed. "Yeah, yeah. I'll let you know. But in the meantime, I'll send some photos, and tell me what you think."

***

I didn't know that when I stepped onto the rich soil of the farm I'd learn a lot about myself in solitude. And I've learned about the trees, their moods, how something as simple as the pattern of the moon can shape the syrup they produce. How the stars above twinkle in a certain way when it's time to start tapping. I began the season this year the day after a full moon. The trees produced more than they ever have. The syrup is sweeter, more golden. Before I plunge the spile into their hardened trunks, I talk to them, warn them about what's going to happen. It takes the shock away, almost like they loosen instinctively, and allow me the privilege of pillaging their sap. I respect them and they seem to yield more when I explain my actions.

The syrup tastes like nothing I've ever had before. It can cure all ills, except heartbreak, and can become a magical potion in the right hands.

CHAPTER TEN

"He said the season only goes for six weeks or so, were you aware of that?" We were digging up an overgrown vegetable patch that had long been abandoned. The ground was rock hard and my shovel kept getting stuck.

"Yeah, of course," Clay said, dismissing me with a look.

"Well, I think we need some kind of plan, don't you?" His nonchalance bothered me. I wanted to know the plan going forward. Secretly, the idea of making maple syrup thrilled me. How a tree produced something so sweet and pure amazed me, and I wanted to be involved from start to finish.

"You're still on probation. How do you know I'll keep you here?" He threw me a sardonic smile.

"Actually, I'm not. Times flies when you're having fun, right?"

"What?" His eyebrows pulled together.

"I've been here over six weeks, Clay, and that probation period slipped past with nary a word from you." For such a trivial thing I felt like celebrating. We'd worked so hard, he hadn't even considered firing me, and the time had flashed past, my farm skills improving, and my body more able to cope.

"Well, aren't you lucky?" he said, a hint of grudging respect in his voice.

"Oh yeah, all my dreams have come true, thanks to your kindness, Clay." I shook my head at his brazen attitude.

"Yep, I'm the lucky one working a solid ten, twelve hours a day with Mr. One-Word-Joe."

"You ever think before you speak?"

Hands on hips, I said, "There's no point being coy about it, you need my help, and I want some answers about when we're tapping."

He let out a sigh, the usual impatient one he did whenever I pressed him for details. He glared at me with those deep, dark, mesmerizing eyes of his, which made my heart skip a beat for some unfathomable reason.

"We'll start getting organized tomorrow, *Miss Need-to-know-it-all.* And if that suits *Your Majesty*, then we'll tap a few days after that."

"Thanks for *emphasizing* all of that like I'm a child." I flashed him a winning smile. "The journals said something about…"

He waved me away. "Forget the journals. I want you to go into town, to the bookstore, and see what you can find about maple trees. All the gear is here, I just need to double check there's nothing missing."

The thought of escaping into town warmed me.

"Take the truck." He tossed me a set of keys.

"The truck?" I gulped.

"Can't you drive?" he scoffed.

"Of course I can drive! It's just I'm used to cars that, umm, are a little more economical size wise." And I only drove automatic, not stick shift. Maybe it was automatic?

"Off you go." He leaned on the handle of his shovel, watching me dither. I threw my shoulders back and walked faux confidently to the truck saying, "Please be auto, please be auto," under my breath.

The door squeaked open and I hoisted myself up. Goddamn it! I pasted on a smile and gave Clay a cheery wave hoping he'd turn back to the vegetable patch. No such luck.

With a deep breath, I turned on the ignition and hoped to God I could reverse out without hitting anything. The truck bunny hopped, and the wheels spun, while I desperately tried to wrench the stick shift into place. I went forward instead of backward.

I gritted my teeth expecting Clay to roll his eyes at my incompetence, but instead he materialized at the passenger door and jumped into the cab next to me. He slid over the vinyl seat, pushing his leg tight against mine.

"Here," he said, placing my hand over the ball of the gearshift, his palm resting on mine. "Push the clutch in."

I was hyper aware of his proximity. He was so close, I could smell the spiciness of his aftershave, and make out the stubble on his face. "Push it," he said again.

I stretched my leg, and held the heavy clutch pedal down. He rolled closer to me. "This is first gear." He pressed the gear upward, my hand moving under the weight of his. "This is second." Turning to me, the dark umber of his eyes shone with a kind of… yearning, or was I imagining it? Time stopped, our hands trapped together. I nodded mutely, in case he was waiting for me to acknowledge I'd heard. There was a subtle shift between us, and I couldn't explain why. "Third, and then reverse." He didn't take his eyes off mine.

"See?" he said, continuing to move our hands. "Can you feel it?"

I gulped. Instead of feeling the red-hot flush of embarrassment, I felt a stab of longing. The planes of his face, strong structured jaw, the fire in his eyes. He bit down on the curve of his bottom lip, and I wrenched my gaze away, worried he'd see something in me, a desire that I wasn't prepared for.

When he moved back across the seat, my denim-clad leg cooled, without the warmth of his pressed against it.

He jumped down from the cab, and said through the open door. "OK, start it up. Drive safe." He shut the door and tapped it twice, as if saying goodbye.

I twisted the ignition and hit the accelerator hard; the truck lurched backward. I reversed in a wide arc, turning the big beast around, trying to steady the thrum of my heart. I was grateful for the distance between us, as Clay's face was etched firmly in my mind. I'd never felt anything that powerful before, and as my breathing slowly returned to normal, I wondered if I'd imagined it. That flash of longing, of what could be, had stunned me senseless.

***

Giving myself a silent pep talk—*you can do this*—I drove Clay's truck into Ashford. It was like driving a tractor; it took all my strength to keep it on the road. There was no power steering so white-knuckled I gripped on tight, and tried not to veer off the road. My muscles contracted and shook with the effort. Laughter burbled out of me imagining Mom seeing me drive such a beast. She wouldn't believe it.

My mind kept drifting to Clay. When he stopped pretending to be fierce, and acted like a normal guy, everything changed. I tried to push the vision of him, face close to mine, our hands touching, out of my head.

On the main street of Ashford I spotted a car bay and wrenched the steering wheel left, scrunching my eyes closed in hope. Probably not the safest option, but when I blinked them open, I was parked close enough to the curb to call it a success.

The Bookshop on the Corner was dimly lit, bathed in a yellow glow from an antique lamp by the door. Lil had raved about Sarah the owner, said she was whimsical, and shy, and knew books better than anyone.

The door sighed as I pushed it open and walked inside. It was like nothing I'd ever seen before. Books were stacked haphazardly on every available surface, as though they'd topple over if you breathed too close to them. Small laneways like a maze crisscrossed the floor, with piles of books flanking each side. It was like finding an enchanted garden, only full of books. The higgledy-piggledy nature of the store was welcoming, and warm. How did they all do it here? They knew instinctively how to decorate their stores so you never wanted to leave.

As I approached the counter, all I could see were a pair of silver ballet flats crossed over at the end of slim ankles.

"Hello?"

The shoes dropped and a twenty-something girl sat upright. She had black bobbed hair, and thick bangs that accentuated her doe eyes. She smiled warmly, almost drowsily.

"Sorry," she said, brushing her hair down, as if I'd caught her napping. "I was halfway through this chapter and I didn't hear you." She held up a book, a bare-chested hero embracing a woman in a glamorous green dress adorned the cover.

"It must be good," I remarked, smiling. Imagine being able to loll away reading in the tranquility of the bookshop—what a wonderful life that would be.

"It is," she said. "But then, they all are to me." Sarah was softly spoken, and small, almost doll-like. "You're looking for…" She took in my clothes, my scruffy old jeans, and thick parka. "Books about maple trees."

"How did you know? Is everyone around here psychic?"

She laughed, and somehow managed to snort, which seemed at odds with her tiny frame. "Sorry, that always happens," she said. "It's my job to know books, but I had a phone call from a rather serious-sounding guy asking me to have a hunt through the store, so you wouldn't *waste time* here." She gave me a sheepish look. "But of course I told him finding good books cannot be rushed."

"Clay called?" My mouth fell open.

She nodded. "He sure did. I told him he's welcome here anytime, but he declined the offer, sadly."

"That's Clay," I laughed. "I've just spent the last few hours trying to get a shovel deep into the frosty ground, and all I can hear is the *twang* it made each time it bounced back up. Farming is hard! A few stolen minutes to read will surely help."

"Won't be long and the ground will thaw out. That should make the work easier," Sarah said, dragging me back to the present. She daintily stepped around books piled perilously atop one another, in columns taller than me.

I smiled in response.

"Follow me, lovely. I have a selection for you in the reading room. I thought you could sit there awhile and see which ones you liked. I'll make you a pot of tea."

In Ashford, no one hurried, they all made a person feel welcome. Sarah was more unassuming than the other girls, quieter, more like me. I felt at ease with her instantly. "Thank you." I followed her through the labyrinth-like store, to a small room off to the side. It had floor-to-ceiling shelves, crammed with books, and a fire in between. It was furnished with old high-back chairs with matching footstools. It was as cozy as it was warm. If I sat there reading, it wouldn't be long before I drifted off to sleep. The room had a languid atmosphere about it.

"Take as long as you like," Sarah said pointing to a glass coffee table where a bunch of second-hand books were stacked. "There's a few cookbooks about maple syrup, and also some about tree tapping, and the traditions behind it. I'll bring you that tea." She plumped up a cushion before retreating with a little wave.

The first book had a maple syrup farm on the cover. Almost as pretty as Clay's farm, with the bare trees, and lush snowfall. I sat down to read. There were recipes for snow taffy made with maple syrup and fresh clumps of snow. There were pictures of children helping make the taffy, their cherubic faces gleeful. There were recipes for maple candies, in all sorts of shapes, but my favorites were the ones that looked like maple leaves.

I read all about the traditions of maple syrup tapping, and how it came about quite by chance. I hoped Clay wanted to tap the traditional way when I gazed at pictures of farms tapping the high-tech way. They showed big, modern properties, where the trees were fitted with brightly colored plastic pipes that ran from the tree trunks all the way down to their factories—it took the beauty away. The trees looked as though they were hooked up for medical treatment, like the life was being sucked from them.

Sarah pottered back in with a pot of lemon-scented tea, and sat in the chair opposite. "Anything take your fancy?"

"I'll take them all," I said, happily. "I see there's a tradition for maple farms, a Sugaring-Off Festival. Once the season is over, and summertime rolls around they celebrate! Maple-syrup-flavored food, music, the whole kit and caboodle."

"Wow, I didn't know that," Sarah said. "You guys should host a party at the farm! That'll draw a huge crowd, I'm sure. We had a Chocolate Festival last year, at Easter time, and we were frantically busy. Brought a lot of new faces into the town, gave us all a much-needed boost."

Could we host a festival? My mind spun with ideas. If Clay consented to a festival, surely he'd sell the syrup he made. It would be good for everyone in town, too. "I missed a Chocolate Festival?"

Sarah laughed. "Afraid so. But here's your chance to host your own party!"

Doubt crept in. "How would I even go about organizing something so big?"

Sarah fussed with a stack of books on a small table, their weight making the wood of the tabletop sag. "Well, we'd all help out. There's nothing like a social event to get the town to rally."

"Do you think Lil and Damon would cater it?" Lil had told me all about their catering business, and how quiet it had been lately.

"Of course! They'd love to do it. You could charge an entry fee, and that'll cover costs. Maybe hire a band?"

"It would be a great way to help spread the word about the farm too. Clay could really build up a decent business…" But would he be keen? He was desperately private, but this would be an amazing opportunity for him going forward, I just hoped he wasn't too stubborn to even consider it.

"Read up on what they do at these festivals and let us know. We can help you hang up flyers, and start a Facebook page, that kind of thing. The sooner you start advertising the better."

"You'd all help out, just like that?" I said, taken aback. It would be a monumental amount of work.

She smiled. "That's what friends are for."

These people, they were different to anyone I'd met. They'd offered their friendship, their trust, without a second thought. I'd always been wary about new people in my life. That same old barrier I put up to protect myself. I didn't let anyone close enough to be able to hurt me. My father had left, as though I was as insubstantial as air. As a child, I'd struggled to come to terms with it. He'd been there every single day, and then he wasn't. So what were we to him? A stopgap until something he determined as better came along? With the Aunt Margot feud, and subsequent alienation of the family, it felt as though people abandoned us like we were yesterday's newspaper.

Could I fall into friendships with these girls, and then leave? Maybe it was time for me to stop worrying about anything other than living in the moment. I was missing out on so much, standing on the edge of life, waiting for something that might never happen.

"I'll ask Clay and see what he makes of the Sugaring-Off Festival." If he said yes, then I'd be committing to staying until around June or July when the weather heated up. At that moment, that appealed to me. It dawned on me that I was genuinely happy here.

"You just let us know and I can knock up some designs for flyers on the computer for you." She grinned.

"Thanks, that would be great. I can't believe you had so many books on maple syrup. I expected you wouldn't have any…"

She poured our tea and handed me a cup. "I'm a book hoarder by nature, so that comes in quite handy. I never throw books away. Their covers can be torn to oblivion, or the pages water damaged but they're still redeemable." She gave a fluttery little laugh. "Though not everyone would agree. But the books, well… they kind of speak to me."

She had depth, such personality, even when sharing her foibles. "What do they say?" I asked curiously.

She held her cup aloft and winked. "*Read me*, usually."

We both fell back into our chairs, laughing.

***

"Don't you think it's ugly?" I pointed to the high-tech method. "Tapping them that way?" I said to Clay, who sat opposite me in the warmth of the cottage. We were flipping through the books, learning all we could about the trees.

"Yeah, I don't like the idea of that. It's not how I imagined it would be. We'll do it the traditional way. It'll be more work, but it seems the right way somehow."

We agreed on something. At last! "While we're at it…" I flipped to the chapter about maple farm traditions. "In June or July, farms host a Sugaring-Off Festival, to celebrate a successful season, and sell some syrup! What do you think? Sarah said she'd help us organize it, and I thought Lil and Damon could cater…"

"No, no way," he said abruptly.

I frowned. "Can you just think about it?"

He let out a long, impatient sigh. "Lucy, what if the syrup doesn't work? We'll have all these strangers here to celebrate my failure. No thank you."

"What if it does work? We can always organize it after we've tasted the first batch." There was something driving me to help Clay. Once I left I wanted to know he'd be OK. If people knew about the farm, and when the syrup was tapped, at least he'd have an income. I was so used to worrying about money, after doing the math for Clay I knew he needed to sell every bottle of syrup he made, in order to last until the next season. The festival entry fee split with Lil and Damon would be another buffer for him. And then the maple syrup sales on top of that.

"I'll think about it."

For Clay, that was as close to a yes as I'd hoped for. I hid a smile. "Great. I'll make a list of things we need to do, just in case." His mouth opened to protest, so I quickly said, "A very small list." And flashed him a cheesy grin.

He shook his head, like he couldn't be bothered arguing with me. "What does it say about the fire pits?" he said, pointing to a passage underneath a picture of the vats of syrup bubbling away.

"There's chapters of information about the fires, and the right temperatures to aim for. I'll leave the books here. You can read them tonight." Then he could sit down, and relax rather than tackle another huge project before I returned. As fit as he was, surely he needed downtime like the rest of us.

"No, you read it." His voice was firm. With a slight incline of my eyebrows I read the piece about when to light the fire for the syrup, and how long it would take to boil down.

"Right, I'll get those ready," he said. "And what does it say about the spiles?"

Again, I read, half impatiently. He could have read his uncle's journals, and seen the sketches, which had all the details about the farm and how to tap the trees. "Your uncle does explain it better, in layman's terms. I'll bring the journals back?"

"Just read these to me. I'm not interested in an old man's musings."

I let out an exasperated sigh. "How can you not be? He gave you this place! Does that mean nothing to you?"

"It means everything to me." His face was dark. "But I don't need to know his private thoughts. Not all of us are as meddlesome as you."

"I'm not meddlesome! I'm interested. There's a big difference." Just when we were getting somewhere he had to throw in a comment like that. "You know people say they've seen your uncle at dusk walking the length of the maples, touching them, gazing up at them, like he used to do."

Clay guffawed. "I don't think so."

"Isn't it a beautiful idea though? Him being so connected here, that even in death, people still see him."

"They couldn't tell who they were seeing from the road. Idle gossip, another reason to stay away from town."

I held in a sigh. "They're good people, Clay. They respected your uncle, and his need for privacy. You're a lot like him you know, except maybe he wasn't as surly as you."

"Yeah? I can't see how they're good people when they sit round, jaws flapping about a dead man. Seems to me like they're bored. And you're no better if you're joining in." His eyes blazed in that special Clay way, but it seemed like bluster to me now. I was so used to it from him.

I lowered my voice to a more reasonable level. "They speak about him fondly, Clay. Almost as if by seeing his shadow, they're keeping a part of him alive. I've only met a handful of people but they *do* care."

"How is that caring though, Lucy? To me that's gossiping."

"What happened to you, to make you so closed up?" I faced him. Trying to read the look in his eyes as they darkened.

He sucked in a breath, like he was losing his patience. "Lots of things, Lucy, and number one was confiding in people. OK? Telling them your weakness, so they can exploit you quick as look at you!" He clenched his teeth against whatever memory his words brought back.

"Your weakness?" I asked surprised, and hoped he'd confide in me. Clay, all six foot, tough-muscled, intensely gorgeous, didn't appear to have any weaknesses, unless you counted his attitude.

He ran a hand through his hair. "Forget it. It's in the past, and the past can stay buried." His voice lost the steely edge.

Breezily, I said, "OK, it's forgotten." I flipped the book closed. "But there's no need to shut out the rest of the world. I'm telling you, you'll need the town behind you if you want to succeed here."

"Would you stop with trying to buddy me up with people? I'm not interested. I can't see how having people know my business can help me. And that's all they want, to know every little thing about a person, so they've got something to talk about other than the weather."

"That's not true!" My voice rose, hearing him talk about the town so blithely when he'd never given them a chance. It rankled me.

"You've been here six weeks, Lucy. How can you know them well enough to say?"

I stammered, trying to think of a way to convince him. "When one of their friends got sick they all took turns running his store. And they all had their own businesses to tend to. They did so well, they went and sold every stick of furniture he had! But they haven't quit there, the poor man lost his wife, and is grieving, so they're trying to work out how to produce an income for him when there's no furniture left to sell. That's just what they're like."

"I bet they're not all like that." He sighed. "What are they going to do to help him?"

I shrugged. "No idea. They're still trying to formulate a plan. He made furniture out of the wood of old boats. Everything handcrafted in his workshop at home."

And just like that he turned away. "Right." I swallowed a sigh. "When do you think the season starts?"

"Monday." He pinched the bridge of his nose. "I surely hope I'm right. I know it's all about the timing." His eyes went wide and for the first time I realized Clay cared. His ambiguity about the trees and how to go about tapping them stemmed from the fact he was worried he'd do it wrong. I was giddy with the thought of being part of a process, a natural wonder, and something I'd never done before. It was only Thursday; the next few days would lag until we could attempt the very first batch of maple syrup!

***

"Monday? You have to tell me in detail how the heck it works, getting the fluid from those lovely trees and somehow turning it into syrup… I mean, I can't even think how that works."

I wandered around the small bedroom, phone cradled against my shoulder. "It's all about the way you boil it down. I hope it works. What if we burn it? Clay won't show it but he'll be devastated, Mom."

"You just take your time, when it comes to the important part. From what you've said about Clay he's not one to rush, anyway. Do I detect a little softening of your heart when it comes to the love god?" she teased.

I went into the bathroom, put the plug in the bath, and turned the hot water on full. "As if," I said. "Well, actually, there's something about him, I must admit. A hot guy is no big deal to me, but I'm getting to know him, and he's a lot sweeter than he makes out to be, but he takes great pains to hide it."

"Honey, he sounds like a great guy. I've got a feeling about him, I don't know why." Her voice trailed off, no doubt she was planning the wedding or something.

I threw a handful of Epsom salts into the steamy water, and laughed. "Oh, please, you sound like CeeCee! She can 'see' everything too."

Mom cackled, loud and high. When she composed herself she said, "You know what? I am going to meet these people one day. I need to give them all great big hugs, for looking after you so great. I haven't heard you this sparkly in a long time. I can't tell you how happy that makes me, honey. I'm grinning like a fool."

I sat on the edge of the bed, smiling, as it struck me how animated I was here, how different I'd become, learning about me, by myself, in a new place. "You will have to visit here, Mom. We'll work out a way to make it happen."

"We sure will," she said, as if she'd already planned it. "I can hear that bath running—you go jump in the tub, and we'll talk soon."

***

I know I was one of the lucky ones. Not everyone has a love affair like we did. Real, heart-stopping, once-in-a-lifetime love. I'll never forgot the moment I saw her. I wanted to paint her, so I'd have her forever. My mouth must've hung open, like a guppy; it was like I was drinking her in. My fingers pulsed, wanting to rush home and pick up a brush, so no detail would be lost, but I couldn't leave, not while she was there. In case I never saw her again. My heart skipped a beat, at the very thought, so I approached her, and told her I loved her, and I couldn't live without her, not caring about the consequences of such an action.

She laughed, and her eyes, those eyes, twinkled and glittered like there was a whole constellation in them. And she said, "Well, why didn't you say so? Shall we dance?" And we never parted again after that night, until she was summoned by God.

Whoever this man had lost, he had her in his heart always. It was a real-life love story; I was blessed to read it. The next sketch was of the couple dancing, the way they held each other tugged at my heart. I almost wanted to look away, as it was so private the way he stared at her, almost like I was intruding. Curiosity won out, and I scrutinized the sketch up close, trying to garner if Jessup shared any facial traits with Clay. They had the same jawline, the same mouth, but aside from that, the rest of their faces were unique to them.

I took my sketch pad out and picked up a pencil. I smudged the thin lines, and attempted to draw the man, but when I appraised the picture, the face staring back was Clay's, with his unfathomable eyes, and complex features. His strong hands, and tense shoulders. I'd seen him smile, and laugh, when he was caught unawares, so I flipped the page and drew him like that instead. It was a revelation—my heart flipped, and I was glad that no one could see me.

There was something about him, some pull he had, and I could admit to myself in the privacy of my room, that I wanted to know him, all of him. Despite the façade, the tough, surly Clay wasn't real. I'd seen enough people pretending in my life to know that for sure. Hanging around hospitals will do that to a person.

Something had happened to Clay that made him fold in on himself, to become the person he thought would keep people away. To hide his so-called weakness. What that was though, was anyone's guess.

CHAPTER ELEVEN

Friday appeared, like any other day, under the cover of darkness. Early March and it was still cold out, snowing and foggy most dawns, but the drift wasn't as heavy. It wouldn't be long, until sunshine poked through gray clouds, and spring woke the flower beds up. I longed for April, when the landscape would change, and I could paint bright-yellow tulip bulbs or the delicate mauve of the cherry blossom flowers.

I dressed in the small room, and made my way straight to the farm.

When I got the cottage Clay was sitting on the back porch, swinging idly on the love seat.

"Good morning," I said, and stuffed my hands in my pockets.

He gave me a half smile. "Hey."

"What's on the cards for today?" I tilted my head.

"Sit, take it easy." He gestured to the spot next to him.

Take it easy? This coming from Mr. Work Work Work? I sat gingerly next to him, making sure our arms didn't brush.

"I love it here," he said, quietly. "Sometimes I forget to stop and admire the view."

I flicked a sidelong glance at him. It didn't sound like the type of thing Clay would say. His tone was mellow, almost mellifluous.

I glanced at the trees. "It's even prettier the way the morning mist slips around each tree in the early light. Almost like it's shielding them."

"Yes…" He crossed his arms, his gaze into the distance. "Today, we'll clean the spiles for the trees. Some of them are rusty from sitting so long. We'll go through our checklist and make sure we're ready to go for Monday."

With a booted foot, he kicked the deck of the porch, the swing swayed softly.

"The journals say the best time to tap is after a full moon, and that you have to talk to the trees and warn them about what's coming so they loosen up, and…" I broke off, thinking how much Mom would get a tickle out of talking to the trees, and planning things around a full moon.

He put a boot down to stop the swing and faced me. "What?" He was incredulous but there was still a peaceful glimmer reflected in his eyes. Like he'd slept well, or something had changed in the hours I was away.

"That's what it says." I threw my hands up. "And it makes sense to me. If someone was going to poke a piece of steel into my trunk, I'd want some warning too. I was going to trek through and have a good old chat with them and see if it helps."

"OK, well feel free to talk to them once you're done for the day. I guess we can check when the full moon is. It can't hurt."

I resisted the urge to jump up and down. I'd expected Clay to clench his jaw and say I was spouting nonsense. I knew he *really* wanted to get this right.

"I already checked. It's on Sunday."

"Well we said Monday, anyway. So it's perfect."

"I can't believe I'm a fully qualified farmer's assistant and we're about to make maple syrup. Can you imagine what it'll taste like?"

"Sweet, I hope."

"I bet it tastes like love feels…" I broke off, embarrassed I said something so weird out loud.

He laughed. "Lucy, I can always tell what you're thinking. Did you know that? Everything you're feeling is written on your face, for all to see."

I blushed. "You cannot!" This was as personal as he'd ever been, but I was horrified. Was my face so open? I'd changed here, relaxed into this new life. My constant frown had disappeared when I wasn't pushing a finger in a doctor's face for some answers. I'd been run ragged at the diner; here was just as hard, yet I felt better than I ever had.

The fresh air, the deep sleep, it was… different. I missed Mom so bad my soul hurt—but each day got that little bit easier. I found myself enjoying it: the trip, the work, and what the future would bring. Sketching again—the way the pencil almost had a mind of its own—boosted me.

While Clay studied me, I thought about the sketch I'd done of him the night before. Had I managed to catch the right curve of his mouth? Without thinking I raised my hand, wanting to brush a finger along his bottom lip, to see what it felt like, to memorize it, before I caught myself and snatched my hand back. *What was I thinking!*

"See?" he said, smiling. "You just *have* to touch me."

"I do not! I was… I was…"

"What?" Humor reflected in his eyes.

Awkwardness shocked me silent, while I desperately tried to think of an excuse.

"Well?" he said.

"I paint, and sketch, and I was…" My throat closed. Now I'd gone too far and I'd have to tell him I'd drawn him last night. What if he laughed at me? He would think I was obsessed with him. Or even worse, what if he wanted to see it? "It ended up being a likeness of you…"

"You sketched me?" He raised his eyebrows, but the mocking tone was gone from his voice.

I blushed. "Yes, but I was trying to draw your uncle. And without much thought, I'd actually sketched you." Urgh. "Probably, because I was picturing the farm in my mind's eye," I added hurriedly.

"You're an artist?" He sounded impressed by the notion. It was the first meaningful conversation we'd had that hadn't dissolved into bickering.

"No, well, I mean…" I blew out my cheeks. Why did I find it so hard to admit that's what I wanted to be? Like I'd jinx myself if I told everyone, and it wouldn't come true. Instead, I'd be working in a dingy diner for the rest of my life. "Yes. I'm an artist, of sorts. I'm still learning."

"You know, I can see that about you now." He gazed at me, like *I* was a piece of art, like he was trying to appreciate it, see something in it.

"Oh yeah?"

"Yeah, you're different, Lucy. The things you say, the way you talk is like art. You just said, '*It's even prettier the way the morning mist slips around each tree in the early light. Almost like it's shielding them.*' I haven't known anyone who speaks like that before."

My jaw fell open. "How can you remember exactly what I said?"

He colored. "I have a good memory, that's all."

"What… like a photographic memory?" There was no way he could have remembered the exact wording, especially something I'd just thrown into conversation.

"No, nothing like that. I just find it easier to remember things, because I've needed to rely on it." His voice tensed up so I let it drop, still amazed at his recall.

"Your uncle's journals are spectacular, Clay. You should see *his* sketches."

He spoke so softly I could barely hear him. "I want to see yours."

"It's not finished," I lied, chastising myself for opening my big mouth. What would he see in the sketch? My heart wide open…

He gave my knee a pat. "Forget it. Work calls."

I flushed at his touch. Seeing him languidly looking at the trees, his expression soft with a type of love he had for the place, it was hard to remember the other Clay. The Clay who'd sat next to me for the last ten minutes was the one I wanted to know.

***

Later that night I burst through the doors of the café. "We're tapping Monday!" I screeched, scaring a small child, who dropped his cupcake, eyes wide in fright.

"Sorry," I mouthed to his mother who smiled back. "I'll buy him another one." Lil waved me away, and went to the display cabinet and pulled out another chocolate cupcake for the child.

Becca was at a table and motioned me over. "You look as if you've gone and won the lottery!"

If anyone knew what Clay's story was, it was his cousin. But from what CeeCee had said, they were as thick as thieves, and it was unlikely Becca would spill the beans about him. The fact he said he had a weakness though, made him more real and I wanted to know what he was implying. We all had a weakness, some more than others, so I wasn't sure why he held on to it.

"If only I could win the lottery," I said. Wouldn't that just fix Mom's life or at least make it a darn sight easier? "Clay says I've become a full-fledged farmer's assistant, and we're tapping the trees Monday." I was breathless, so I sat, and plonked my backpack on the floor.

"Gosh," she said. "You're the first one to stay on the farm so long. I knew it the moment I clapped eyes on you that you were the one!" Her eyes twinkled.

"The one?" I asked.

"The *chosen* one." She did some jazz hands and the usual Becca histrionics, like she was an actress. "Let me order some gingerbread coffees and we can have a proper chitchat."

She ordered at the counter and then returned to the table, tossing her curls over her shoulder.

"So," she said, clasping her hands in front like she was praying. "I've been meaning to drop past and see how it's progressed but, honestly, people come into the salon, and they get to talking and the day races away. By night-time, I'm not so eager to drive down that dark road, all those shadowy trees scare the life out of me. I've had to make do with Clay coming to my house for dinner and hear about all the latest goings-on at the farm."

"Maybe a weekend visit, then? You'll be amazed at how much it's changed. *I'm* amazed. Clay never stops working."

She chewed on a piece of gum so hard I thought her jaw might dislocate. "Oh, he's always been like that. One of those people who just *has* to be doing something. There's no sitting down, no relaxing for him. We're so different! My idea of heaven is watching a chick-flick marathon, and not moving from the sofa, unless I need more chocolate. I don't think Clay knows what rest is."

The street lights flicked on outside. "He said he doesn't sleep much. I wonder why?"

Becca raised an eyebrow and dodged the question like a pro. "Anyway," she said. "You must come see me at the salon. Your hair is wild, though it does suit you, all tangled and bed-head like that." She tapped a finger to her chin. "Some girls spend an age trying to achieve that look. What's your secret?"

"My secret? I'll never tell." It hadn't dawned on me to worry about my appearance, especially working outdoors. There was no point doing my hair or my make-up only to get to the farm and have the outdoors muss it up. Plus, I was more of a lip balm and pinch-your-cheeks-rosy kind of girl.

"Three gingerbread coffees, and three slices o' chocolate meringue pie, with a generous helping o' Chantilly cream, and some strawberry coulis. Don't mind, if I do," CeeCee cackled and sat with us, pulling a plate toward her.

"Thanks, Cee," I said, my belly rumbling just gawking at the piece o' pie in front of me.

"How's it going there? You still lovin' that place?" CeeCee asked, before taking a sip of coffee.

I swallowed a mouthful of pie, the sweetness of the meringue and the rich chocolate almost making me cry out in delight. "My body aches in spots I never knew I had. But today was a good day." I thought back to the morning, sitting by Clay on the love swing, when he was unguarded and real. "We're getting somewhere. Tapping starts Monday, and I can't wait to see what happens."

Becca hit the table so forcefully the plates jumped in fright. "What the hell is in that pie?" she yelled. "I've never tasted anything so good!"

CeeCee laughed. "You'll get used to Becca's dramatics."

Becca gave me a toothy smile. "Seriously, though," she said between mouthfuls, "Clay's raving about you. Reckons, with your help, he just might be able to make that place a success."

"Raving about me?" Somehow I couldn't see Clay raving about anyone, or anything.

She nodded. "Oh, yeah, he is. He was all *Lucy read up on how to tap the trees and explained it all; I know we can do it.* And *Lucy said she's an artist, and I want to see her work,* and *Lucy has this crazy laugh, like a hyena.* Lucy this, Lucy that…"

My mouth hung open so wide, I almost had to pick my jaw up off the table.

CeeCee turned to me. "Sounds to me like someone's been bitten by that old love bug again. Rife round here at times." She guffawed, and hit her knee, amused at her own antics.

I tried to cover my surprise by eating, but choked on a piece of cake. Becca jumped up and patted me hard on the back. "Sorry." I fumbled with my napkin.

Becca sat back down, and winked. "I think CeeCee is on to something. You've turned a shade of red that's so bright I'm almost sunburnt just staring at you!"

I took a huge gulp of the gingerbread coffee, which burned all the way down, doing my best not to snort it up my nose at what Becca had said. "No, girls." I swallowed, tried to compose myself. "You're wrong. So, so wrong. Clay hardly speaks to me, and when he does it often ends in a petty squabble."

CeeCee exchanged a look with Becca, her face crinkling into a wide smile. "Aw, now ain't that the sweetest thing? When two people pretend that little spark of love ain't there? Them there's the fireworks, you see? It's Cupid saying, here you go… celebrate!" Her voice turned wistful. "Some folk read the messages from the cherub all wrong, thinking, oh lookie here, I need to douse this fire 'fore it spreads." She tutted. "Love ain't that hard. You just gotta recognize it. And I surely do." She looked me straight in the eye. "Do you?"

I dropped my fork, which clattered to the floor. "No." What was this crazy talk? My belly somersaulted so hard I hugged myself to stop the sensation.

***

"So, what's the problem? You're starting to feel something for him, but you're fighting it, because it doesn't make sense? Is that what you're saying?" Mom's voice was heavy with confusion.

I sighed, it wasn't clear in my mind so how could I explain? All I knew was when I watched Clay something inside me flickered on, something I'd never felt before. "I don't know what I'm saying!" I laughed. It was crazy. I was crazy. "He's the most infuriating person I've ever met, so what the heck am I thinking? And… I really don't know a thing about him when it comes down to it."

"I bet you're painting him a lot, right?" In the background, I heard the usual blare of a TV.

"In oils." And they were magnificent. I had far too many canvases with Clay's face adorning them. Michelangelo would be proud of this specimen. He put David to shame.

It was Mom's turn to giggle. "This is the best thing you've ever done. How about you send some of those to the Van Gogh Institute? After seeing the photo of him you sent, phew…" she pretended to be hot under the collar "… they'll choose you first thing, no questions asked."

"Mom! You're saying use his looks to get me in!" And I bet it would go a long way too in their decision. But there's no way I'd ever part with those paintings. They were too private.

"Well why not! After all, it's your brushstrokes that bring him to life!"

I fell about laughing, missing Mom, but loving our conversations. It was almost as good as being with her, in fact better, because now we had something else to talk about other than my sad life in Detroit.

CHAPTER TWELVE

Monday morning, I was back in the café with Lil, jittery, and not paying much attention on account of it being tapping day.

Lil touched my arm to get my attention. "Now that the oats and honey mix is cool we can add it to our dough mixture and knead it." I shook the maple daydreams away and tipped the contents of the bowl she passed me into our dough mix.

Lil said, "Time to get your hands dirty."

We broke the mixture into two and kneaded it. We were making honey oatmeal bread rolls for the breakfast crowd. The town was lucky to have the café, everything baked from scratch, the menu endlessly rotating.

"So what happens next?" I grabbed a pad and pencil. I had started taking notes of the recipes we cooked together.

Lil kneaded like an expert. Her dough was already together and smooth, whereas mine was still a globby mess. "We let it rest for an hour in a warm spot and the dough will rise and double."

I tried to copy Lil, the way she rolled the dough into itself with her nimble fingers. I looked almost like a surgeon with my blue latex gloves on. My hands were still a blistered, calloused mess after farmwork.

"Then section into rolls, and bake. Easy!"

I groaned. "I'm going to miss these coming out of the oven as well!" Most things we cooked took longer than thirty minutes or so to bake, and I'd have to head to the farm, missing them coming out of the oven warm and heavily scented.

Lil laughed. "I promise I'll save you some. I really mean it this time!"

Whatever we made sold out during the hours I was away, or Lil ate the rest because she claimed the jellybean made her do it. Secretly, I was thrilled to spend the mornings soaking up her knowledge, and enjoying the friendship. And while the produce at the café was heavenly I went for the company more than anything.

"Have you been to the Maple Syrup Farm, Lil, besides the applecart out front?" I asked Lil, copying her as she put the dough in a bowl and covered it with plastic wrap, setting it aside next to the warmth of the oven.

She nodded. "I used to play on the farm when I was a child. A group of us used to tear through the trees and try our luck fishing in the lake. Jessup knew we were there but never said anything. One day, we turned up and there was an old tractor tire tied by rope to a tree. He'd made us a swing."

I slipped my gloves off and threw them in the bin. Lil motioned for me to sit while she made us breakfast, our morning as routine as the sun coming up. "That was so sweet of him." There seemed to be no end to the mysterious man. Again I wished somehow I'd had the chance to meet him.

Lil took flour, butter, and milk and whisked it in a bowl. "A gentle man, an old soul, from what I saw."

"In the journals, he talks a lot about the maples, and how they're his friends in a way."

Lil cradled the bowl under one arm and continued stirring it. "He *was* friends with those trees. As kids, we used to spy on him. He'd croon lovingly to them like they were real people. Once I'd climbed a tree, and got stuck there for hours, when he came and sat at the foot of it. I didn't want him to know I was using his 'friends' as a playground. He spent hours sketching."

So they were definitely Clay's uncle's journals. *Jessup*. A man who loved and lost, and lived in solitude for the rest of his days.

"It's so sad. In a way, I miss him, and I didn't even know the guy." How could I explain the connection without sounding like a fool?

With the clang of the frypan, and the element lit, Lil dolloped a pat of butter in. When it sizzled she poured batter in. "Pancakes with berries and cream," she said when I gazed at the mix. "Maybe the maple trees were enough for him. He surely did make the best syrup I've ever tasted."

"It's like I recognize his artwork, or maybe it's just I feel his pain. I don't know."

Lil flipped the first pancake. "What does Clay say about it all?"

I grimaced. "Doesn't seem to care either way."

"Men." Lil shook her head. "So today's the big day? Rested after a weekend of relaxation and ready to tap?"

I blew out a breath. "Yep. I'm nervous—I don't know why! I think because Clay's edgy about it too. Doesn't want to mess it up."

"It'll be in his blood. His uncle was a master at it, so I'm sure he will be as well. Those kinds of things seem to stay in families. Tapping trees isn't as hard as it looks, it's just a lot of work."

"I might just have a bottle of maple syrup for you soon, if all goes well."

Lil added more pancakes to the plate. "Well then, we're going to have to scout out more maple syrup recipes. You're going to need to learn to cook with it."

"Speaking of which," I said, "Sarah found me a pile of books about maple syrup farms, and we read all about the traditions, one being a summer Sugaring-Off Festival. Lots of maple-flavored food, music, and fun. Clay said he'd consider it, if the first batch is good."

Lil's eyes widened. "Now you're talking! So what's the plan?"

I shrugged. "I haven't really got one yet. But I was hoping you'd consider catering it, if Clay says yes."

"Are you kidding, I'd love to! We need to start planning... I know the syrup's going to taste great! We need to find some recipes." Lil wiped her hands on a tea towel, and took a notepad from next to the phone. "So, the first thing that springs to mind is some maple bourbon barbequed ribs, can you imagine how great that smell will be for people wandering around the farm?"

My mouth watered just thinking of sticky, sweet, fall-off-the-bone meat. "That's a winner, for sure, Lil. How many people do you think we'd need to cater for?"

"Hundreds," she said grinning. "The Chocolate Festival drew a huge crowd, and if you want to have your party in summertime, then I'd say even more would attend. We better think of some recipes that will feed the masses!"

"What about slow-roasted beef? With some kind of maple marinade..."

Her eyes lit up. "Yes! We could use Damon's rotisserie—he can be in charge of that. And the desserts, well, that'll be the fun part."

We abandoned our pancakes, and instead discussed various recipes, narrowing down a shortlist. Lil's face was animated, the thought of catering for hundreds of people inspired her, rather than scared her. I was swept along in all the planning, only once or twice thinking of Clay who hadn't actually agreed to it as yet. It paid to be organized though, especially for an event this size. There was no harm in making a plan.

***

Once I arrived at the farm, I dashed straight to the maples. Hazy morning light filtered through, landing in soft shards on the velvety ground. Feeling energetic, and a little crazy, I dashed from one trunk to the next, running a palm over and warning the trees of what was to come. If Clay saw me now, he'd peg me as downright cuckoo. The old man, eccentric, or just sensitive to his environment, had loved these trees. I wanted to follow his method, and if that meant explaining to these magnificent maples about what was to come then that was easy enough.

Laughter spilled out of me, as I ran. "Sorry," I said, breathlessly. "We'll try to be gentle. Sorry. Sorry. Sorry." I imagined the maples nodding, respectful that they knew their fate. It was like Jessup was standing behind me, in my shadow. My skin prickled, and all at once I felt as weightless as I ever had. For that brief moment in time, it was simply me and the astounding beauty of the trees, the light, and the feeling that life in all its forms was miraculous.

I kept on, my words tumbling out. There were so many trees to talk to.

***

"Ready?" I asked.

Out of all the maples we'd selected the ones with thicker trunks and decided on one tap per tree, rather than the standard two. We couldn't hide the fact we felt a certain level of guilt drilling into the majestic trunks. The trees we'd chosen were southward-facing, which meant they'd get the most daytime sun. Clay had asked me to study the books I'd got from Sarah and then grilled me endlessly about them.

"Ready," Clay said, holding a drill a few inches from the tree, pausing and scrunching his eyes closed.

I patted his back. "Well, what are you waiting for? We have hundreds to do today."

He narrowed his eyes, drill poised midair. "It... this is going to sound crazy, but I feel like it'll hurt them." A blush bloomed up his cheeks. I almost fell over in surprise. Clay was worried about the tree's feelings? Mr. Cold Heart himself?

"I've 'told' them what's coming," I said, unable to hide my grin, "as per your uncle's stipulations. I've warned them, crooned to them, hugged them even. We're tapping the day after a full moon... I think we're all ready." I too felt that same guilt, but I wanted to get it over and done with, fast, like ripping off a Band-Aid.

His mouth was a thin line, as he put the drill up against the trunk. "You warned them? When?"

I laughed, remembering the buoyancy I felt earlier that morning. That one snapshot of time where I was euphoric, and energized, lingered still. "Today, before I woke you up."

He cocked his head. "I was awake," he said, "I was waiting for you..."

"Well I was here, wasn't I? You'll thank me later when the syrup tastes sweeter."

"I bet it will." Something changed in his face; he didn't clench his jaw so often. He probably thought I was a little screwy, and felt sorry for me. "You like it here, don't you?" he asked.

Was he just dillydallying for time? I hadn't expected to love it here as much as I did. The farm felt different to any place I'd been, like I belonged here, and I had finally found my way home. I'd traipsed over every corner of America with Mom and nowhere had felt like this. It would take an aeon to put my past into words for Clay, so I just I said, "Yes, I love it here." He was a man of few words anyway.

A tendril of hair blew into my face, making me blink. Clay brushed it gently behind my ear, his lips parting like he wanted to say something. But he didn't. We stood mute, staring at one another for too long to be comfortable. Something had shifted. We both recognized it.

The trill of a bird overheard broke the moment. He shook his head as if dislodging a thought.

"Right," he said, his voice thick. "Where were we?"

I stepped away from him, needing a minute to catch my breath, as my mind scrambled with confusion. Nothing had happened, and yet... I was on fire with the thought of him. The guy who said so much with just a look. I was almost liquid, as a lushness spread through me.

"The trees," I mumbled, pointing, trying to stop the erratic beating of my heart. "It's time to tap them."

Clay turned away from me, and ran a hand slowly over the trunk. I'd never been so envious of a tree in all my life. The buzz of the drill rang out, as Clay pushed his weight against it. The shavings from the bark were a tan color, which meant the tree was healthy. If the shavings came away darker, like the color of chocolate, then we knew the tree wasn't right for tapping.

"One down," I said. There was no way I would have been able to drill into their beautiful trunks, marring them. On some trees you could see circular scars where they'd been tapped before, and had tried over time to heal.

"Put the spile in," he said. The mood changed, when we weren't staring directly at each other. It was easier to rally myself and pretend it was any other day.

I gave the tree a reassuring pat. "Sorry, Persephone."

He arched a brow. "Persephone?"

I rolled my eyes, an attempt to go back to our usual banter. "If you'd get over yourself and read your uncle's journals, you'd see they're all named. According to his squiggly diagrams this beauty is Persephone." I pointed to the next tree. "That's Athena, then there's Venus, and Artemis…"

"I get it," he cut me off.

"He named them after goddesses, and wrote about how each is unique. Isn't that the sweetest thing you've ever heard?"

Clay forced a smile. "Real sweet. Now can you put the spile in?"

That was as close to agreeing as I'd get from him. "Sure, let's get these babies in." The spile was the conduit that took the sap from the middle of the tree and dripped it into the galvanized bucket.

"This won't hurt a bit," I joked, and with a deep breath pushed the spile into the hole he'd drilled, all the while saying, "Sorry, sorry, sorry."

I hooked the bucket handle over the spile, and made sure the lid was firmly closed so nothing could infect the liquid before we'd had a chance to collect it.

"Let's take a photo," I said. I took my cell phone from my pocket and snapped a few pictures of the tree before taking a sneaky one of Clay so I could send another one to Mom. "Our first ever tap. I'm pretty impressed."

I swear he smiled. "Impressed enough to do your happy dance?"

I blushed to the roots of my hair. I had performed a number of happy dances out of Clay's sight when something compelled me to celebrate. Or so I'd thought. "You saw my happy dances?"

"Every one of them."

I pictured myself under the trees, dancing like some kind of wood nymph wannabe. "Oh my God."

"It was like..." he scratched his chin "... watching an interpretive dance."

Maybe my dancing was a whole lot better than I gave myself credit for. "What was your interpretation? A contemporary dancer?"

He guffawed, and quickly clapped a hand over his mouth. Once composed he said, "Well... at first I thought you'd walked into a spider's web, and that you were terrified, but then it kept happening, so I figured that maybe you intended to ah... move like that."

I was mortified. There was nothing to do except backtrack. "Why were you spying on me anyway?" I swatted him on the arm.

"I thought maybe you were low on sugar or something at first. And since you're an employee I felt it was my responsibility to watch over you."

I moaned. "You think I'm unhinged!"

He laughed, a full-fledged, deep sound that made his chest rumble. "I think you're *expressive*! It's like your body reacts before your brain catches up."

Well I'll be, Clay laughed. And not just a little bit. The proper, blood-pumping, belly-hugging laugh. Not only had I changed since arriving in Ashford, but so had Clay. He was almost a joy to be around. The tranquil air here had helped heal us both, or maybe it was the maples and the fact we were excited and on edge with nerves that made us react so differently. "Let's get these spiles in."

***

I let out a yawn, completely bushed. We'd tapped three hundred trees at least. Each tap it was easier not to let the guilt get to us and we eventually got faster, and more productive as the day stretched on.

Clay yawned in response, as if it was contagious. "Enough for today?" he asked.

"Yes." I nodded gratefully. Hopefully we'd tapped enough to make a big enough batch for the first harvest. According to our calculations we'd have plenty of sap to boil. We estimated thirty liters of maple sap boiled down to one liter of maple syrup, so it was best we harvested extra, since the season was so short. He needed something to sell, after all.

I was itching to go back to the first lot of trees and see if the buckets had filled but fatigue won out. We made our way haltingly to the cottage. My hands ached from the work, and my back wasn't faring much better. Clay looked as bright as always, as if he didn't just work for almost twelve hours straight.

"You must be starving," he said as I took my coat off and dropped it in a messy heap by the front door before flopping on the sofa.

I was always starving, a fact Clay had noticed. "Nope, too tired to eat. Wait. That was a lie. I could eat a horse and chase the jockey. Do you want to come into town? There's this new pizza place, just opened—we could share a pizza? I promise I'll only eat my half, unless you eat too slow, then all bets are off."

"Not for me." He folded his arms and leant against the side of the sofa.

"Why? Surely you need to get out once in a while?" He picked up my coat, and folded it. He was one of those people who liked everything orderly. "Clay, I'm about to wear that coat again, so there's no point picking it up."

He gave me a pointed stare. "There's a coat hook for a very specific reason."

I laughed, happily ignoring his jibe. "So pizza yes or no?"

"Nope. But I'll drive you into town. You worked hard today."

I clapped a hand over my mouth before saying, faux seriously, "Is that your version of a thank you?"

"Get in the truck." And again he smiled, not widely, but enough that I saw the white of his teeth.

"If I didn't know better, I'd say you were happy, Clay."

He lobbed my jacket at me. "Maybe."

"See? What was the point in folding it?" Honestly, he had to dot the i's and cross the t's. The only thing I was pedantic about was art, and planning ahead. Things like clothes, and dishes, and general tidiness bored me silly. Clay was the opposite, everything had a place, and he couldn't relax until it was in it.

The ride into town was mercifully quiet. Clay drove with one hand on the wheel and his other arm along the door frame. The radio played a country and western song, which I hummed, half to keep myself awake and half because I was unsure about how to make conversation.

Lights from town twinkled ahead. Store fronts lit up gray evening, like little beacons of wonder. The old truck rumbled down the main street.

CeeCee from the Gingerbread Café was on the sidewalk, closing the A-frame chalkboard to take it inside. I gave her a wave, as we drove past. She flashed me a smile.

As we neared the pizza place there were clusters of people lingering by outside, under big tables, or by benches set up along the sidewalk.

"OK here?" Clay said pointing to a car bay just further along.

"Perfect." I jumped down from the cabin and stood on the curb.

"See you tomorrow," Clay said. Before I could say anything, he inclined his head and rumbled away.

The scent of freshly baked pizza wafted over, making my mouth water in anticipation. I turned on my heel and went inside, shrugging away any thought of Clay. You couldn't get blood out of a stone, and it was time I learned to give up on a lost cause.

I ordered and went back outside, finding an empty table. The owner, Maria, had given me a steaming cup of coffee to sip while I waited and I drank it greedily even though it burnt all the way down. My eyelids were set on closing, and I forced myself awake with the mantra: pizza, shower, bed.

My bones cracked as I folded my stiff body into a sitting position.

"Lucy!" I turned to the familiar voice.

"Hey, Becca!"

She sat at the table, nursing a cup of coffee. "I meant to get back to the farm earlier to catch you before you left, but I smelled pizza, and the restaurant being new, I couldn't resist."

I laughed. "It smells divine." The scent of wood-fired pizza permeated the night air. It would be hard for anyone to resist. I did wonder, though, if it would take some of the Gingerbread Café customers away. Lil was always saying how tough it was to stay afloat. But the café was closed at night, so maybe it would add to the town, and not affect Lil. I hoped so, for her sake.

She pushed a stray curl back. "So how did the great big tapping marathon go?"

I let out a groan in response. "I've never been so tired in all my life. But it was great."

She tutted. "Long day, though. Sheesh, that boy works you too hard." She said it with a smile and I didn't doubt she'd already been on the phone to Clay.

I nodded. "We were in the moment, really. It was only when we finished the fatigue caught up."

"How was Clay? Not too grumpy, I hope." Becca took a sip of coffee, and gazed quizzically at me.

"Grumpy?" I raised an eyebrow and Becca tittered. "He was good today, happy. I asked him along for pizza but he said flat-out no."

Becca squirmed. "He'll get there."

Get where? Why wouldn't he make friends? There was being shy, and then there was being outright hostile. Clay was somewhere in the middle. "Why does he avoid town?"

Becca's name was yelled out. "Sorry, that's my pizza. How about we meet up for a proper chat soon? If I don't catch you at the farm we can meet back here for pizza and wine, or at my place?"

Again, his secrets stayed hidden. "Pizza and wine, a match made in heaven. Let me know when you're free." I waved goodbye as she tottered on high-heeled boots to grab her pizza.

My name was called shortly after Becca's. I took the box and trundled home. The lights were out so I crept to my room, placing the pizza on the buffet. I tried Mom's cell phone, and got her message bank. The pizza remained uneaten as a jolt of foreboding hit me. She'd expected my call, specifically asked for it. Maybe she was tired. Or not having a good day. Though usually she'd text at least to tell me. I opened the pizza box. And then closed it. I couldn't shake off the feeling something was wrong. I tried Aunt Margot's number, and it rang out. Dammit! Why did that woman even have a phone when she hardly answered it!

I sent Mom a long text and hoped by the morning I'd have a reply. I switched the light off, the thought of eating no longer appealing. What if something had happened to her? It was crazy—we'd had plenty of days we didn't speak but I couldn't shake the ominous feeling that settled heavy in my chest.

CHAPTER THIRTEEN

The next morning, I dashed past the café, and told Lil I'd take a baking rain check. She rushed out with a gingerbread-man cookie, and a blueberry muffin. "For the road," she said, winking. I gave her a warm smile, and promised I'd stop by later. I was ravenous after no dinner, and bit into the muffin. My phone buzzed. *Please be Mom.*

Pulling it out of my pocket, it lit up.

"Hey, honey! Sorry I worried you. The new medication I'm on makes me ditzy, well ditzier than normal." Her croaky laugh rang out.

Relief coursed through me at the sound of her voice. "So you're OK? Nothing's happened?"

"I'm fine, precious! Don't worry about me! You promised you'd go off and explore, and phoning home's only going to halt that enthusiasm. I want you to be free."

I walked quickly, puffing slightly as I listened. "I am free, Mom. C'mon. I worry when I don't hear from you and you know it. You wanted me to call you and, I don't know, I just had this awful feeling for some reason."

"Put it out of your mind, honey. I'm fine. I'm sleeping more, that's all. The new meds, they're gonna take time for me to get used to. So I don't want you panicking if I don't call. I'll text, and that'll be enough until my body sorts itself out. OK?"

My eyes stung. I knew she'd do this eventually—try and distance herself from me so I'd forget Detroit. Forget the merry-go-round of our lives. The hardships, the humor, the health battles. I was adrift without her.

One day, she would be gone. Is this what it would be like? This emptiness? I took some shallow breaths, grieving that day when I'd be alone in this world, without her.

Did she make me promise to leave, so I'd make some friendships, and learn to live without her, my one true friend, and the only person I ever loved? A bleak, gray cloud of loneliness settled over me. No one would ever be able to replace her, not a friend, not a location, nothing.

"OK... but I'm not going to stop calling or texting. If you don't answer, fine, but I'll try again the next day."

"I miss you just as much, baby, trust me. I'm dreaming of you though. I'm seeing you surrounded by trees, and love and light, and I know I've made the right choice."

"Love and light?"

She cackled. "So I'm a little mystical? I have to go, baby." A clattering sounded down the line.

"Where on earth are you, Mom?" I could hear people speaking, muffled, not the usual quiet of our apartment.

"Oh that's just the TV. Send me some more pictures, and we'll talk later. I love you."

"Love you too, Mom."

As I trudged to the farm with a heavy heart, I focused on the best times I'd had with Mom. In each and every memory was her face, her smile, head thrown back, shiny white teeth flashing. The sound of her laughter, like chimes.

I tried to shake off despondency, and live in the moment, like she'd do. It was like I was swinging between intense highs and lows. I'd never be able to shake the worry away, and being so far from Mom exacerbated it. Walking down the driveway at the farm I thought of her. She'd point out the birds, and know what species they were by their call. There was no point dragging my feet, despite the gloom I felt. Besides, I was excited to see if the maples had produced anything overnight. I wanted it to work, for Clay's sake. When he spoke about tree tapping, he changed. He relaxed his shoulders, and unclenched his jaw.

"Let's go," he said, when I stepped up onto the porch. With a nod, I followed him to the barn, and jumped into the truck, grateful for once he wasn't a big talker.

While the sun splintered the horizon we drove through the clearing between the trees, parked, and went to inspect the sap buckets.

"They're full!" I said, gazing down at the clear liquid.

If we'd put the tap in at the wrong angle, or the tree wasn't as healthy as we'd thought, the buckets would have been empty. It was a mix of science and a little luck and we'd done the job right the very first time.

"We better hurry," he said. "We don't want them to overflow."

We went to high five—but Clay stopped, grabbed my palm and inspected it. "Lucy, God, haven't you been wearing the gloves? Look at your hands!"

I snatched my arm back. Even with gloves on, after pushing in spiles the day before, my hands had copped another beating and were red raw with grazes. They didn't seem to heal, not when the work continued each day.

"It's OK. Come on, let's get the buckets emptied." Shoot, the last thing I needed was an argument with him.

"You can't work like this!" He gave me a hard stare.

"I'll put my gloves on now. It looks worse than it is." With my head buzzing, I'd forgotten to hide my hands.

What if he said I wasn't fit to work? I turned to walk to the trees, but he pulled me back by the shoulder.

"I'll empty the buckets, you drive the truck forward as we go. Will that still hurt, holding the steering wheel?"

"Really, I'm fine, I'm used to it now. It won't hurt to drive."

He grunted. "You've been working with your palms like that? It looks like you rubbed them on a cheese grater."

I smiled. "This is new."

He tilted his head. "What?"

"This caring side."

With a kick of the ground he said ruefully, "Can't have you reporting me to the farmer's assistant association, now can we?"

I gave him a playful shove. "OK, it's not called farmer's assistant. How was I supposed to know? What am I actually called?" In light of everything, his concern warmed me. It was exactly what I needed after the strange call with Mom.

"A farmhand." He laughed.

"A farm*hand*?" We doubled over laughing at the double meaning. "That should have been my first clue, then."

"Just be careful," he said, motioning to my palms before striding off to empty the first bucket into a drum we had on the back of the truck. "If it hurts, you let me know."

"I will," I said, surprised by the care in his tone.

Once we collected the sap, we'd begin the boil process, which turned it into thick golden syrup. The fire pits were set up behind the barn, with great big pots that looked like cauldrons. The thought of filling them with the maple liquid and stirring them while it reduced made me grin like a fool. I remembered Clay's uncle's ponderings about making maple syrup, and how much he loved it. A shiver of sadness went through me as I thought of him doing it all alone.

Clay jogged from the trees, grabbing buckets and emptying them, while I idled in the truck a few feet behind him. When he ran toward a tree with his back to me, I goggle-eyed him as the world around me drifted away. That body, that fire in him, was enough to make me heavy-lidded. He was mellow, happy, like a kind of peace had found him these last few days. Whatever shadows had followed him here were slowly evaporating.

With a bucket in his hand, he turned and faced me. We locked eyes. There was a question in his gaze, like he was trying to read me, or recognize something in my expression. My hands trembled. I wanted him to stare at me like that forever. But I wasn't staying in Ashford. This time I was the one doing the leaving—even though a part of me wanted to stay. Would he miss me? I'd miss him, and this place.

***

Clay drove the truck slowly as if we carried a newborn baby inside. He didn't want to waste a drop of liquid that was now all safely tipped into a barrel in the bed of the truck.

With a chain and hoist, he rigged up the barrel, and slowly poured the contents into one of the vats. He then reversed the truck to the next vat and did the same, until all the vats were full of liquid.

"Go up and relax on the porch," Clay said, with a half smile. "It's too hot near the fire pits."

"OK." I retreated up the steps, and fell into the swing.

From my vantage point, it was like watching a raincloud being made. The steam from the bubbling vats mushroomed up and out, eventually dissipating as it rose in the sky.

It took an age for the liquid to burn down into thick syrup. I sprawled out on the soft cushion, and closed my eyes, every now and then peeping one open to see Clay's face, scrunched in concentration as he stirred the liquid in the vats and checked the temperature. His skin shone with perspiration, his muscles flexing hard, as he went from one vat to the next, the heat scorching his skin red. It was his face I focused on, despite the searing flames under the vats and the cloudy air from the fires. Clay looked happy. It was like he was meant to be here, in this place, this farm, always. Without knowing why, I had a shiver of comprehension—Clay needed this place just like the old man did. There was something here, something tenuous that calmed them, and made them whole again, despite what they'd faced. I felt it too.

***

As dusk colored the sky ocher, I stretched, my body snapping back into place. Clay had left me snoozing for hours. There hadn't been much for me to do while he stood over his syrup, like a wizard.

The porch creaked, as Clay made his way over.

"How's the syrup?" I asked, brushing my mussed hair back into place.

"It should be just about perfect." He stared at me intensely, his gaze traveling to my hair, my mouth. Absently I touched my bottom lip, and he blinked and looked away.

The thought of us producing a bottle soon was mind-blowing. We'd achieved so much for two people who knew nothing about maple trees when we first stepped onto this fertile soil.

I followed Clay to the vats, and stood a few paces behind. He pulled on thick gloves to protect his hands from the heat. I shuffled from foot to foot, eager to see what was hiding beneath the lid.

The vats, with their cauldron-shaped, blackened bottoms, looked like something you'd cast spells over.

I silently prayed that the first batch would be a success. Clay lifted the lid, and peered inside. "Can you pass me the candy thermometer?"

Maple syrup peaked at a certain temperature and if you left it too long or it went too high the batch would be ruined. Once the temperature was right, we would filter the syrup to remove any sugar sand that had crystalized. That had to be done while the syrup was still molten so Clay had to be cautious, and take it slowly.

I found it by the first vat and raced it back to Clay. Our fingers brushed, and we locked eyes once more. He mumbled, "Thanks," and dipped it in to check the temperature.

I leaned close, and scrutinized the inside of the vat. It had reduced so much there were rings around the edges, as it had slowly evaporated to a thick syrup. The stately trees had provided for us. It was almost like we were some mystical beings with the saccharine scent of the syrup permeating the air, and the steam from the vats encircling us.

"Well?" I couldn't help prodding a finger into his back. "Is it ready? It *looks* ready."

"I can't believe it," he whispered. "It *is* ready. We somehow managed to make our very first batch of syrup. Now we just have to bottle it."

"It's like magic." Manna from heaven. Mom would've got such a kick out of watching it made. Could she even travel this far these days? Even if we had the funds somehow... which we didn't. The thought of her never leaving Detroit again was heart-wrenching. A seasoned traveler and her last stop was a town she'd declared too gray to be pretty.

"Lucy..." Clay said. "What's wrong?"

I averted my eyes. "Nothing." How could I explain? Everything was right, and wrong, and I couldn't fix it.

I couldn't make Mom better. The yin and yang of life struck me, and I couldn't formulate an explanation quick enough or easy enough without blubbering like a baby.

Clay didn't say anything, just stared at me with those hazy, deep-brown eyes of his. He stepped forward and embraced me. My arms remained folded and prodded into his chest, and I held myself stiff. I had to, or I'd dissolve into messy tears. The way he'd sensed my sadness only made it worse. People cared about me here. And I guess that was beauty. Mom's type of beauty.

"It's OK, Lucy," he said with so much feeling, I held my breath. His scent, washing powder, the woods, mingled together with him, and I wanted nothing more than to stay in the safety of his arms.

***

I watched Clay from the corner of my eye. He was so complex. We each knew nothing of each other's pasts, but obviously there were layers of baggage that shaped us into who we were, and somehow the universe conspired to throw us together. I took comfort in it. And got back to the present moment. Bottling the syrup.

We'd moved everything we needed to the barn and were ready to pour the liquid into leaf-shaped bottles.

I fastidiously cleaned a workspace. The silver bench top sparkled so much you could eat off it, and we had to make sure nothing contaminated the syrup when we poured it.

"If this works, then it was worth it. All the long days, the longer nights..." His voice petered out.

"It was worth it anyway."

We glanced at each other, our eyes twinkling with excitement. "Ready?" I asked. The liquid had thickened, and the color was perfect, but somehow seeing it in the bottle, the way it would go out into the world, was even more thrilling.

"You go first," he said, motioning to the funnel.

"No, this is your farm, the first ever bottle of maple syrup should be poured by you!" I rummaged in my pocket for the phone. "I'll take a photo."

"No photos." He went to the sink to wash his hands.

"Why, in case I sell it to a celebrity magazine?" I cocked my head.

"Very funny. Right, let's get this done."

He placed the funnel into the first bottle and tipped the syrup in. It oozed slowly down, its amber color catching the light, as if it were real gold. Screwing the lid tight, he held it aloft and inspected it. It was as precious as a gemstone, the vibrancy of the color and the thickness of the syrup.

"I didn't think it would work," he said, his voice wistful.

We were silent, unable to speak as we stared at the bottle like it would solve the meaning of life. It was so much more precious than an adornment for pancakes. All that love, and work, bottled, just like that.

"Your turn." He passed me the funnel. "Maybe we can take a few photos then?" There was a playful hint to his voice.

"Lucky me," I teased. "OK, here goes." My hands shook, and I laughed nervously to cover it up. Clay gave me a wide smile as I poured my first ever bottle of maple syrup.

"Photo together?" I asked.

He moved beside me and looped his arm around my waist and I snapped a shot.

"There," I said, and dropped my gaze to the floor.

"We probably shouldn't celebrate just yet," Clay said. "What if it tastes terrible?"

My hand flew to my mouth. "What if it does? No," I said firmly. "It couldn't look that pretty and taste ugly. Impossible."

Clay poured a dab of syrup on the tip of his finger and pushed it between his lips. My own lips parted in need. "Taste it." His voice was husky.

I stared at Clay's full mouth. My breath hitched in my throat.

"Don't you want to try it?" His gaze burned into mine. The air around us hummed with a sense of urgency.

"Yes..."

Clay reached for my hand and poured a dot of syrup on the tip of my index finger. I lifted it to my mouth, and licked the circle of sweetness, my eyes never leaving his. The moment was charged with our silence.

His gaze traveled to my mouth. With a low moan he said my name. All I wanted to do was touch him. I stepped forward, an invitation. With one swift movement, he cupped my face and pressed his lips against mine. The sweetness of the syrup was all there was between us. We kissed urgently, as though it would the first and last time. The intensity of it stole the breath from my lungs. When we parted his gaze burned into mine.

"Lucy..." His voice was throaty with desire. I ran my hands over his T-shirt, wanting to feel the warmth of his body more than anything before. He grinded against me, and kissed the soft skin behind my ear, and down to my neck, making me shiver. The world around me dimmed, as my lips found Clay's.

I could feel the rhythm of his heart, quick and steady, pressed tight against him. The desperation, the breathlessness, was interrupted when my phone shrilled. I jumped, as if scalded, and the moment was broken.

I couldn't ignore it, in case it was Mom and she needed me. Clay watched, as I answered the call.

"Mom, hi! No you're not interrupting anything." I mouthed a sorry, but he'd already turned and gone. My mind swirled. I touched a finger to my lips, trying to focus on what Mom was saying.

"Sorry, Mom, can you say that again?"

"I said, why's your voice all husky like that?" she asked.

I crept to the barn door to see where Clay had gone. "Sorry, you caught me in the middle of… pouring the first batch of maple syrup."

Mom talked, as I tried desperately to work out just how that had happened and what I was supposed to do about it. One thing was certain, I'd just made things more difficult.

***

We spent the afternoon studiously trying to avoid each other. I wasn't sure if he regretted the kiss, but the tension was palpable. When we were in the same room, I blushed as we bumped hips, or knocked arms. I busied myself by the front porch, lacquering the new banister Clay fitted. He disappeared, out of sight. All I could hear was the drone of a power tool somewhere in the distance.

When nightfall approached, I packed all the tools away, and cleaned all the paintbrushes, then went to find him to say goodbye. The fluoro light in the barn shone out in the night. I stood just out of Clay's vision, near the open door. Wrapping my coat tighter against the chill of evening, I watched him sand down a piece of wood. Dust motes danced, circling Clay like fairy powder.

I inched closer to the open door. He was focused on the wood, sanding the top of it to get it even. He ran his palm over the top, almost lovingly, to check for imperfections.

His muscles swelled with the effort. Stars twinkled overhead in the inky night, almost like they were flashing encouragement. *Kiss him.* But I couldn't. Instead, I let butterflies swarm inside me, a constant fluttery feeling whenever I was near him. It was the sweetest thing, my own secret.

CHAPTER FOURTEEN

Turning the corner from the bed and breakfast the next morning into the main street of Ashford, I was stunned to see so many cars parked down the length of the road. Even though the sky was still dark I checked my watch, wondering if I'd overslept. Six a.m. to the minute. A few townsfolk milled out the front of the Gingerbread Café. Something was wrong! Why were they all assembled so early? Were CeeCee and Lil OK? I jogged the rest of the way, and fell through the door. The café was full. People hovered by the fire, or sat glumly at tables. All eyes alighted on me, their long faces evident in the gloom of the morning.

Out of breath, I managed, "What? What is it?" When I found CeeCee in the crowd, I breathed a sigh of relief. She was OK. I went to her.

"Sit down, sugar plum," she said, making room for me next to her. "Everyone who don't know already, this is Lucy. She works at the Maple Syrup Farm just outta town, and the pretty little thing is stayin' with Rose at the bed and breakfast. Y'all say hi now."

The locals greeted me with a wave and a mumbled hello. Some sat slumped, others holding their heads in their hands. I scooted to the chair next to CeeCee.

"We're having an urgent town meeting," CeeCee said, facing me. "The bank is foreclosing on Walt's store. And that just ain't right. Poor man needs time to get back on his feet again. So we brainstormin' ways to raise enough money to keep him afloat. There's gotta be something we can do!" While CeeCee tried to remain stoic the panic in her voice leaked out.

"Right," said Lil, giving me a wave across the table. "So…" She tipped her pen to a pad in front of her. "The ideas so far are a raffle: each business donates a prize. That's easy, Sarah said she'd organize the draw, and we'll all sell tickets. What else?"

Rose wandered in, looking as elegant as ever, her hair tied neatly in a bun. "Sorry I'm late, folks." She pulled up a chair behind me and patted my back.

A man with a curly mustache and gray hair said, "What about a car wash, or a quiz night?"

"I see your hearts are in the right place folks," a small brown woman, with sharp features said, "but how long can we keep this up? We don't know when Walt will make furniture again, let alone be back in the store… Don't get me wrong, I'm not saying we don't help him. But maybe we need to figure out something else we can sell for him. It doesn't have to be furniture but something that keeps his business ticking along. There's only gonna be so many quiz nights and car washes we can do before people get tired of them. There aren't that many of us, after all."

The crowd murmured. "Good point, Rosaleen," Lil said. "Maybe we can organize this first lot of fundraising to keep the wolf from the door, and then look at your idea. What kind of things could we get our hands on? If not furniture, then what?"

People drummed fingers on tables, or rested back on chairs.

"We could sell *second-hand* furniture," Sarah from the bookshop said. "When I go to book auctions, in big old warehouses, I always see a bunch of stuff like that. Maybe, if we got it for a steal, we could revamp it, or... I don't know... That won't work, will it?" Her face pinched, and she fussed with her black bangs.

"It's a nice idea, cherry blossom," CeeCee said. "But I 'spose we gotta be practical. As much as we gonna help Walt, none o' us will survive if we running round after two businesses. We need something sorta simple where we can all chip in with a bit o' our time and the like. But what?"

All eyes were downcast. The air in the room thickened with their sadness.

Lil stood. "How about I make us some breakfast? That might help kick our brains into gear."

"I'll help, Lil." I joined her in the kitchen, donning an apron. CeeCee gave me a warm smile, softening the worry from her face.

"Thanks, Lucy. Toast some bread; I'll scramble some eggs, and fry bacon. We've got cherry tomatoes in the fridge. We can roast them up with a splash of oil. Maybe we'll think better with full bellies?"

A good-looking man with curly hair and a checked shirt wandered over. "I'm Damon," he said holding out his hand to shake. "Lil's husband."

"Lucy," I said. "Nice to meet you." He had sweet brown puppy-dog eyes, and somehow he and Lil matched with their easy smiles, and relaxed natures.

He inclined his head. "How's about I get the coffee sorted?"

Lil kissed his cheek and without them talking you could see the love that radiated off the pair. Clay's face flashed into my mind. And it was only then I noticed the time. I was late and I'd be even later by the time I walked there. My heart seized—what if he thought I wasn't coming after the spontaneous kiss yesterday? I'd explain when I got there; he'd understand. Or would it be awkward, and the old Clay would greet me with a scowl?

"Right, folks," CeeCee said. "What kinda things don't Ashford have? Something new might draw in a crowd, 'cause right now, we need help fast. The bank ain't gonna dillydally no more."

I sliced knotty loaves of bread as the locals chatted behind me, and I thought Ashford must be one of the sweetest places on earth, that the whole town gets involved to help one of their own.

***

After hugging the girls, I left the café, hurrying down the long road out of town. Damon had offered me a ride, but I didn't want to take him away from the meeting. As time went on, the worry for their friend increased, their voices raised in frustration. I hoped they'd figure out a way to save Walt's store in time.

As I approached the last store in town Becca walked around the corner, her hands deep in her bag, looking for something. "Oh, Lucy! Oh my goodness. When can we catch up?"

Oh my goodness? Did she know about the kiss? Surely not? Clay didn't seem the kiss-and-tell sort. "What about after work today?" Who knew what the day might bring? After yesterday's escapade, I might be leaving a lot quicker than expected.

"Great! Let's meet at mine? I'm just up the road." She pointed. "The little pink cottage, with the huge oak tree out front."

"What should I bring?"

She waved me away. "Just yourself. I'll grab pizza, and wine, and a chick flick or two."

I nodded and kissed her cheek, before continuing on.

As I wandered my thoughts drifted back to Clay. Was the kiss accidental? We'd been in celebratory mode after making maple syrup. In the quiet of morning, remembering his lips against mine was intoxicating, like I was drunk with a yearning that was wholly new.

I blinked away the memory so I wouldn't arrive flushed. The gravel of the driveway crunched under my boots as I made my way to the maples. Clay would be collecting the sap, so I hurried to the clearing, looking for the truck.

By the lake, he dashed from one bucket to the next. He must have heard me coming and glanced over. With my hands pushed deep into my pockets, I ambled over to him, trying to read his expression before I said anything about yesterday.

He stopped, dropped the bucket by his side, and bit his lip. I shuffled my feet and waited for him to speak.

"You're late."

I hid a smile, having predicted that those very words would fall from those luscious lips of his. "Sorry, there was an emergency town meeting, and I helped the girls at the café make breakfast."

"Yeah?" He raised an eyebrow. "What was the meeting about?"

"The bank is foreclosing on Walt's furniture store. They're trying to work out a way to save it. Those big meanies—I see why you avoid town. Imagine having friends like that, hey? I mean who needs enemies, right?" I couldn't help but tease him and was rewarded by the ghost of a grin.

"I hope they find a way," he said, and walked to the pick-up truck to empty the bucket.

"Me too," I said.

The bucket lid clanked, as he walked over. He stood a half step from me. I held my breath, wondering what he'd say.

"You think we can get to work now?" He was so close, I could reach out and touch him. His expression was neutral but his eyes darkened.

"Er… yes."

It was like I was exposed in the clearing of maples. As if he was staring so deeply into my eyes he could see my soul and knew I was spellbound. He was *too* good-looking. The kind of guy who would break your heart as quick as look at you… and yet… and yet… My pulse sped up, as I gazed at his face once more. And just like that, he said, "Let's work, then."

The world went back to spinning, and I tried hard to pretend that the kiss yesterday meant nothing. It *was* nothing. He was just a guy with a huge chip on his shoulder to match an equally big ego. He was gruff, and rugged, and *not* for me.

He kept on staring, so I said, "About yesterday, that shouldn't have happened. It was the excitement of the syrup, and…" The lie escaped only to save my pride.

"Let's forget it happened." As if he was talking about a dropped hammer.

He trudged off. I mentally castigated myself as I walked in his shadow. I couldn't help it though—when he locked eyes with me, my heart beat a different rhythm. "It wasn't really memorable, anyway," I said to his back.

He spun to face me. "It wasn't?" Again he dropped the bucket, and stepped forward, wrapping his hands around the small of my back, like he knew exactly where his arms fit on my body. "What are you doing to me?" His voice was thick. Before I could reply, his mouth was hard against mine. I closed my eyes and kissed him back, any other thought floating to the ether, vanishing, until I came up for air.

"What are we doing?" he said.

This was only going to complicate matters. "Maybe we should forget it happened, Clay? Again, I mean. I'm leaving, and you're…"

"I'm not ready for this… whatever it is."

I raised my eyebrows. "I'm pretty sure I said forget it first, Clay. So there's no need to be sorry, because clearly, I am not interested in you either." Truth was, I felt something for Clay, some unequivocal, heart-stopping, breath-taking desire that I had absolutely no control over, and it irked me. He was barely able to hold a conversation, so how could it be plausible?

"You just can't stop, can you?" he demanded. "I don't want to feel like this, but it's too goddamn late."

I gave him a shove. "Shut up and kiss me, and that's the very last time," I said.

He brushed his lips against mine, softly this time, cupping my face, like he didn't want to let me go.

***

"S-o-o," Becca said later that night, clutching a glass of red wine. "Tell me honestly, you love him right?" She flicked her hair, and laughed. There was something so fun about the way Becca didn't take life too seriously.

Music played quietly in the background inside Becca's small cottage. We had just gorged ourselves on a cheese pizza and I was almost too full to talk. Especially about Clay. But wasn't this what girls did? Eat junk food, drink wine and chat about guys? The thought made me smile, but I couldn't confess about Clay just yet. I didn't know how I felt, and I wasn't sure what his motivations were either. "What is it with everyone?" I blustered. "We are colleagues, erm… associates, ah, just friends, sometimes. And other times, we're enemies."

Becca refilled my glass and flopped back on the sofa, pulling her feet underneath. "I don't know, Lucy. Clay has clammed up. Last night I couldn't get a word out of him! And I mean, let's face it, he's not usually a big talker anyway."

"Last night?" I blushed. "So he didn't say anything?"

She pointed a finger at me. "Aha! Something happened yesterday! I knew it! He was a bumbling incoherent mess! I kept asking him about the syrup, and just the word provoked a coughing fit."

I blanked my face. "Nope, nothing happened..." *Nothing happened today either...* I bit my tongue to stop the truth burbling out in one big fat confession. If it had been Lil I probably would have confided in her, but Becca was related to Clay, and was intent on playing matchmaker anyway. The less she knew now, the better, just until I decided how I felt.

She knitted her brow. "Shame. You know, Clay's more like my brother than a cousin. And I'd love to see him happy. With you. It's not too soon to plan the wedding, is it?"

I rolled my eyes. "Don't make me throw something at you, Becca."

"So pink for the bridesmaids?"

***

As soon as I arrived home I texted Mom. "Mom, I'm in a bind. I kissed Clay, well a few times, and now I'm not sure what to do. Xoxox"

The tips of my fingers hovered over the buttons on my phone, wanting to ask about her health, her appointments, but I knew she'd avoid the questions anyway. Part of my promise was to pretend the world was perfect, but it was hard to break the habit of worry.

I hit send, and was rewarded with an instant reply. "WHAT! Tell me everything!"

Smiling, I imagined her in bed at home, propped up on pillows, the filmy light from the phone shining on her face. "We made maple syrup! And I guess, feeling proud, we kissed! And then the next day, we kissed again. But why would I tangle myself up here, when I am all set to leave? Besides he's a moody jerk at times."

"Moody jerks are the lifeblood of romance. You go for it, honey. I'll text you tomorrow. Sleep tight. Xoxoxo"

Before I took my sketch pad out, I read another passage of the journal.

My paintbrushes lean against each other, collecting dust. The canvas stays bare, propped up on the old wooden easel. I'll never paint again, not without my muse. Instead, I sketch, bringing her to life on the page. If only it was that easy.

My eyes widened. He never painted again? I had to find out who he was. He spoke as if painting was a career and not just a hobby.

CHAPTER FIFTEEN

A week later, the vats were bubbling away, white clouds rising up, making the air foggy. We retreated to the porch, waiting for the sap to reduce. Clay took my hand in his. We hadn't spoken about what was happening. I didn't want to sully it with talk of leaving. And at that moment, I didn't care whether we had something or nothing. I hadn't been able to contact Mom again for a few days now, and Aunt Margot's phone kept ringing out. It felt cruel, like I was being ignored, but mostly, I worried they were hiding something from me. I wanted to rage against the world at times like that. Where were they? I'd promised myself if I didn't hear back I'd call the doctor and demand some answers.

"So you see we didn't need the old man's journals to make the syrup work," Clay said, eyes on the vats. His voice irked me, the way he discounted his uncle so easily.

"How do you know that, Clay? Reading your uncle's journals has been an eye opener. For my own life, and maybe for his. His story being read means he mattered, right?" He merely shrugged. When he had that look of feigned disinterest I wanted to lob something at him. "I think you should read them. I'm telling you now, you could learn a lot from him, just like I've done."

"Why do you keep pushing me? I'm not interested in the old man, or his crazy ramblings. You talk like he's gospel or something, like I need saving!" His voice rose, only angering me.

"Why are you so goddamn stubborn? I'm telling you this because you're making the same mistakes he did! He shut himself off here, and the only friends he had were trees! He had a very good reason—she died—but what's your excuse? Huh?" Heat radiated through me. "I just don't get you, Clay! When you open up you're like sunshine on a cloudy day, but then it's almost like you catch yourself being happy, and you shut down. I want you to read the journals, and see if you recognize yourself in them!"

"And then what?" he spat. "Pretend to be someone I'm not? Would that make you happy? I don't know what you're trying to get outta this, but I'm not changing, if that's what you're hoping! This is who I am and if you don't like it, then that's bad luck! A few scribbles from some old man I never met won't change anything." His posture was rigid.

I dropped his hand and jumped from the love swing. "I never said I wanted you to change. I'm only worried that you'll end up like him, when there's no goddamn reason for it!" I blinked back tears, frustration coursing through me.

"There is a good reason for it, Lucy, but it's none of your business!"

"Of course it's not! Nothing is my business… I am nothing to you, I guess?" My words came out in angry bursts. "You're not emotionally available, Clay. It's like you're numb. Dead to the world and all who inhabit it. I wanted you to read the journals, but I won't ask again. Surely a dead man's memories should amount to something…"

He gave me a hard stare. "I don't see how it means anything! He is *dead*, Lucy."

I glowered at him. "Do you want to know what the journals are about?"

He crossed his arms over his chest. "Why? What does it matter?"

"How can you be so insensitive? The old fool, or whatever you call him, left you this farm. You're an ungrateful jerk, Clay. I bet he wouldn't have left you anything if he knew how icy cold your heart is!"

"Oh, yeah?" His lip curled.

"Yeah! You're selfish, and pigheaded, and..."

"Dyslexic," he spat, his eyes blazing.

"And, rude, and stubborn!" I stopped short. "What? What did you say?"

"I'm dyslexic, Lucy! I find it hard to make sense of words. There—you happy now? Let's dredge up everyone's secrets and have a group hug? Would that satisfy you?" His voice was guttural with fury.

My shoulders drooped. "I didn't know." What else could I say? I rubbed my face. My anger ebbed away and was swiftly replaced with guilt. What had I done? I'd pushed him to this point, with something he hadn't wanted to share. A shamefaced blush bloomed up my cheeks. I thought back to all the times we'd stared at books, and he'd ask me to read the passages. The way he committed things to memory, like he depended on remembering.

"See what dwelling on the past does, Lucy?" he yelled, his fists curling. "I lost everything, *everything*, because I trusted people I shouldn't have. And I wound up here, saved by a man I didn't know. Given a second chance, and a place where I could hole up, and forget. You go around thinking the world's this sunny place, where people are good and wholesome, but it's not like that, Lucy! Not in the real world." He stalked off into the barn, cursing as he went.

That's where he was wrong. I knew what the real world was like. I knew the depths of despair, and heartache. My heart sank, watching him storm off. I wished I hadn't pushed him to breaking point.

In the distance the maples were a more solemn color. It was like they changed with our moods as much as they invigorated us. They were attuned to us too and felt the dips and changes in our psyches.

This kind of beauty, the quiet majesty of the maples, would fix the most damaged heart. His uncle had proved that much already. But could this place fix Clay? I swung back and forth, wondering if he was too broken.

***

"Jesus mother o' Mary! There you be! Come inside quick, I got some good news!" CeeCee hurried over, wrenching my arm.

I laughed, relieved to run into her smiling face after the tense day at the farm. Clay had ignored my attempts to talk, saying he wanted to be left alone.

"What is it?" I asked. CeeCee's hands were quaking. She played with her apron strings, unable to stop fussing.

"God's gone and heard our prayers. I can't even believe it myself!" She put her hands together like she was praying, and looked to the ceiling. "Seems someone's been *real* busy." She grabbed a scrunched-up tissue from her pocket and dabbed at her eyes. "This morning some folk left a pile o' furniture—handcrafted, no less—out the back of Walt's store. Whole town's in a tizzy over who made it. No one's ownin' up to it. It's a real-life mystery. Ain't that the greatest thing you ever heard?"

It took me a moment to unscramble CeeCee's words—excitement made her speak rapidly. "What?" I said, surprised. "That's the best news I've heard in a long time!"

She chuckled. "You gotta see this for yourself!" She grabbed my elbow and marched me across the street, flinging open the door of Walt's store. One of the locals I recognized from the town meeting was by the front counter, and welcomed us in. They must have been back to taking shifts to help out.

When I saw the furniture I stopped in my tracks. Beautifully carved tables, buffets, dining-room tables and chairs. I walked to a table and ran my hands over the polished surface of the wood, just like Clay had done, when I'd watched him out of sight by the barn door. I recognized the markings in the wood, and the shape of the table, octagonal. The chairs were a work of art, with grooves and patterns worked into the legs. The cushions were royal-blue velvet material, the very same that he'd just re-covered the old sofas with.

"Well," I said, a lump in my throat. "Miracles happen, don't they?" A rash of goose bumps broke out over me.

CeeCee patted my hand. "They sure do. Whoever did it just gone and saved Walt. I wish there was a way we could say thanks." Her eyes glittered with unshed tears.

"I'm sure there's a way we can find out…" My words petered out. Instinctively I knew he wouldn't want anyone to know it was him. The ground shifted almost imperceptibly. He wasn't who I thought he was; he was better.

"I think," CeeCee said, "it'll come out soon enough. Rosaleen's not gonna let this slide 'til she finds out who it is. But 'tween us, I got my suspicions." She winked.

I hid a smile. She *always* knew. CeeCee had a way of reading people's minds. "I'm sure you do, CeeCee. I've got mine too, but some secrets I'm not so sure need to be shared."

"Well, then, we're gonna have to find somethin' else for Rosaleen to clutch on to ain't we?" she joked, pulling me back across the road. "Let's celebrate. How does a piece of pie sound?"

***

"The town's buzzing, Clay. Did you know that?" We stood by the open barn door, the breeze whipping my hair backward.

"About what?" He turned away. I grabbed his arm and forced him to look at me, clamping my hands around his bicep.

"About the furniture." I touched his chin, forcing him to look me in the eye.

He ran a hand through his hair and shrugged.

"I saw you, Clay. I know that wood was from here. What you did… it saved him." It was hard to even think about the grieving Walt and all this friends in town who'd wrung their hands worrying how to stop the bank foreclosing. Now they were all celebrating because of an off-the-cuff comment I'd made to Clay, who'd decided to help save a man he didn't know.

I pushed past him into the barn. In the corner sheets were draped over mysterious shapes. I ripped them back, exposing dining-room tables made out of oak, varnished to a shine. There were chairs to match. Small coffee tables, bookshelves. "You made all of this for Walt?" I couldn't hide the surprise. Clay wasn't who he portrayed; he wasn't selfish, he was *selfless*. The long nights where sleep eluded him, he must have come out to the barn, and worked through till late. "These are beautiful, Clay."

"Leave it be."

"*Why?* Why can't you just admit it was you, and it was a sweet thing to do? Why do you have to be the tough guy?"

He lifted his chin. "It's not about being the tough guy, Lucy. You just don't get it."

It was hard to read his expression in the dim light of the barn. "So explain it to me?" What kind of person couldn't understand gratitude? Why was he so messed up?

"It was nothing. I make furniture all the time. I wanted to help, that's all. I didn't do it for any other reason, and I don't want anyone to know it was me. Period."

"Why?"

He sighed. "I hope it helps. I know what it's like to lose everything."

I reached for him, but he brushed past. "Can we do some work?"

"You're a good guy, Clay. No matter how much you try and hide it." My heart beat that little bit faster, staring at him, and he wrestled with his response. Clay wasn't such an enigma. He was kind and considerate, but for some reason didn't want anyone to know it.

"Clay…"

***

While taking a different route back to the B and B, I couldn't resist trying to catch my mom on the phone. It had been so long since I had heard her voice. No matter how old I was, I still looked to her for reassurance, especially after the conversation with Clay.

"Finally!" I said as Mom answered her phone. "I was about to send out a search party."

She managed a small laugh. "Oh, you stop that worrying, honey. I was sleeping. I told you these new drugs are sending me straight to the land of zeds."

"When Aunt Margot didn't answer her phone I got worried."

"You called her?" Mom said, concerned.

I bit my lip. I'd forgotten the cardinal rule: I was not to bother Aunt Margot. "Yeah, sorry, Mom. But you do have to understand, I'm so far away, and when I can't get hold of either of you for days, I panic."

Her tone softened. "OK, but try not to call her, honey. I don't want her feeling all beleaguered. I'll make sure I call you when I'm fresh instead."

"Good."

"So how's farm life? And that gorgeous hunk of a guy?"

I laughed, continued walking through the woods and filled Mom in on what had happened since we last spoke, including all the details about Clay, and his desire to be alone on the farm.

CHAPTER SIXTEEN

Mid-April rolled around and with it the end of the tapping season. We were busy with plans for the Sugaring-Off Festival, which Clay had grudgingly agreed to, knowing he needed the visibility the festival would bring, otherwise it'd be a long and frugal year for him.

We'd cleared the land by the lake, and mowed the lush green grass, which seemed to grow overnight now that the weather had warmed. Daisies grew wild and free in bright-yellow bunches, and bees buzzed gaily around them, making me yearn to make honey. How hard could it be? I could picture Clay dressed in beekeepers' garb, pilfering the sweet nectar they made. Maybe one day, he could do it. I made a mental note to tell him.

I'd left the barn, where I'd been sorting a string of tangled fairy lights, and headed to the porch for my water bottle. Clay wandered over.

"What are you doing?"

"Taking a five-minute break, boss. You?"

He stroked back my hair. "Why don't you take today off? I'm going to fix up the old applecart, give it a lick of paint."

"A day off? Did you bang your head this morning?" I couldn't hide my surprise.

He gave me a lopsided grin. "You've worked hard, Lucy. Harder than I ever imagined."

I rested my head against his shoulder. "Well, you won't hear me argue," I said. "I'm might go sit by the lake, and soak up the sunshine."

Clay stood, and dropped a kiss on the top of my head. It was something so simple, but it spoke volumes to me. It was loving, unlike the passionate clinches that sometimes overcame us.

I went into the cottage and found my backpack, hefted it onto my shoulder, and trekked to the lake at the back of the farm. The water was flowing freely, its gentle waves lapping against the embankment. I found a shady patch of grass to sit on and took my sketch pad from my bag.

I sketched the maples, their long languid trunks, their marks and scars. Each tree unique as a fingerprint, the names Jessup gave them easy to recollect after spending so much time with them. I drew an elderly couple, legs entwined, hair splayed out, as they embraced under the leafy canopy.

Twigs snapped, and I turned to the sound. *Clay.* I bristled.

It was too late to cover the sketch; he'd seen it already. I closed the book anyway, and squinted up at him, half annoyed he didn't warn me of his approach, and hoping he wouldn't mention the picture. He'd know it was us I had recreated. But it was the us of the future. If he'd looked long enough he would have seen the gnarly, arthritic hands of age—the seventy-year-old Clay. And the elderly me, beside him, trapped for eternity on the parchment. Did it mean I wanted to grow old with him?

"Finally," he said crouching next to me. "I get to see a masterpiece."

He prised the book from my hands, my protests falling on deaf ears, but left it closed. A ray of sun shone, landing in a soft shard on the sketchbook in his hands. It sparkled under the light, and I thought of my mom, and her love of signs from the universe… What if he liked what he saw? What if he didn't? Did it matter? I knew him well enough now to know he'd be supportive, that under all that gruffness Clay was more genuine than almost anyone.

"Why are you so scared, Lucy?" His gaze burned into mine. "About showing your art to anyone?"

I stiffened. "It's private."

"But why?" he probed. "Come on, you've grilled me. Answer me this one thing."

I swallowed back my fear. "Because it's the only thing I can control. It's the only thing in my life where *I* get to decide its fate. And I don't want to fail at the *one thing* that's mine." How could I tell him…? With my mom, I had no say, I had pleaded with the gods, all of them, to spare her. I'd prayed, and bawled, and begged, and she continued to deteriorate. She would leave soon; I felt it like a whisper on the wind. And I would have no one. Who would I be without her? How could fate be so cruel as to try to take away a woman so vital? My art was like a friend—that shadow who was always there for me, a way to help deal with the pain. And if I failed at that, I would be alone. But how to say all this without Clay reassuring me it would all be OK? Because I didn't want reassurances. They were just hollow words.

"And you think me seeing a picture will somehow hurt you? I would never hurt you, Lucy. Ever." His voice was husky with emotion.

"But how can you know that, Clay? None of us know what's going to happen. We can make promises, but that doesn't guarantee things won't change. Life is fickle… love, health, happiness, it can all change in an instant."

"Do you see what you're doing, Lucy? Because life can change, you don't really live it. You hover on the outside looking in, trying to protect yourself from future hurt *that may never happen!* You say I hide, but you hide too."

My mouth hung open with surprise. "I don't hide, Clay. I'm here, aren't I? In a strange place a million miles away from home—"

"Stop," he said, twisting his mouth in frustration. "Don't sit there and give me the same old lines you use to convince yourself. I want to see your work. I want to know why you take such pains to keep it secret, and then volley a bunch of words to hide behind."

"Fine," I lifted my chin. "Be my guest," I said, my mouth suddenly dry.

Clay knelt down, and leaned his face close to mine, his voice almost a whisper. "I'm not going to judge you, Lucy. I get that this is your secret. The thing you turn to when you need to make sense of the world. But I want to see it. It will be like looking through your eyes, seeing life the way you do."

My heart hammered. He knew exactly what my art meant to me. "That's the part I like to keep to myself, Clay. What if we look at the world differently?"

I'd painted us in the *future*, for crying out loud. Something a love-struck teenager would do. I wanted to kick myself for making it so obvious.

"So what if we do? I know you better than you think." He gave me such a heart-wrenching look, like he missed me, like I was gone from here already.

His face was inches from mine, his breath on my lips, I could almost taste him. "You don't know anything about me, Clay. And I don't know much about you."

"What do you want to know, Lucy?" For the first time, he looked open, interested, and not held so tight by his own past.

I wanted more. I wanted to know everything about him—what he liked, what he loathed, what made him unable to sleep, what he'd lost that made him hide here.

"Have you ever been in love before?" I'd meant to ask about his past, but the words tumbled out before I had a chance to stop them.

"And that, I am not prepared to talk about," he said.

"Of course not," I sighed.

He sat on the shady patch of grass next to me and flicked open the sketchbook. My spine hardened.

Instead, I thought of us. I was leaving; none of this mattered. What I had here was nothing more substantial than the wind. Clay was all bluster, and when it came time to get to know him, he flicked the switch, and avoided it. And begrudgingly, I kind of understood. We both had parts of us we didn't want to share. There was no point knocking down the invisible wall that stood between us.

"This is us?" He pointed.

I mumbled, "Yes it is."

He didn't say anything, just held it closer and surveyed it like he was looking for clues. "When we're old." He said it so wistfully, with so much hope, I turned to him. A smile lit up his face. "I love it, Lucy. I really, really love it. Sometimes, you know love when you see it."

"And you see it there?"

"I see it on their faces, in the way they hold each other."

We fell against each other, and I heard his breathing quicken. His gaze burned into me, and I thought if I never felt like this again my life would pale.

***

Our legs were tangled in sheets, as Clay ran a finger along my back. "So the institute, it's a six-month course?"

"Mhmm," I mumbled sleepily.

The fan spun overhead, making shadows dance around the room. "You should apply. They'd accept you, I'd bet on it."

I stiffened in his arms. Did he want me to leave? I tried to mask the hurt I felt. "Whether I apply or not, I'm leaving here after the festival. You'll get all the time in the world to be alone."

"I didn't mean that, Lucy." He clenched his jaw.

"You don't owe me an explanation," I said, trying to make my voice light. I rolled from bed, dragging the sheet with me. He'd said the very first time we'd met he didn't want a girlfriend, said it on a number of occasions, that he wasn't ready for that after whatever the hell had happened to him. It stung though, that feeling of rejection. I hadn't been searching for love either, but had stumbled on it, and I couldn't tell anyone. Again, another goodbye was going to darken my days.

"Come back to bed." He patted the empty space beside him.

"No, I have to go," I said, dropping the sheet and searching the floor for my clothes. It was mid-April, and I'd already decided to apply for the institute. Clay's words only steeled my resolve to be accepted.

***

In the cupboard, rows of canvases lay stacked against each other—paintings I'd done since I arrived in Ashford. Some soft watercolors, others intense and dramatic oils. One by one I leaned them against the wall where the light was bright, and knelt down to scrutinize them.

The first was called *Wake me this way*. It was the imaginary little girl, her rosebud mouth the same color as her cheeks, her blankets ruched up under her chin. The open window, the full moon a speck in the distance, landing in soft shards on her face. The scent of Lil's fresh bread melding its way in light and glittery, like fairy dust, pulling her from her dreams.

The second painting made my heart tug. I'd called it *Friendship*. Lil had an arm draped over CeeCee's sturdy shoulder, their shiny white teeth showing, as they laughed over a joke. CeeCee's brown crinkled face shone and she had one hand over the soft swell of Lil's belly. Their unconditional love for one another radiated from the canvas, and for the first time ever, I couldn't find fault with my work. I narrowed my eyes and leaned closer. Surely there was something I could have improved? But I couldn't see anything. Maybe it was because I'd managed to capture how they felt about each other.

The third and final painting was of Clay, and I'd called it *Unrequited*. At the time of painting it, we hadn't even kissed. My stomach somersaulted as I gazed at it. I could never part with this painting. When I left, I'd always have this reminder of Clay, and the times we shared here, in Ashford. There he was, gazing at me with that fiery look in his eyes, his full lips parted like he was about to kiss me, his strong jawline begging to be touched. I'd never met a man so magnetic, so irresistible. And I felt heartbreak, honest and real, that one day he would love someone, and it wouldn't be me. Some girl would come along, and find the key and unlock *all* of him. As a desperate kind of envy washed over me, I hoped he'd be happy, with or without me. I loved him enough to wish him that.

I picked up the little-girl canvas, and the one of Lil and CeeCee. I'd send them to the Van Gogh Institute and hope they accepted me. Paris was calling.

CHAPTER SEVENTEEN

A few weeks later, I walked the familiar road to Ashford, taking note of the yellow buttercups that sprouted in the bright spring day. I'd spoken to Mom earlier and she was cheerful, and sprightlier than I'd heard her for a long time. With the sun warming my back, and Clay on my mind, I felt as happy as I'd ever been. I was dressed like the real me: denim cut-offs, a cheesecloth singlet, and bangles galore. The town was busy. People sat outside soaking up the golden rays, and shielding their eyes as they spoke. I smiled and waved to them all, stopping here and there to chat before placing flyers for the festival on their tables with a backwards wave.

The paint was still drying on a canvas that I'd just *had* to paint, aptly named *The Darling Buds of May*. Ashford sure was a pretty town in springtime and with the new month colorful flowers were abundant. People here tended their gardens, and even helped plant seedlings along the roadside. I walked the length of the main street, asking storekeepers if I could hang flyers for the Sugaring-Off Festival in their windows. The faces were mostly known to me now, give or take a few. And everyone pulled me by the elbow for a chat, so instead of it taking thirty minutes, it'd taken me two hours.

"Hey, I wondered if I'd catch you today!" Henry said, standing on the stoop of the travel agency. "Have you got time to shoot the breeze for a minute?" He gave me a questioning look.

"Yes." I laughed and followed him inside. Each local had used the same term to ask for a chat. "While I'm here, can I give you some flyers to hang in the window for the Sugaring-Off Festival?"

"Sure," he said amiably. "I've heard all about it! The town's buzzing with it all."

I took a couple of flyers from my backpack, and handed them over. "I hope you can make it."

He gave me a big smile. "Of course—wouldn't miss it for the world. Besides, Lil's cooking and it's all you can eat— you got a sure-fire winner there, and then there's the maple-syrup-flavored *everything*. Lord, I wish it was June already."

I laughed, again. The sentiment had been similar with the other locals I'd encountered. Lil's cooking was famous around here, and they were mighty sure there was no limit to the amount they could eat.

He turned his computer monitor to face me. "After our talk about Paris, I've been keeping an eye out for flight specials like you asked, and one popped up today! It's a round-the-world trip, for only a fraction more than what you'd pay to go to Paris. It's a new airline, and they've got the most amazing specials. I'm half tempted to close up shop and venture off myself!"

"Around the world?" My eyes widened.

He grabbed a pen and pointed to the screen. "So, that basically means it's open-ended. You can pick four destinations; you just need to nominate the countries you want to go to."

"Wow, four countries. I could dash off after I've been to Paris. See some of the world." I thought of Mom's book, the places she'd loved in her twenties. Greece, Sri Lanka, Australia.

Henry nodded eagerly. "Check out the price." He pointed to the bottom of the screen.

My eyebrows shot up. "Wow! Why is it so cheap?"

"It's their first day of trading so they're calling them birthday prices!" Henry was jiggling around, as nervous excitement got the better of him. "The only catch is, you have to book the first flight within six weeks of today. As I said, the other flights can remain open, as long as you choose the destinations."

I hugged myself, thinking hard about what to do. Every dollar saved was a bonus, but leaving in two months? That would be right after the festival, meaning I'd be in Paris mid-June.

I'd be leaving Ashford. And Clay. And all the friends I'd made here. Was I ready? Part of me wanted to stay here forever.

What did I have with Clay? He'd never asked me to stay. And would I? Would I be the girl who gave up her dreams for love?

"There's only a few seats left, so whatever you decide we have to be quick."

My mind reeled with so many emotions.

He refreshed the screen. "Oh, golly, now there's only two left."

"Let's book it then," I said decisively, taking my purse from my bag. I tried very hard to ignore the fact my heart seized at the thought of saying goodbye.

"Great," Henry ran a hand over his balding pate. "So Paris it is? Six weeks from today?"

I rubbed my face. "Yes. Paris." The city of romance. And art, and culture, and… people other than Clay.

I was really going to leave Ashford.

"You're going on the adventure of a lifetime, Lucy. If I was younger, I'd be off again too." He lifted his cane ruefully. "These days, the memories have to sustain me. So thank God, there's enough of those here." He touched his temple.

"You're right," I said, his sentiment convincing me. I had to travel while I could. Who knew what the future had in store for me? I'd forget this place, one day. Maybe the pull I felt here, I'd feel everywhere. I left the travel agency with heavy steps.

***

At the cottage the next week Becca was bouncing around the room, her skirts swishing as we discussed the festival. "Oh," I said. "I almost forgot! I had Tiffany make these! I thought we could sell them on the day, a little keepsake for guests." I handed her a box of maple-leaf charms made out of silver.

"Ohhhh," she breathed. "These are so pretty! I bet you'll sell out early. You've done so much to help Clay, I wonder sometimes how he'll go when you leave."

I steered the conversation back to the festival, not wanting to talk about leaving yet. "He's helped me too. What if no one turns up?" I went from moments of wild panic we'd be overrun, to worry that we'd spend a fortune and only a handful of people would arrive.

Becca waved me away. "Everyone's talking about it already. Don't you worry. Besides, the rumor mill won't miss an opportunity to meet the mysterious Clay."

Clay chose that moment to walk into the living room and rewarded Becca with an eye roll. "Yay," he said, heavy with sarcasm, and flopped on the sofa beside me. "I can't wait for the Sugaring-Off festival." He slapped his forehead. "I'd love nothing more than the farm being overrun with strangers. It would bring me joy!"

"Yeah, people celebrating your successful season, eating delicious food, listening to a live band, *buying* your maple syrup, *paying* to attend. It sounds horrible, doesn't it? I don't know what we were thinking! I mean, *what's to like*?" I threw him an icy smile. "He's super excited Becca, as you can see."

She fell onto the recliner and folded her arms. "Clay, will it kill you to mingle?"

"Probably," he said.

"Let's change the subject!" Becca picked up a bottle of maple syrup. "You guys are a great team." The syrup was a darker amber than our earlier bottles. The later it was in the season the stronger the syrup tasted of maple.

"You haven't tasted it yet," Clay said.

"Oh, please. I know how good it'll be. Lots of people are excited about buying it. Hey, can I take some for Missy?"

Clay nodded. "Sure."

I chewed a fingernail, wondering when I'd tell them I had booked a flight. Each day it was a little harder to fathom, and I'd try and get the words out, but they'd catch in my throat.

"Great," Becca said, then knitted her brow. "This might cheer Missy up. She's been so down in the dumps, I haven't seen her in town for a few weeks." Missy owned the salon where Becca worked.

I was grateful for Becca's chatter. It was so much easier to focus on her than my erratic emotions. "What's wrong?" I asked. I knew a lot about Missy. Locals at the café spoke fondly, but I'd yet to meet her.

"Lil and CeeCee seem to think she's having some trouble getting the baby to settle. She's got colic, or something that keeps her up half the night. Missy's usually coiffed to perfection, but she came to the salon a few weeks ago and looked downright bedraggled. CeeCee shooed her straight home and followed her there."

"Poor Missy," I said. "Where's her husband? Can't he help some nights?"

A shadow crossed Becca's face. "He's working double shifts at the dairy to help keep things afloat. With the salon's takings going to my wages, I guess they don't have enough to make ends meet. Sometimes the takings aren't even enough to cover my wages so Tommy adds to it. I feel awful about it."

"Don't be too hard on yourself, Becca." She fiddled with her cup, and averted her eyes. "You need a wage, and I'm sure Missy knew it was going to be tight while she was away. It's not your fault." I felt for Tommy—a new baby and double shifts wouldn't be easy. And Missy, being up all hours with no notion of what to do to fix it all.

Becca sighed. "I know, the guilt gets to me, knowing she's on her own most nights, while Tommy works himself to the bone. Both of them plus bubs aren't getting enough sleep. I just feel bad, that's all."

I knew how tiring double shifts could be, let alone adding to it with other strains. "Maybe we can offer to babysit one night or something? They can just go ahead and sleep." I took a sip of coffee.

"Yeah, I've offered but Missy is breastfeeding, and has trouble expressing enough to last if she was to go out. She's really struggling all around."

"That's so hard." I'd heard Missy was this vivacious, lively woman, who made everyone laugh with her self-deprecating style of humor. "Why don't we have the festival planning night at her house… make it more of a girls' night? You can do her hair, and paint her nails, something to lift her spirits. Lil and I can bake, fill up her freezer? I'm sure we can all try and rock the baby to sleep or something? If we keep our talking down to a whisper Missy can go ahead and snooze."

Becca clapped her hands together. "That's such a great idea! Why don't I ask the girls, and we can all go?"

"Perfect."

Clay groaned. "I might just stay here, if it's all the same."

I laughed. "And miss the girls' night? Are you sure?"

He grinned. "I'll try my best not to feel left out when you go. I'm going to make dinner," Clay said, retreating from girl talk with a wink.

"What's got into him?" Becca whispered, watching him retreat. "He's like another person!"

I gazed into my coffee cup hoping my face wasn't as pink as it suddenly felt. "No idea."

"Is that so?" She lobbed a cushion at me. "Well, secrets are hard to keep in small towns." She waggled her eyebrows.

I grinned. "They sure are."

"If your taskmaster is finished working you to the bone today, I can drive you back to town, and we can see if Lil's still at the café and if they want to arrange a night for Missy."

"Oh, that's OK." I waved her away. "I think we've got more to do. We've spent half the afternoon inside." I bit my lip. Of all the things I could have said!

She pulled a face. "Is that so? Doing what?" she asked, a teasing tone to her voice.

I coughed into my hand. "Just…" I had a mental blank and the only thing that sprang to mind was, "I'm leaving… in five weeks."

Becca's face fell.

Clay leaned against a door jamb, his expression black. "What?"

I silently cursed myself. "I've booked to go to Paris. You know, world travel calls and all that."

Clay folded his arms so tight his veins popped out. "Oh yeah?" A muscle along his jawline pulsed. "Sorry to have kept you so long then."

What was I supposed to say to Becca? She'd put me on the spot. We hadn't told anyone about our relationship, or whatever the heck it was.

"Are you angry at me?" I asked him.

His eyes glinted with a type of ferocity. "Why would I be angry, Lucy? You can just come and go as you please. There's nothing keeping you here, is there?"

I blinked, surprised at the hostility in his voice. "Clay, that's a stupid thing to say and you know it! You're the one who said go and apply for the institute! I can't just give up my dreams on a whim!"

"I'm a whim?"

"What institute? Who's a whim?" Becca's face moved back and forth between us like she was watching a tennis match. "Is this some kind of lover's tiff?" She scrunched up her nose in confusion.

I scoffed. "Absolutely not! Steely heart over there wouldn't be capable of love! It might offend his reclusive sensibilities!"

"O-O-O-K. It is!" Becca somehow found it amusing, while Clay and I continued to glare at one another.

"So are you leaving, Lucy, or not?" Becca asked. "I was teasing you to see if the old rumor mill is true and you are indeed sneaking kisses under the maples at twilight, but now I'm just confused."

I colored. People had seen us all the way from the road?

"Well?" Becca asked, cocking her head, her face not as bright.

"Yeah, I am, Becca. The ticket's booked and paid."

The room was static with silence, and I couldn't help feeling I'd hurt them deeply.

***

"How was I supposed to know what to say?" I pulled weeds from the garden bed, tossing them into a pile.

Clay was on his haunches next to me, his aftershave wafting over, making me want to bury my face in his neck. "Leave it, Lucy. It doesn't matter."

I held up a hand. "It doesn't matter. *It?*" I never knew how he really felt. Was he angry I hadn't told him first, or upset that I was leaving? He shut down, and was frosty with his attitude.

He grabbed a shovel, and dug into the garden bed, his muscles flexing. I'd miss those arms around me, more than he would ever know. "Why can't we talk about it?" I put my hands on my hips.

"What's the point?" He glared at me. "I think we should just forget about us." He motioned from me to him where our hearts were. "It'll be easier." He dropped the shovel to the earth with a sigh.

I scrunched my eyes closed. He was hurt. Eventually, I said, "I don't want to forget about us, Clay." I stepped into his arms, and he held me tight, his heart beating against my face—a sound I would never forget.

"The farm sure will be quiet when you leave," he said, his voice light.

What had I expected? Him to beg me to stay? I knew Clay wasn't that type of guy.

CHAPTER EIGHTEEN

"There's only two weeks to go until the festival! We've sold over two hundred tickets already, and there's more orders coming in every day. At this stage I'm worried about finding enough space for them all, but Lil says they'll bring picnic rugs, and we'll have plenty of tables and chairs…"

"You've always been great at organizing things, honey. I'm so proud of you," Mom said slurring her words more than usual.

"Have you seen the doctor lately?" I broached.

"Yeah, yeah," she mumbled. "I'm fine. My voice has taken a hit, that's all. I sound worse than I am. Have you heard from the institute yet?" I'd told Mom about applying two weeks before the cut-off for submissions. I'd had to pay extra for express freight, so not my finest choice.

Outside on the porch of the B and B, Rose walked out carrying a basket of laundry to hang on the line. She hung sheets and pillow slips. With the warmer weather the B and B had its first flurry of guests.

To Mom, I said, "Not yet. Can you imagine how many people submit? I don't think I stand much of a chance against people who've had years studying art at college."

She scoffed. "You had the best, darling. You had Adele all those years, teaching you one on one. Besides you've got a natural talent for it. I know they'll choose you. I can feel it in my bones."

"Well, how can I argue with that?" I laughed.

"What have you decided about Clay?"

I sighed. "Nothing. It is what it is, a vacation romance, complete with fireworks that will end as soon as I leave here."

"You never know," she said, "what life has in store."

"Go on, tell me what the tarots say about us then…"

***

The next afternoon, we took a break and headed into the cottage to escape the heat. After much pestering, Clay had finally agreed to listen to his uncle's musings. "Get comfortable," I said to Clay, flipping open the journal.

Clay sat at the dining-room table with an exasperated sigh.

"Let's hear what the crazy old man has to say," he said and folded his arms.

I glared at him.

"What?" he said. "I mean it, let's hear it."

"Clamp that mouth of yours closed then." He mock saluted.

I read aloud:

All these years later I still think of her when I wake, and when I sleep. She haunts my dreams, my days, as though she's waiting for me. Love doesn't end when a person dies. I don't know what happens when you leave this world, but I know we'll meet again. Maybe we are reborn, and our paths will cross in the next life and our love story will continue. It has to. I hold on to that when the pain of losing her comes for me.

I put a hand to my chest. "See? Isn't it beautiful?"

"Yeah, so he missed her, I get it." He shrugged.

I tilted my head. "I think, between these pages, there's a message here. Like there's answers about love, or life, and the key to happiness. Maybe this is one of the greatest love stories of all time."

"I don't think so, Lucy. The greatest love stories don't end in tragedy." He folded his arms, and rocked back on the chair, his face void of expression as if he wasn't touched by his uncle's words at all.

"Yes they do! The *best* love stories are tragedies. *Romeo and Juliet. Tristan and Isolde.* Stories like that teach us to love whole-heartedly, no matter what it costs, because what if it's fleeting? Would you rather not love than to love for a little while? Real love that overshadows everything else and makes time stop, and nothing else matter?" I didn't say it out loud, but I was clinging to the idea, because that's how I felt about Clay, and maybe the brief time we had together would be enough to last me forever.

"Love is *too* hard. And this journal proves it. Besides, *Romeo and Juliet*, and *Tristan and Isolde* are fictional stories, right? This is *real*."

"Fiction comes from somewhere." I closed the journal, running a hand along its cover. "Most people would die to find a love like he describes."

"Was it worth it, though? He spent the rest of his life missing her." How could he not get it? Clay obviously didn't feel love as deeply.

"Of course it was! Because he loved her with *everything*: his soul, his heart, his mind, his body. She was his world, so the *real* world faded to black. Don't you see? He found another kind of beauty here. And he could see her here, feel her here. He wasn't hiding, he was seeking salvation the only way he knew how."

"Maybe," he conceded.

"He loved a girl so fiercely he couldn't function without her. He's a hero, really. A proper *real-life* hero, who worshipped a woman above all else." My tone was clipped as I tried to convince him. "And there's more—look at these sketches."

The thin pencil lines were smudged, you could just make out the whorls of his fingerprints. Even gone, his mark was still here, the very essence of the man. The picture was of the lake, flowing freely, the sun shining, like it was now. The tapping over, another season upon us. As always, she was there, this time lying on a rug, hand shading her eyes. The length of her long hair fanning out behind her.

"Do you know anything about your uncle?"

"No."

"Well, you're not going to be much help when it comes to solving this riddle."

He sighed. "Lucy, sometimes I want to strangle you. He'd dead. What does it matter?"

"And sometimes I want to beat you over the head with a baseball bat, so we're even. It matters because… because…" I faltered. "It's walking in his footsteps here, making maple syrup, talking to his trees. He was someone special, and for some reason I want to find out what happened to him. I want to know he was OK in the end. He sketched so beautifully…" My voice petered out. Like me, he chronicled his days with artwork, with his sketches in the journals. His heart was right there on the page for all to see.

Somehow it shaped my confidence as a painter; he didn't hide from his feelings. Some of the sketches were raw and angry scenes—a crumpled, mangled car, a scream so loud it was like I could hear it. We were the same, kindred souls, who used our medium as a coping mechanism. Why couldn't I share my art with the world? Those who needed it, those who recognized something in it and related, would understand, and those who didn't, did it matter?

It was an epiphany. The time I'd spent here had made me stronger physically but also emotionally. I'd learned so much about myself, and what I wanted and needed in order to be happy, and to fulfill my mom's wishes for me. And to fulfill my own.

Jessup had shown his very soul to me with his work, his musings, and there was a desperate beauty in it. It was timeless, and forever. He and the girl were gone from this world, but part of them would always remain because of his art.

"He died here, alone. That's what happened to him," Clay said, flippantly.

"I don't understand why it means nothing to you!" Clay was so caring in one way, and so narrow-minded in another. Surely, his uncle's life meant something? Just because he didn't know him, did that mean he didn't matter? It hurt to think one day Mom would be gone, and it would be like she never existed, except to me, and the space she left in my heart would be a gaping wound that no one could replace. Would I be the only one to miss her?

***

We were clearing the last spot of land, ready for the Sugaring-Off Festival. To the left of the lake was a grassy patch that would be perfect for the guests.

"Let's start there." Clay pointed to a clump of logs that were overgrown with weeds. "I'll go and get the truck," he said. "We can hoist the logs into the bed, and use the chipper later."

I was already using a scythe on the tall growth as he walked away. With the sun on my back, it was tempting to roll over and lie there squinting up at the bright-blue sky. Instead, I moved to another section, where the weeds were taller than me. I stepped forward ready to launch the scythe and tripped over something. I brushed the long grass aside. It was a rusted-out chainsaw. Why would there be one all the way back here? I parted the weeds and came to a copse of trees.

My breath hitched. It was like something out of a fairy tale. A tiny little cottage stood there like something out of "Hansel and Gretel". How could we have missed this? I suppose these trees weren't maples so we'd never bothered to walk this far over before.

When Clay returned I waved him over excitedly. He jumped out of the truck and jogged over to see what I'd found.

"What?"

"You're not going to believe this, Clay. There's another cottage." I gestured into the distance.

"Where?" From where we stood all that was visible was the long grass, and the leafy trees. Maybe the snow had a part in shielding it from view when we'd edged close before.

I pointed. "Behind here, follow me."

I pushed the grass back, and stepped into a dark clearing. And there it was. The windows were covered in a dusty film, so I brushed it away and peered in. Pitch black inside.

I wandered around to the front door and nudged it open.

It was too dim to see much.

"I'll get the torch from the truck," Clay said jogging away.

Too excited to wait, I stepped into the cottage, groping the wall for a light switch but finding none. The floors creaked underfoot, as I strode around.

Clay raced inside, the torchlight trained directly on my face, blinding me before he realized. "Oops," he said and directed the light away, so it landed on one of the walls.

"Shine the torch over here," I said. With the light trained on the wall, shadows danced around the room. "Clay... look at these."

Paintings. Two of them. They *must* have been Jessup's. Though I remembered in the journals, he said he hadn't lifted a brush since he arrived here. The woman's eyes were a deep dark brown, with swirls, minuscule flecks, in so many different hues, it was like reading her past… almost like a code, if only I knew the symbols.

My heart stopped, sure I was staring at the work of a master. To see the woman brought to life in color was awe-inspiring. It was as though I knew her, knew him, from the journals, and now they were brought to life by oil paint. At that moment I so desperately hoped the Van Gogh Institute would accept me. I wanted to learn, to absorb as much as I could so I could paint like this one day. My skin prickled as I stepped closer. I knew this work from somewhere. I'd seen it before; I was sure of it.

"Why would he hang paintings here? And not inside the cottage where he actually lived?" The space was empty, other than one lonely chair.

"I don't know," Clay said. "But we can use this cottage." His eyes lit up. "We could sell the maple syrup from here. It won't take long for me to fit out. And I can install some lights." He flicked the torch to the bare ceiling. "What do you think?"

"I think these are magical." I couldn't drag my eyes away from the paintings.

"They're creepy." Clay dismissed their exquisiteness just like that.

My eyes went wide with surprise. "How can you say that? Look at the detail… Somehow he's captured what they feel for each other. Can't you see it?" It was like I could read their minds, their love poured from the canvas. This timelessness was why I painted. These two people were gone—maybe joined again in the next place, but a part of them would always be here, trapped, frozen in time on the canvas.

"I'll sheet those walls, and install shelves for the bottles of syrup." He paced around, face eager with the prospect of more work.

"What about the paintings?"

"They're not really my thing," he said. "Let's call it my gift to you."

All I could do was shake my head. How could he not see what I was seeing? "Are you sure you want to give them away? I don't know, I get the feeling they're priceless, somehow."

He scoffed. "Yeah, Jessup, a maple syrup farmer... I don't think so. They're all yours."

I turned back to them, wanting to take in every tiny detail. "Thanks, I might ship them home to Mom for safekeeping." But could I part with them, even just until I got home? They were beauty personified.

"I'm going to grab a measuring tape, and size up what I need," he said, the paintings forgotten as easily as that.

"I'm have to catch up with the girls at Missy's, so I might head back to the B and B early..."

He kissed the top of my head. "I'll drive you, and that way you can take these with you now."

When the paintings were safely in my room, I couldn't help but stand there agog, and stare. While Jessup's sketches had been extraordinary, the paintings were on another level. I tried to call Adele in Paris, but got her answering machine. I left a quick message, and hoped she'd call me back soon. The room was silent, bar the beat of my heart, which hadn't slowed to its normal pace since I'd laid eyes on the paintings. I had an overwhelming feeling my life was set to change, and I didn't know if it was for the better or not. Was it because of the artwork in front of me?

CHAPTER NINETEEN

"She's adorable!" I softened my voice so as not to scare baby Angel, as Missy passed her swaddled daughter to me. Angel's tiny face peeped from the white blanket. She had a small tuft of auburn hair the same color as Missy's.

"Why thank you, Lucy!" Missy said. "She melts my heart, but golly, she seems to be a night owl. Sleep doesn't come easily for any of us."

Missy slumped back on the couch, and yawned. Not even make-up could disguise the dark circles under her eyes. I glanced back at Angel. She blinked up at me, openly curious for such a small thing.

"She'll get there," CeeCee said. "Babies ain't all the same. Some take a little longer to get themselves 'climatized, that's all."

"I hope I'm doing it right, Cee. It's easy to sit here and worry over every little thing, sometimes. You know, at mothers' group, all those babies sleep through the night already... The moms all rave about how easy it is, and I'm the only one who says differently. I get to wondering what I'm doing wrong." She squeezed her eyes closed as if she was fighting off tears. I wanted to give her a great big hug, and the kind of advice CeeCee would, but I had no idea what to say to make her feel better. I'd never even cuddled a baby before today.

"You pay no mind to those other mothers," CeeCee said, her voice rising. "I got half a mind to go down there and ask them why they don't support you more! Seems to me, it's one big competition, and that ain't right. No baby is perfect, they just babies, so I think they're stretching the truth sayin' otherwise."

Missy gave Cee a shaky smile. "I know, Cee. But they're all energetic, and happy. I drag myself there for Angel's sake so she can meet other babies, and socialize like the books say you should, but I could easily stay home and sleep for a week. Maybe it's because I'm so much older than them? Right now I feel ancient." Missy's eyes shone with tears. It was so hard sitting there not knowing what to do. At least we'd stock up her fridge, and freezer, and she'd be able to have an early night while we crooned to the baby.

CeeCee waved her away. "Don't you even think such a thing. You're doing a great job, Missy. She's got the colic. There ain't much you can do but ride it out. Sleep deprivation is tougher than almost anythin' so you doin' just fine."

Missy sighed. "It's so hard to see sometimes when my brain is foggy. I'm just so thankful I've got you at the salon, Becca. I don't know what I would've done otherwise."

"I'll stay as long as you need me to," Becca said. "I'm absolutely loving it here." I'd forgotten Becca was only staying in town while Missy was away. Ashford would be a tiny bit duller without her sunny nature.

"At this rate," Missy said, "I don't think I'll be coming back. Not for a while."

There was a knock at the door. "It's only me!" Lil walked in, her tiny little belly poking from under her shirt.

Everyone chorused hello, and Lil sat beside me on the couch and peered down at Angel. "Hello, beautiful girl, it's your Aunt Lil." She spoke baby language to her and pulled some hilarious faces. I found it almost impossible not to laugh. "What?" she said searching my face. "Too much?"

"Ah…" I said, "Angel seems to like it." The baby was gummy-smiling back at Lil.

"Where's Sarah?" Becca asked.

"She's on her way," Missy said. "Got held up with that delectable man of hers, I'd say."

There were murmurs all around. Ridge apparently was quite the hunk. Sarah called him her book boyfriend come to life, but I hadn't met him yet. He worked away, his visits to town infrequent. It gave me hope about long-distance relationships, the way Sarah raved about him.

"Until then, how about we make a mess of Missy's kitchen? I'm going to make some of the recipes we'll have at the festival, so you can all tell me what you think." Lil patted my knee.

"Pass me my little bundle o' joy," CeeCee said, beaming. I handed Angel over as delicately as if she was made of glass.

Missy piped up. "I gotta say it, I can hardly wait to taste the food you all make with maple syrup. I reckon I gained ten pounds at the Chocolate Festival, and now there's maple syrup—a girl's got no chance living in this town!" She guffawed, and her whole body relaxed.

CeeCee said, "Those infamous curves of yours Missy are a touch on the skinny side. You need plenty of maple syrup to put Vol-into-Uptuous, you hear? Can't have you sashaying around town skinny! People'll think we ain't feeding you right! They know we your best friends. And what's that say about our cookin' if you done lose too much weight?" Her body shook with her deep rumble of laughter.

Missy slapped her leg, and hooted. "So, if I'm too skinny it will look bad for you? Well why didn't you say? I would have eaten a helluva lot more these last few years!"

I grinned at them. "Does that apply to me too?"

"Well, sure!" CeeCee said. "You part of the gang now!"

My heart was fit to burst. I'd never had friends like these.

Lil grabbed my hand and pulled me into Missy's kitchen. It was all pine-covered, but sassy like Missy herself, with touches of red, from vases, to sparkly chandeliers, and picture frames.

She took two aprons out of her bag, and threw one to me. "OK, so I thought we could start off real simple, and stuff that Clay might be able to sell all year round too. So some maple sugar pecans—how does that sound?"

"Perfect! You know, he only really has to work four months a year. Unless he makes enough maple syrup to sell all year round. I have no idea what he'll do the rest of the time. He can't sit still, that guy."

"He'll find something to do. There's always someone who needs a hand." Lil smiled as she tied her apron. She reached for a cookie sheet under the bench. She knew her way around Missy's kitchen. "Take that parchment paper and line the sheet."

She switched on the oven while I did as instructed. "Now spread out the pecans."

I crunched into a pecan before spreading the bag evenly on the sheet.

"Now all you do is drizzle over a cup of maple syrup, a dash of cinnamon, and a pinch of salt. It's that easy. Then you bake for ten minutes, and it's done. I thought we could make some sweets like this for a goodie bag for them all to take home—what do you think?"

"Great! Then they won't forget the farm in a hurry."

Spinning on her heel, Lil put the sheet in the oven, and then went to her purse again, this time pulling out a writing pad. "Yell out if you don't like the sound of any of these, but I thought to shine the light on maple syrup we'd make them all, then we'll have every taste bud accounted for."

"OK," I said, marveling at how considerate Lil was being—after all, she was the caterer, not me.

"So, to go with our savory meat dishes, I thought of maple grilled corn, maple coleslaw, and tomato and watermelon salad with a maple dressing. That way, the boys can be on the grill, and we can handle the other stuff in the kitchen. The salad we can pre-make and just add the dressing on the day…"

The syrup would be used in such a way, that maple would be the hero of each and every dish. "They sound amazing, Lil."

She flashed me a smile. "Wait until you taste them. I'm so glad I'm pregnant, because I am going to claim I'm eating for two, and eat even more than usual!"

I laughed. The scent of the maple-covered pecans permeated the room, rich and nutty.

"Now, the best bit—sweets. I have about a squillion ideas, but I think the most popular would have to be maple and apple ice cream. I can ask Sarah to help serve it. We've got an ice-cream cart that we can use, and people can just wander on over and choose the type of cone they want…"

"Perfect, Lil! Please tell me we're making that to try now?" I gave her a hopeful look.

She raised her eyebrows. "I had a feeling you might say that!"

Lil took out the ingredients to make ice cream and went patiently through each step with me.

***

We'd eaten and tidied the kitchen. Missy's freezer was stocked with the meat dishes we'd made to test the recipes.

They were so mouth-wateringly good, I couldn't wait for the guests to taste them.

We settled back in the living room and talked quietly. Missy had escaped for a nap while CeeCee crooned to baby Angel, attempting to get her to sleep too. Becca had called it a night, because she had to be up early to open the salon. That just left me, Lil, and CeeCee, until there was a rap at the door.

Sarah from the bookshop arrived, stumbling inside with a huge bag of books. "Sorry I'm late! Honestly, I spend more time on Skype with him than I do in real life. Our paths don't seem to cross much anymore."

"They don't?" I asked.

She shrugged. "I guess it's always been like this, but lately, it's harder for me. Like I'm waiting, all the time, like we've stalled."

"Have you told him, sugar plum?" CeeCee asked gently.

Sarah forced a smile. "No, not yet." She waved her hand. "Anyway, never mind, I still have my books. So what's been going on? What did I miss?" She looked to us one by one.

Lil sagged against the sofa. "Lucy just told us she's leaving not too long after the festival. She's off to Paris."

"I can't imagine you not being here no more," CeeCee said.

I swallowed back a lump in my throat. "Me neither." Their faces fell, and it was hard not to do the same. I was supposed to be thrilled with the thought of traveling, but instead, I was torn between wanting to stay, and wanting to pursue my art. Even if I didn't get accepted into the institute, I would still be with Adele, who was a brilliant teacher.

"Well," Sarah said. "We better make sure we give you the time of your life before you go. We sure are going to miss you."

"Right," Lil said, clearing her throat. "Let's go through your checklist, and see if we can't scratch a few more things off."

I took my notebook from my bag. "Chairs, tables, crockery," I said. "Vanessa from the community center said I could borrow theirs for a small hire fee. So I've booked them."

The girls nodded. "Decorations." My brow furrowed. "I have so many ideas, but really it all comes down to cost."

CeeCee spoke up. "Balloons are cheap an' easy. Kids love 'em, too. How 'bout we buy a bunch in the same kinda colors as the maple leaves? All those reds and oranges?"

We spoke in hushed tones as the moon rose high in the sky. A feeling of gratitude washed over me, not only for their help with the party, but their friendship too. I hoped no matter where I went, or ended up, they'd keep a part of me in their hearts, always.

"You know, the town's gone crazy with wanting to pitch in because of what Clay did for Walt…"

I inhaled sharply. "How did you know it was Clay who made the furniture?"

Lil moved around the bench and sat beside me. "Rosaleen, of course. Town gossip, and late-night street trawler. She saw him. She sees everything, that woman."

I threw my head back and laughed. "Is she the one who caught sight of us under the maples?" I didn't add "kissing passionately"—I was still shocked people knew.

"Actually, no." Lil laughed. "That was Jimmy the bus driver. Said he saw you on many occasions, and didn't know where to look, until CeeCee hollered, 'Maybe look at the road, Jimmy, like you 'sposed to!'"

"It's true what they say, then. No such thing as a secret in a small town."

"If the grapevine's quiet, someone will go ahead and make some up… It's not all rainbows and butterflies, but I guess it'd get boring if it was."

CHAPTER TWENTY

The Sugaring-Off Festival was only a week away and our nerves were high. That day at the farm the afternoon came around quickly, as we'd raced to complete tasks. The hours spun by in a frenzy as we fitted shelves to the cottage, and hooked up lighting. Overnight Clay had sheeted the walls, and flicked a coat of paint over them.

My time was fast running out, not long until the farm was crowded with people, and not long until I'd fly to Paris. Both made me jittery with nerves. I hadn't broached the subject of leaving with Clay again, half fearful I'd see nothing in his eyes. I'd rather go thinking he'd miss me, than getting a simple wave goodbye.

"Done," he said, placing his drill on the counter. The shelves were up, and ready to be filled with bottles of maple syrup, which would sparkle under the tiny downlights Clay fitted.

He was extraordinarily gifted when it came to measuring and fitting cabinetry, and anything mechanical, or electric. "So numbers make sense to you?" I asked, as I swept the floor, ridding it of sawdust.

"I can read a tape measure, if that's what you mean," he said absently, as he surveyed the newly fitted shelves.

"How'd you run a business before, with all the paperwork and stuff?" I was intrigued how he managed it, and hoped he wouldn't see it as prodding.

He let out a long breath. "I had a business partner."

"Oh?"

"Yeah, oh. Can you drop it?" He slid me an irritated look.

"Why?" I put my hands on my hips. "Why can't I know you better?"

He shook his head. "I like you, Lucy. You like me. Isn't that enough?"

Like?

"No, it's not enough." There were times where I wanted to sit down with Clay and pour my heart out to him. But his resolve to keep the past private only steeled me to do the same.

He scowled. "What do you want? You're leaving, right? I don't hear you saying you're coming back anytime soon. You want me to give you the grisly details of my life—will that make it easier for you to walk away?"

"Why do you think I'm always searching for a way to leave? You haven't asked me to stay, Clay. You haven't asked a damn thing about me."

"Because *you're* leaving, Lucy." His voice dropped. "And the more I know about you the harder it'll be to let you go."

"Clay…"

"Do you think I'm with you just for the sake of it?" He cupped my face and stared deeply into my eyes, his gaze penetrating.

"I don't know what to think, because we never talk about it." I wrapped my arms around his waist, thinking of Paris, and the fact he wouldn't be there. The best part of my day was seeing Clay, the way he gave me a warm smile, and kissed me until I was breathless. Even if I wanted to return when the year was up, I couldn't. I was going back to care for my mom, and nothing would change that.

"I'm not one to sprout about how I feel, Lucy, but I thought you understood. I don't do one-night stands, or short-term relationships. But this happened. And what right have I got to tell you what to do? I know you have to leave, and I know you've got ambitions loftier than making maple syrup. I won't stand in your way."

I blinked back tears. "So… it's goodbye for us, after the festival?"

"I don't know what to say, Lucy. But if you stayed, and gave up your dreams, things would be different," he said. "You'd be bitter about it."

I gave him a sad smile. If this was love, wouldn't we refuse to part?

"It's unbelievable the universe would throw us together if it can't work."

"Who knows what might happen. I'm a patient man, Lucy." Would he wait? I'd be back in Detroit. Could we commute between the two places, or would our feelings dilute as time apart blurred the way we felt into a distant memory? Sarah saw Ridge every few weeks, and they were struggling with that. This would be way harder.

"Come here." He led me outside into the sunshine and pulled me to the grass, our legs tangling. He kissed me, his lips soft against mine.

Hours later, using our clothes balled up as pillows, watching the sun set, he spoke. "You wanna know about my past, here goes… I built up my business from nothing. It was just me and my tool belt, and a few odd jobs here and there."

"So you were always exceptional with your hands?" I grinned.

He kissed the top of my head. "Always. Well one summer I met an old friend from the neighborhood. He'd just landed a job as the engineer on a huge industrial building site." As Clay talked, he stroked the top of my shoulder, sending shivers down the length of me. I turned to face him, and put my hand on his chest, our nakedness feeling totally natural.

"I worked for him for a while, doing fit-outs of each office. When it comes to work, if I'm stuck reading plans, someone explains them and I can memorize them, all the numbers, all of it."

"Who explained them?"

"My girlfriend, Dahlia."

I tried to push the queasy feeling of jealousy away. Even her name was exotic.

"That company, my old friend, liked the way I worked. I never missed a deadline, and the finishes were always spot on, because I'm a perfectionist, I guess. Eventually they offered me bigger contracts, so the business grew. I employed staff, and got a partner. Someone who could organize all the paperwork, the taxes, all the stuff that makes my head spin. I stayed hands-on, because that's all I've ever wanted to do. Life makes sense to me when I can turn a length of wood into something beautiful, something functional."

I didn't interrupt, just watched the expression in his eyes change as he spoke. "We made lots of money, those first few years." He paused, a flash of anger crossing his face. "Life was good. Dahlia eventually joined the business and worked in the office. We gave her a slice of the pie. We landed the biggest contract we'd ever had. It was huge! I thought we'd taken too much on. We scrambled to find more carpenters, and I spent my nights checking their work to make sure it was up to standard. I was fanatical about it. I wanted it to be right. Dahlia and I became ships in the night. Things changed. I felt distant from her, and I didn't know how to fix it, or even if I wanted to. The pressure had got to me, and all I could think of was finishing the job, and having a break. It almost killed me: the deadlines, the errors, shipments of wood going missing. It was like a black hole of stress."

"That sounds awful," I said frowning. "I can't picture you being so caught up with making money." Here he was a million miles away from luxury. He only ever seemed to want to make enough to get by.

He faced me. "It was never about the money for me. Sure, I wanted to be comfortable, but at that level, I was drowning. But I didn't want to let anyone down. I hated it. Dahlia and my business partner, Jerry, knew I was dyslexic. It's not like I can't read, but it takes me so much longer to process everything, I lose my way, and it's frustrating. They handled the finances, the paperwork, and all of the payments, so I looked after the technical aspects, and the staff."

My heart sank, guessing what was coming. I stroked Clay's chest, felt his heartbeat speed up as he recalled his past.

"Finally, the job was finished. It was all approved by the builder. It was like the weight had been lifted and all I wanted was a break. The money had been transferred for the job. That night, after locking up the office, I went home to find Dahlia gone. All her things, gone. I wasn't upset; I was mostly relieved. We didn't have to end it with a messy blame game. The next day, I was up early, and in the office. I'd planned to meet Jerry and get all our contractors paid up. But Jerry never showed. I knew then— and probably the signs were always there, but I was too busy to see—that the money was gone. He and Dahlia had skipped town, taken the money, like something out of a B Grade movie." He laughed, a hollow sound. "I'd actually signed a bunch of paperwork days before, giving them my share for a pittance, if you can believe that. I hadn't taken any notice of what they pushed in front of me. Why would I? I always signed whatever they asked."

"Oh, my God, Clay. How could they?" Shock made my eyes widen. "Why would they be so cruel? It wasn't as if they didn't have their own stake in the business."

He shrugged. "All that for the sake of my share… The worst thing was having to dodge the phone calls from the guys who'd spent the better part of three months working on that one job for us. I had no way of paying them. In the end, I sold my apartment, and used the money from that. I sold it for a lot less than it was worth, so they didn't have to wait any longer than they already had. I was almost thirty, and worked fourteen years as a carpenter, and I lost everything. My business, my house, my reputation, and of course my girlfriend, but it's not like I mourn that part."

"And then you inherited the farm?"

"Yep. A few months later I got the call from my uncle's attorney. I'd grappled with leaving, but my name was mud, so I figured I'd come hide out in sleepy old Ashford and forget about the world, and the people who inhabit it. Until this bossy blonde strode up the driveway, and I *knew* things would change."

"Bossy?"

He laughed. "And nosy."

"Oh yeah? You don't want to know what I thought of you when I first walked in."

He guffawed. "*Nice drill you have there*? If I remember correctly, a euphemism if I've ever heard one."

I blushed, and covered my mouth to stop the laughter. "I can safely say, it's one of the best drills I've ever had."

"Is that so?" He rolled over, pinning a leg each side of me, and leaned on his forearms, gazing into my eyes.

"Maybe I need another lesson on how to use it?"

He let out a moan, and bent to kiss me.

***

I think I'd just about exhausted Clay by the time I left the Maple Syrup Farm. He wanted to drive me back to town, but I'd grown to love the walk, especially now the sun followed me a few steps behind. My body twinged at the memory of his touch, and sometimes I wondered how I'd ever be able to function normally again. I was still reeling about Clay's confession and angry on his behalf. It explained so much about him, and his need to be alone. The way he couldn't easily trust people anymore.

The Gingerbread Café was still open, so I poked my head inside.

"Sugar plum," CeeCee said waving me in. "Well lookie here. Care to tell me why you all flushed like that?"

"Sunburn," I deadpanned.

"Don't look like sunburn to me." She waggled a finger at me.

I laughed and followed her to the silver prep bench, hefting myself up on a stool. "Where's Lil?"

"She's taken off early, with that fine thing o' hers from across the way."

I smiled at the way CeeCee spoke. *That fine thing* was Lil's husband, Damon, but she never used his Christian name.

"You in a bit of a conundrum?" She stared me down, making me blush.

I folded my arms and leaned on the bench. "How do you always know?"

She smiled, her brown face crinkling like paper. "Well, you see, you're all flushed up with love, but right there—" she poked me between the eyes "—you got the tiniest little wrinkle. So spill…"

I sighed. "Why is life so messy sometimes? I'm meant to be 'finding' myself but somehow I've managed to find someone else, and I have to leave. I made a promise to my mom. And I want to go, I really do, but I also want to stay. How can I please both parts of me?"

"You ruled by your head and your heart, cherry blossom. Findin' yourself is as easy as listenin' to 'em both and deciding what's best. You ain't the stranger who walked in all that time ago lookin' like a deer trapped in headlights. I see a beautiful girl, flushed up with love, and confidence. Art school won't go forever now will it?"

I mulled it over. Mom wanted me to be happy—it was as simple as that. But I knew she wanted me to further my art, and after being here, and finding Jessup's journals, being inspired by him, so did I. Mom had complete faith I could make a career out of it. I think her real motivation was she'd know I had something else I loved in my life other than her when things changed.

"There's always a solution to every problem, if you look hard enough," CeeCee said. "And if it's meant to be, he'll wait."

Would he though? I'd changed so much in the last few months, but so had Clay. Was our relationship, or whatever it was a stepping stone for things to come? Or just a bridge to cross? Only time would tell. "Long distance—it will have to be if he does wait, Cee."

"You never know what might happen… You just go on and things will work out, mark my words. You need a gingerbread milkshake," CeeCee said. "Always makes things clearer."

"Thanks, Cee." I leaned my elbows on the bench, and cupped my face, watching her work. She ambled around the kitchen, grabbing milk and spices, and whipping some cream in a handheld blender. When she placed the drink in front of me, my mouth watered. Spicy, nutty, and dolloped with so much cream, it'd fill me up if I managed to drink it all.

"Lil's been baking up a storm, practicing a bunch o' new recipes. What else you lovebirds got to do for the festival?"

I blushed at the term, and then guilt crept up and tapped me on the shoulder. Clay and I had spent the better part of the last few days lying entwined, on the soft green grass by the lake when we should have been working.

"Oh," I said. "Fix a few garden beds. Pick up the bain-marie. Confirm with the band. Buy napkins, and the decorations…"

"Never you mind," CeeCee said. "'Tween all of us, we'll get it done. You know Walt said he'd come, and I'm just about giddy with happiness for him. Lil and Damon went to visit, and you know what… he was working on some furniture. Things might just be looking up for our Walt."

"Oh that's great news, Cee."

She put her hands on her plump hips. "I was thinkin' we could introduce him to Clay, maybe they can bond over furniture or some such, and it might bring him outta the house more."

"Might get them both out more," I said.

"Two miracles in one day?" She laughed. "It's happened before."

***

Back at the B and B, I dialed Mom's cell. It rang out, so I washed up, brushed my teeth, and called her again. This time she answered, but a coughing jag got the better of her.

"Sorry, honey. Dang cough. How's things? It's late."

"Were you asleep?"

"I can't sleep in this awful place... sometimes—" She broke off, suddenly.

My skin broke out in goose bumps. I *knew* she was keeping something from me. "*What place?* Where are you, Mom?"

Silence hung between us. I listened hard—voices, TVs in the background. My heart beat so hard, I could feel it in my ears. "Mom..." I tried to keep my voice level, hoping my first instinct was wrong. "Do not tell me you've moved into *that* place, please." I spoke through clenched teeth, as realization hit me hard.

"Honey..."

I stifled a sob. "Aunt Margot was never there, was she?" That explained all the dodged phone calls, Mom allegedly asleep when Aunt Margot was hundreds of miles away in her own house.

She sighed, rasping. "It's for the best."

"The best?" I spat the words. My brain was about to explode. I couldn't believe she'd do this. The one thing we'd always vowed would never happen. Her moving into the state facility. Aunt Margot must have paid a paltry amount to make it happen, and wiped her hands, probably thinking she was a savior. My chest seized. "Why, Mom? WHY?" The sobs escaped as I thought of her in that place, where there were too many beds crammed into the rooms. Where it was understaffed, and busy, too noisy for her, and she was too easygoing to ask for what she needed.

"It's not so bad. Now I want you to listen to me. Lucy, this would have happened anyway. You'd work yourself into an early grave the way you were going, and I won't have it."

"No!" I let the tears fall. Part of me wanted to scream at her for doing this, and the other part wanted to curl up and sob. Our family of two that had been split up the middle. "No way, Mom. I'm coming straight back. I'm leaving..."

"Oh no you're not, Lucy! I won't have you wasting your life anymore! I forbid you to come back! You hear me?" Her voice rose. She'd never yelled at me before. "You made me a promise and you're going to keep it!"

"So you lied? This whole trip was built on a lie? The promise was for nothing! Just like yours was!" I couldn't comprehend why she'd do such a thing. Facilities like that meant the end was near, and it goddamn wasn't.

"What?" she asked quietly.

I took a deep shuddery breath. "I know you broke a promise to Aunt Margot, and that's what started the fight."

Silence met me.

"Mom?"

"How'd you know about that? Did she tell you?"

"No, of course not. I've overheard you arguing about it. So what was it, Mom? You can break your promises, but I can't break mine, even when it means you're *there*, in that hovel of a place?"

She sighed, a long crackly sound, and guilt rushed me, thinking how this would affect her later. "Aunt Margot wanted me to stop traveling when I had you. She made me promise after your father left, that if I wanted to travel I was to leave you with her, so you could get a proper education, have some roots. Of course, I promised her. Because I didn't think we'd leave." A cough caught her unawares, so I waited for her to stop, all the while trying to envisage myself being raised my Aunt Margot.

She continued, her words slurring slightly. "I thought we'd have the dog, the cat, the car, the job, live in the 'burbs… but I just couldn't do it. So I packed us up and left, and Margot got as upset as I've ever seen her. She said some pretty horrible things to me, and I lashed out too. Every day, I regret what I said to her. Nasty things, that I tried to take back, but couldn't."

"What did you say?" I couldn't imagine my mom saying anything hurtful; I'd never heard her raise her voice until today.

"I told her..." she paused, catching her breath "... that she wasn't going to steal my child just because she couldn't have her own. It was cruel, and mean, and I still don't know why I said it. But she was so intent on you being raised the 'normal' way, that I couldn't stand it. What's wrong with doing things differently? She backed me into a corner, and told me how unlucky you were to have a mother like me, someone so selfish—that only my wants and needs were met."

I ran a hand through my hair, my mind spinning. I knew Aunt Margot had frowned upon our travels but I didn't think it was that serious. My feelings toward her softened a little, because she thought she'd had my best interests at heart.

"I don't know what to say, Mom." I'd never thought Mom was selfish for wanting an alternative lifestyle. I'd always admired her for it. I could see, though, how Aunt Margot railed against it. Living simply, sometimes with only a penny or two—it was probably frightening for her to imagine.

"Why didn't she adopt, or try another way, if she wanted children?"

Mom tutted. "Victor wouldn't. Downright refused. So Margot then took a shine to redecorating her house every six months or so... I think she wanted to be a mom so bad, it almost killed her. It killed our relationship."

"So let me get this straight... you called her and asked for help?" Now the secrets were out I had to know how they'd managed it, and what I could do to fix it.

"I've been writing her for years, keeping her informed of our progress, and one day, she wrote me back, after all that time. She wanted to help you, Lucy. She always has. So I told her all about the Van Gogh Institute and we came up with this plan. Though, of course, she tried to make all these demands, like you go off to college here and that kind of thing. I said I would only agree if the deal was you get one year for yourself, with no strings attached."

"And what did she have to do with it? Did she pay for the facility?" It hurt to even say the word.

"Yeah, she did. And I asked her to come visit me, but she's still mulling that one over. I guess a fight that's carried on this long can't be resolved that quick. You know how much I hate asking for help, but we both thought your future was important, and it was time for you to be young, while you still are… so here I am."

I clutched the phone, as tears spilled, for her, for me, for Aunt Margot. We'd all had things to overcome in order to survive. What a team we'd make if we'd been more open with each other. "It's not fair, Mom. We agreed you'd never, ever go there. They can't look after you there, not like I can."

"It wasn't fair on you." Her voice softened. "I'll be OK… I really will. When you're a mom, Lucy, you'll understand better. I love you more than I can put into words, and if that means I lose a bit of sleep here, then it's worth it for you to have the life you should."

"But how can I, now I know you're there?" The thought of me traipsing around, laughing and smiling each day, while Mom was cooped up in a gray room, the sound of so many TVs blaring, depressed me.

"Because it's only one year! I have friends here, now. I'm quite popular you know." She laughed, and it sounded real.

"Like who?"

"Like Curt, and Stevie, and Craig. There's Meryl, and Dianne... I mean it, they're great people, honey. They understand what it's like to be me; it's kind of like one big support group."

"So Aunt Margot never came and stayed at all?" My voice dropped. I was hurt they hid it from me, and while I understood their motivations, it didn't make it any easier.

"No, honey, but she paid for someone to move our stuff into storage, and clean the place up."

The paintings we'd found at the farm flashed through my mind. I was suddenly glad I didn't send them to a vacant apartment.

The fight left my body, and I slumped, unsure of what to say, or do. "Are your friends nice?"

"They are, and they are sick of hearing about my pretty daughter the painter, I'm sure. Did you hear back yet?"

"Not yet."

"You will," she said, her voice certain. "Soon."

"You sure you're comfortable there, Mom?"

"I am, honey. As good as gold, knowing my baby is out there living life. That's the best feeling in the world, and I get to have that every day for a whole year. Nothing's better."

I wasn't convinced. She needed to be at home, somewhere quiet, someone safe. When she wasn't well, she'd have the privacy and the dignity that afforded.

"I'm going to try and get some rest now, most of my roommates have turned in, so it's lights out. I'll speak to you soon?"

We said our goodbyes, and I clicked off the phone, wondering how she'd managed to keep that from me for so long.

***

Sleep eluded me; I spent the better part of the night tossing and turning, my mind unable to stop spinning. I flicked on the bedside lamp, and snatched up the last journal.

No one knows I'm here, except my sister, and she'd never tell. I've changed my name. I get word from her that they're looking for me. My work is now worth triple, apparently. They want to know where the last two paintings are. Those paintings, I could name the price. What's money, though? The only person I'd give those paintings to is God, and that's only if he brought her back to me for one more day. I'll never leave here, not until I'm carried out. And no one will ever know.

I gasped. The paintings. I wrenched the covers back, and jumped out of bed. They were standing inside the closet, against the wall out of harm's way. They must have been worth a ton of money. Or was Jessup a crazy old man, like Clay said?

Hastily, I snatched up my cell phone, and took two quick pictures and texted them to Adele in Paris. She hadn't responded about the sketches but maybe she'd recognize the paintings. I kneeled down and took a close-up of the signature, which was scrawled in red paint: JDS.

Jessup… what? With shaking hands I sent the pictures to Adele with a text asking her who she thought JDS was and to respond urgently. In the meantime, I crouched in front of them. Were those earlier feelings of recognition with the sketches because he was someone well known? Someone famous enough that he had to hide out in sleepy old Ashford in order for the world to forget he ever existed?

My phone pinged. Adele!

"Is this some kind of joke?"

My hands shook too much to text, so I dialed her number.

"Lucy, what's going on?" Her voice was high-pitched with excitement. "Where are those paintings?" Her words tumbled out in haste.

"Here with me. In my room in Ashford." I tried to keep my voice level, but it shook regardless.

"What? Are you kidding me? Please tell me you're not playing some kind of prank."

"No." She must know! My hands quaked. "Who is he?"

She screeched right down the phone. "JDS is none other than Jeremiah David Sampson. And those two paintings are the ones that went missing when he did. Don't you remember? It was all over the news for months... His wife, she died in a car crash. And he never painted again. Ever since there's been conspiracy theories about where exactly those two paintings ended up. They were his last, and in an exhibition at the Steinwick Gallery in New York, but he took them back, and was never seen again. And neither were they."

My palms were sweaty. I absently ran a hand down my jeans. "I must have been a child when that happened. But I knew his work was familiar. I recognized it."

Adele cut in, "The eyes, he was famous for the way he made them a story unto themselves. I should have realized when I saw the pictures you sent of the sketches, but I thought maybe it was someone simply copying his style. And I hadn't had a chance to get back to you because a friend had a crisis so I've been in Provence for the last few weeks."

"The eyes... yes! That's what I was drawn to as well. So Jessup was Jeremiah? And no one knew he was here except his sister?"

"I don't know about his sister, but all I know is, people looked but they couldn't find him. He vanished."

"His nephew, Clay, inherited his farm, but I don't think he knows about this either. He gave me the paintings like he was giving me a quart of milk..."

Adele gasped, shell-shocked, like I was. "They were there the whole time? I mean… I just can't believe it. And Clay *gave* them to you?"

"He did, not knowing they're worth a lot of money." My heart raced and I tried to stay focused. "If you could read the things Jessup wrote about his wife, gosh, it's heartbreaking. Without her, nothing mattered to him. He said the only person he'd sell those paintings to was God, and that's only if He gave her back, for one more day."

"Wait, so you have the journals, too, admitting who he was?"

"He alludes to it."

She blew out a breath. "But his handwriting, they'd be able to analyze it. There'd be no question those paintings are genuine. And his sister, they'd be able to trace her."

"You can make out a fingerprint on one of the sketches, where he's smudged it. What would the paintings be worth today, you think?" I stuttered saying the words.

"I'd have to check, but, Jesus, I imagine a truckload of dosh. They're *the* missing paintings."

Tingles raced down my spine. "Don't tell anyone, Adele, but can you do some investigating and let me know?" I gulped back guilt. If I sold the paintings I could help Mom. I could hire round-the-clock care; I could damn near buy her a whole ward to herself when she needed treatment. It would solve every single problem. My blood pumped, just thinking of the future and how perfect it could be. "I can sell them."

"OK, I'll keep it between us. But are you sure they're yours to sell?"

Clay.

Mom.

She needed me; she needed a *solution*. "I'm sure," I said too quickly. "He gave them to me."

"There's no harm in doing some research I guess. I'll see what I can find out and call you tomorrow. Put them somewhere safe, for God's sake."

"I will. Call me as soon as you know anything."

She let out a long, slow breath. "This is just unbelievable... I can't even—" She stopped. "Right," her voice was businesslike. "I'll call you as soon as possible."

"Thanks, Adele."

We rang off, and I sat there bewildered. The paintings *were* mine. Clay had said so. I dreaded to think what he would have done with them had I not been there. Maybe used them on a bonfire, or dumped them with the rest of the trash.

My eyes were drawn to them again. Imagine owning them, having them propped on a living-room wall, being able to gaze at that kind of beauty every day. I pinched the bridge of my nose, as a headache loomed.

If I sold the paintings at an art auction, I'd get more money than I'd ever dreamed of. A mystery that plagued the art world for so long would be solved, and someone wealthy would then own two of the most sought-after masterpieces in the world.

I bit my lip. But Jessup hadn't wanted anyone to know. It was *his* secret. It wasn't mine to share. Imagine if Clay found out that I knew the paintings were worth so much money, and on impulse had thought of selling them without even asking him. I would be as bad as his ex-girlfriend, and business partner, doing a midnight flit all for the sake of money.

My body slumped.

I couldn't do it. Not to Clay, not to his uncle, or Clay's mom, who kept her brother's secret all those years. And while it would solve all my problems, it wasn't right. And I knew Mom would agree. She didn't raise me to go around and break people's trust, just for my own sake.

Defeated, I climbed back in bed, and switched out the light.

Jessup had lost so much, and yet, he found a kind of peace at the farm. It was easy to see how, the way the sun drenched the meadows, and the light reflected off the lake, the view as pretty and inspiring as art itself.

The inner art critic in me fought against that. Wasn't it a waste of fine work, for them never to be seen again? Wouldn't I be doing the world a favor if I sold them? There was no question my mom would improve if we could afford better health care. She'd never fully recover, and our main battle was time, and how much she had left—wouldn't it be wonderful if she could enjoy that time in comfort? A house of her own by the beach, where she could watch the waves from her porch. Nurses there twenty-four seven. Healthy food, sunshine, laughter, love.

Why should she suffer due to our finances? Surely that wasn't fair. Out of all the people to find the paintings, maybe it was a sign, fate, that it was me.

I pulled the comforter up, and lay in the dark with my eyes wide open.

CHAPTER TWENTY-ONE

The next morning, I woke bleary-eyed, having barely slept. My head throbbed from a headache that had taken residence in my temples and slowly increased like someone playing bongos inside my brain. Guilt. It was a guilty headache.

In the light of dawn, I realized the paintings were not mine. Even though Clay had given them to me, he had no idea they were worth so much money, and I would never break his trust like that. It was only my desire to save Mom that tempted me. I'd wait for Adele to call, and then explain the whole story to Clay and he could decide their fate.

I carefully bound all the journals together, and put them in my backpack. They would have to be returned too. They were the missing link, and proof of who Jessup was. I had an inkling Clay would keep his uncle's secret. He knew better than anyone what it felt like to want to hide out, and I couldn't imagine him desiring the kind of attention he'd get if he decided to share his uncle's story.

Besides, his mother had been involved in the cover-up, and I doubted she'd want to be grilled by reporters the world over. She made a promise to her brother, and I respected that. I'd made one with my mom, and as hard as it was, I was trying not to break it.

With heavy legs, and a throbbing head, I pulled on some clothes, to head to the farm. Despite everything, I still had to prepare for the Sugaring-Off Festival, so many people were expected to attend. Hopefully being busy would take my mind off it all. A cloak of regret hung around me... Even though no one would ever know, I was disappointed in myself for even thinking of selling the paintings without Clay's knowledge.

I wasn't that kind of person.

I crept from the B and B, and headed to the Gingerbread Café. There wouldn't be many mornings left baking alongside Lil. It was almost time to head to Paris.

***

"So, the jazz band have confirmed," Lil said, smoothing down her apron. "They've waived their fee, since it's all about celebrating the art of maple syrup." Lil smiled. "Our social lives are pretty quiet round here, so the townsfolk love this kind of community event. We used to have a lot more on throughout the year, because Janey and Walt were the driving force. Without her things have fallen away, a little." Her eyes went glassy. "Anyway—" she fanned her face "—this is going to be brilliant for the town, and for the Maple Syrup Farm. Who knows, Walt might actually take up the reins again, after this."

"Wouldn't that be great?" It was hard not to draw comparisons between Walt losing Janey, and Jessup losing his wife. Jessup never really got over it, so maybe Walt would take a long time. Though, with everyone in town looking after him, things might be different.

"All we have to do then is make the food. Some I'll do the day before, and the rest we can make fresh that morning."

I nodded. "Great, Lil."

She inclined her head. "What? What is it?"

I shrugged, my lip wobbling. For the first time ever I had someone to confide in other than my mom, but the list of things bothering me was so great I didn't want to burden Lil with it all. "Spill," she said. "Don't make me beat it out of you."

I averted my eyes. Unbeknownst to the entire town, they'd had a famous painter living among them.

"We all have secrets, Lucy. Some we spread; some we don't. You know—" Lil leaned close to me "—sometimes, things are kept hush-hush though... depends on exactly what a person's hiding." She winked.

I held in a gasp. There was no way she could know about Jessup, or what I had discovered. My cheeks bloomed anyway. "I hope you're right, Lil, because I almost made a very bad decision. I almost broke Clay's trust, all because it would help my mom, and now I feel like the world's worst person."

"Almost? So you didn't then?"

I shook my head. "I didn't but I was sorely tempted." I wanted to tell Clay about the paintings first, in case he did want the secret kept. That was the least I could do in the circumstances.

"Well, put it out of your mind." She shook my shoulder. "I think you're getting upset because you're leaving soon. Is that what it is?"

The doorbell jangled and CeeCee wandered in. I forced a bright smile and we got back to our to-do list.

***

Alone, trudging to the farm, I dialed Mom's doctor. He'd known us for a while and knew we'd wanted to avoid the state facility. Now I knew where she was, I couldn't function properly. It was like my life had been flipped upside down and a part of me worried Mom was still keeping something back.

The doctor answered abruptly, "Dr. Hoffley."

I walked to the shade of a tree and sat down. "Hi, it's Lucy."

The doctor sighed good-naturedly. "I've been expecting a call from you. I thought it would come with a few choice words, yelled down the line."

If it was another time I'd laugh. I'd lobbed some curse words at the poor doctor when he'd given me news that seemed so ridiculous that it couldn't possibly be true. "It's your lucky day. I'm too tired to be angry."

He sighed. "Look, Lucy, I know you wanted to avoid the facility as long as you could. I get that, believe me I do. But with your mom, things are going to deteriorate. You won't be able to care for her, Lucy—"

"Yes I can!"

"Let me finish," he said, softening. "You couldn't. She's close to needing round-the-clock care, Lucy. I know you don't want to hear that, but she needs suctioning, her breathing monitored, all those kinds of things, with machines you don't have at home. She'll last longer in care—she will."

I clenched my jaw, unable to speak. Tears rolled down my face. Pulling my knees up, I thought of the bleak future without my mom. It was really going happen, sooner than I thought.

"I know this isn't what you want to hear, and I'm sorry, Lucy." When his voice came back, it was gentle, and I was thankful the doctor was honest with me. It couldn't be easy for him either. We'd had some battles over the years, but he knew it was because I loved my mom, and it was because I was scared. He'd given me his private cell number once, when we were going away for a weekend, in case anything happened. He was a good guy, and I tried not to call him unless it was an emergency. "How long?" I finally said.

"You know I can't say, it's anyone's guess. Could be a year, maybe two? But with extra nursing help, someone there for emergencies, you'll have longer with her. I've discussed this with Crystal, and she told me about your trip. As hard as it is, I understand why she's making you do it."

"A year or two…" I whispered. "What about the people who live for decades with it? Why not her?"

"She's a fighter, you know that. Anything could happen. She's not giving up. She never will."

"If anything changes, can you call me?"

"Of course. And just think of all the news you'll bring home with you. That'll be as good as any medicine for her."

"Thanks, Doc. For everything." I hung up, and fell back against the grass, sure I was going to die of a broken heart. Everyone always leaves me.

***

Roses scented the air from garden beds at the entrance of the farm. Their red heads stood tall and proud, green stems reaching for the sky. Clay stood next to me, wearing his uniform of jeans and no T-shirt. When he stretched to cut back an overhanging branch, I could see why his tan went all the way down. His jeans hung low, and for a moment I was lost, staring at his body, a wondrous and appealing sight, one I'd now run my hands over too many times to count. He moved to the roses, handling them carefully so he wasn't stabbed by their thorns.

I blinked away my sun-drenched desire and said, "What are you doing?" Their beautiful red petals fluttered to the ground as though the flower was crying.

"I'm deadheading the roses so more grow."

My mouth dropped open. "Why? That's an absolute waste of something so beautiful." An unreasonable amount of anger coursed through me, and while I knew deep down I was being illogical, I couldn't help it.

He dropped the stalk. "What?"

"Why should that flower be sacrificed so more can grow? That's hardly fair on *that* flower is it?"

He shook his head. "That's how it goes, Lucy, if you want healthy roses. It won't be a waste. You can put them in a vase."

I stood in front of the roses, protecting them. "No, Clay. Don't cut them."

He tilted his head. "Are you for real? We're neatening up the garden, including the flowers... otherwise by Saturday, there'll be a bunch of half-dead roses on display."

I folded my arms, not ready to let it go. "They'll still be half alive."

He gave me a puzzled look. "Is this even about the roses? What's gotten into you?"

I double blinked. "I just... I don't know." What sense did it make to cut one off because some of its petals had begun to brown? Maybe I was being irrational, but it hurt to think of the flower dying earlier than nature intended because it was less than perfect. Truthfully, I was comparing it to my mom. Someone so pretty, so vibrant, cut down in her prime, when she still had so much more to give. Just because she couldn't cope on her own, did that make her less worthy to live? No. So why should anything suffer, even a rose? The conversation with the doctor had almost ruined me. I couldn't think through my haze of grief.

I should have told Clay about my mom. My life and my past. But I'd held back, what was the point? I was leaving, and this time I was certain I was. There was no way I'd let anyone leave me again. It was too painful. From now on,

I had to protect myself against hurt. Telling Clay would only make matters worse.

"Lucy, you can trust me, you know." He gazed at me like he knew my secrets, and loved me anyway. When he took me in his arms, I almost crumbled. He sensed it was more than protecting roses. I could trust him, but could he trust me? I let myself relax into his arms and scrunched my eyes closed, feeling grief-stricken and disgusted with myself.

***

Clay made me a cup of coffee and sat across the dining-room table, staring so solemnly at me that I almost cried. My heart was awash with so many emotions, it was hard to rein them in and harder to make sense of them.

Everything had built up. My shoulders tensed, my back ached, just like it had when I first arrived at the farm. Though, now the pain was not from physical work, but from holding myself together so tightly, so nothing spilled out.

I was leaving the only guy I had ever loved. I was leaving my mom in a place that I'd vowed she'd never go to. And my new friends. And all the experiences I'd had here. Would they fade over time, the memories? The love, would that dim?

"Lucy," Clay said leaning forward, staring deeply into my eyes. "Is everything OK?"

I forced a smile. "Yeah, I'm fine, Clay."

He raised an eyebrow. "When a girl says fine, it doesn't mean fine, it means something is wrong."

"You've had a lot of experience with girls, then, I take it?" I don't know what made me say it. It's like I wanted to fight to distance myself from him to make it easier to leave.

He frowned. "Do you want to talk about it, or not?"

"Not."

"Fine," he said.

"Is a guy's fine the same as a girl's fine?" I played with the handle of my mug, avoiding eye contact.

He snickered. "No."

"Right." I rummaged around my bag, and produced a notebook. "We still have to pick up the chairs, and all the stuff from the community center."

"I can do that this afternoon."

"OK, and the decorations… I can pick them up from the grocery store and we can hang them on the day." I'd found a selection of glass jars with scented tea-lights, hanging on thick twine. We planned to loop them around the branches of the maples, the small candles lit, and safe against the wind, in their glass housings.

Bonnie had found me LED fairy lights too. Clay had fixed wire in a zigzag pattern, and tied it between trees, so all I had to do was twirl the fairy lights around the wire, and they'd shine down on the tables beneath. If the day yawned into night-time, and partygoers stayed, then there'd be enough light for the merriment to continue.

"The food's being sorted; the jazz band has confirmed. I think that's about it, then."

Clay reached out and linked his fingers through mine.

"I'm sure it'll be bedlam on the day, but for now, that's all the major stuff done." So much remained unspoken, but by the look he gave, one full of longing, and a touch of regret, I knew he was marking the festival as a day closer to the end of my stay.

"Lucy… why can't you tell me what's wrong? I've told you everything about me, and here you are, pretending everything is fine, when you're all tensed up like you're about to explode. Do you think I don't care? Or won't understand? What's holding you back from telling me?"

I let his words sink in, toying with spilling the whole damn story.

"I just have to go to the bathroom," I said. I'd freshen up, and then I'd confide in him. It was impossible carrying these burdens alone, and I wanted to tell him about the paintings, and what I'd discovered. I stood, hitting my knee under the table. "Ouch." Tears stung my eyes, and I was grateful the bump gave me an excuse for it. "Excuse me," I said hurriedly. I escaped to the bathroom, and washed my face. I dabbed at my skin with a towel, hearing the buzz of my phone. I scraped my hair back into a ponytail, and rushed out to answer but the sound stopped.

Clay had his finger on the screen. He looked up. "I was trying to hang up," he said. "That's the loudest ring tone I've ever heard." With one last swipe at the screen, he hit the wrong button and a message played.

"Oh, my God, Lucy... The paintings are worth millions. Millions! I do think you should tell Clay. You can't sell them without him knowing! Anyway, it'll be a worldwide sensation..." I froze at the sound of Adele's excitable voice, before my brain caught up, and I hit the end button.

"Clay, I can explain..." He glared at my phone like it was poisonous, before making eye contact with me. My legs almost gave way. His face was contorted with anger, his eyes fierce.

"I trusted you, Lucy!" His words reverberated around the room in a big boom.

My face dropped. "I was going to tell you. I was going to give them back to you. And the journals." I moved to him, to touch him, cool him down.

"Yeah?" He was so angry he snarled. "I don't believe you!"

"Clay. Let me explain..."

"I won't let you do anything!" He smashed a palm down on the table, making the contents jump. "So… who was he?" He clenched his teeth so tight, a muscle ticked along his jawline.

Clay didn't know. His mom had kept her word all those years, even after his death. I wondered if she knew the paintings were here all along. "He was a famous painter called Jeremiah David Sampson. But when his wife died, he died too. He hid out here, for the rest of his life, and never picked up a brush again. Before he disappeared, he took two of his most sought-after paintings from a gallery, and the art world has never given up searching for them. They're the ones we found in the little shack, and they're worth a lot of money." I spoke in a rapid burst, trying to calm him down and convince him.

"And you knew, since when?"

I cringed. "Last night. And I was going—"

"You're just like them," he spat. "All you see is dollar signs."

"I'm not, Clay. I'm really not." I so badly wanted to take him in my arms, but fury radiated off him. I could almost feel the heat of it.

"So, your friend lied?" He glared. "You never contemplated selling them?" His voice was heavy with doubt.

"Well… no. Yes, but I can explain." He pushed past me and stalked out. I reached for his arm, pulling him back.

"Clay, it wasn't for the sake of just money. It was for my mother." He wrenched his arm free. "Can you listen?" My voice was beseeching.

"Your mother? How about my mother? I bet she'd like her own brother's paintings, don't you? I gave you those paintings as a gift, Lucy! I can't get over the fact you weren't even going to tell me. You were all set to sell them without a goddamn word to me!" His face went puce with anger.

"It was a knee-jerk reaction, Clay." I threw my palms up. "My mother's not well. She's in a state facility and it's awful. Yeah, I contemplated it! Sure, why wouldn't I dream of creating a better life for my mom with the time she has left! But I didn't go through with it! I would never lie to you. I wouldn't have gone through with it. For one brief moment, it was the answer to my prayers, but I wouldn't have... I promise you, Clay." My eyes filled with fresh tears as I faced Clay, his granite expression firmly in place.

"I can explain it better, if you sit down."

He glowered at me, the full force of his fury hitting me hard. "If your mom is so sick what the hell are you doing here? And then dashing off to Paris? Doesn't sound as though you're doing it too tough, Lucy."

I held a frustrated scream. "I made her a promise, Clay. She wanted me to apply for the Van Gogh Institute, and to start living my own life. She thinks working double shifts in a diner, and then caring for her isn't living. Reluctantly I agreed. But she did all of that so she could move into the facility while I was gone without me knowing... the thing we'd always promised we'd avoid, because *she* wants me to be free. She must think it's an obligation to care for her. We can't afford a better place, one where she'll have correct treatment. She's got ALS, Clay, so no matter what, she's not going to get better. But I wanted her to have at least some quality of life and she won't get it where she is now."

His expression darkened. He didn't believe me. I suppose the jaunting off to Paris thing made it hard to swallow. Why had I ever agreed to this trip?

"Bring the paintings back, Lucy."

He spun on his heel and walked out, slamming the door behind him.

CHAPTER TWENTY-TWO

How had I made such a mess of things? Despondency sat heavy in my belly, making me nauseous. I didn't want to explain the paintings to anyone, but I had no way of getting them back to the farm. I couldn't walk all that way, carrying both of them.

Lil was the only one who had an inkling so I called her on my cell.

"Lucy! Hey we've—"

"Sorry, Lil, can you come pick me up at the farm?" My voice broke. I gulped back the summer air, and tried to settle down.

"Sure." Her voice softened. "You OK?"

"Not really, but I'll explain when I see you."

"I'll be ten minutes—sit tight."

I'd searched for Clay, but couldn't find him. His truck was still in the barn. A property this size had plenty of spots to hide out, and I only hoped he'd cool down and see reason.

Ten minutes later, Lil's truck chugged down the driveway, her long blonde hair blowing out through the window. I opened the door and jumped in, Lil giving me a sideways glance. "What happened?"

I wiped angrily at the tears that wouldn't stop flowing, and explained to Lil as we drove back out on the main road. "Right," she said when the whole sorry story was explained. "So he thinks you were set to make a mad dash with the paintings, even though he gave them to you?"

I played with a balled-up tissue. "He didn't know they were worth anything when he gave them to me."

"I know," she said, her voice level. "But, Lucy, surely he understands anyone in your situation, with your mom and everything, would have thought the same, if only for a fraction of a second? The thing is, you *didn't* do it."

I leaned my head against the window, and stared, numb, as the meadows rushed by. "That's the thing, Lil. I *did* think about selling them and not telling a soul except Adele. I don't know what I was thinking. And he won't forget that, not after what happened to him before. I've ruined everything."

Lil patted my jean-clad leg. "What do you want to do?"

"If you don't mind, I need to take the paintings back to him, and then I guess I'll see if he's ready to talk? If not, I'll head back to the B and B."

"Sure, I can drive you back. Don't worry, Lucy. Once he's had time to think, he'll understand."

I gave her a wobbly smile. I knew Clay better than anyone, and I knew this he would not forgive, no matter what excuses I had. I cursed myself for being so stupid, and calling Adele before I'd even told Clay. He had every right to be mad at me. It was a foolish thing to do.

More than anything, I wanted to talk to my mom, and tell her what had happened. But how could I? It would only worry her—the amount of trouble I'd caused. All because I wanted her to have the life she deserved. What was left of it, anyway.

***

With the paintings safely tucked behind the seats, Lil drove me back to the farm. Our chatter had fallen away, as we approached the front gate. The sun was sinking for the day, the orange of it spilling across the hazy sky.

I sensed Clay wasn't in the cottage. Everything was too still. It was like the farm was holding its breath, waiting for him too.

"Need help?" Lil asked. I shook my head no, just in case Clay was inside. It bothered me, leaving something so valuable in the cottage for anyone to find, but surely he wasn't far away. The irony hit me hard. Maybe he was waiting for me to leave.

I pushed open the door, and called his name. As expected, no response.

I propped the paintings next to the bedside tables in his room, the only place where sunlight wouldn't affect them because thick curtains blocked out the light. The sweater he'd been wearing was thrown onto the bed in a messy crumple, which was so unlike Clay. I snatched it up, and buried my face in it, just in case I never got to inhale his scent again. I folded it and placed it on the buffet. Caressing the leather covers of the journals one last time, I put them in a neat stack on the bedside table.

With a heavy heart, I headed back outside where Lil was patiently waiting, her eyes questioning. I shook my head, and her smile dropped.

***

Back at the B and B, I studiously avoided Rose, begging off with a headache. I wanted to be alone. For a moment, I wished I still had the old man's journals. I'd found his musings a comfort. I'd miss reading his scrawls, and eyeing his sketches. Even though he was gone, he'd felt like a friend. I'd gotten to know a version of him, one not many people would have known. And even though in reality he was someone famous, I would only ever think of him as Jessup, the man who loved a woman above all else.

If Clay didn't want to see me, then in two days the Sugaring-Off Festival would be a disaster. He wasn't a people person, and had asked to make sure I dealt with the crowds while he helped out behind the scenes. I'd joked that it was time he showed his face and stopped the gossip, but he'd just given me a rueful smile, and said, maybe.

I tried to call him, but his cell rang out. Eventually it was switched off.

The day had taken its toll and I fell into a restless slumber. When I woke early the next morning, murky dreams were just out of reach, my head clearing, as the hazy memory of sleep evaporated. And then it all came rushing back. Clay. The farm. The festival.

I threw back the covers, and dressed quickly. I wouldn't take no for an answer today. He would hear me out and if he decided he couldn't handle it I'd leave directly after the Sugaring-Off Festival, instead of a few days later, as promised.

I'd put too much work in to walk away, and leave it all on his shoulders, but he'd have to hear me out, goddamn it. I didn't want to let Lil or CeeCee down, or the plethora of townsfolk who'd donated their time.

I breezed past the Gingerbread Café. Lil was there, hands deep in a bowl, mixing something sweet.

"Any word?" she said, when the jingle of the doorbell announced my arrival.

"Nope. And he's not answering his phone, either. I'll head there anyway."

She nodded, giving me a sad smile. "What about the festival? Should we cancel it? I was going to bake today, and have everyone get there early tomorrow to help you set up…"

I mustered a determined look. "No, the festival will go ahead. I'm not letting my mistake ruin the amount of effort everyone's put in. Plus Clay needs it. Everyone within a fifty-mile radius will know the farm is back up and running."

"Great." Lil's face brightened. "Let's make it a huge success then. And don't worry about Clay. I'm sure he's realized by now, and is probably waiting for you at the farm. I'll make a start on our menu, and you meet me back here whenever you can."

We had the menu planned like we were going into battle, cook times and the order in which we'd do everything was neatly written out, and now I was throwing a spanner into the works, by racing back and forth. "Let's hope he's there, otherwise, I'll have to work through the night to get it all done."

She waved me on. "Go see, and it'll be all hands on deck, if we need to."

With a curt nod, I waved as I rushed out of the café, mentally checking off things I had to do, and putting them in order of priority. It helped assuage the guilt about Clay, and allowed me to focus on not letting the town down.

At the farm there was a slight breeze, the glorious red maple leaves fluttered hello. I smiled at the thought Persephone and her friends were happy to see me. If I hadn't read the journals, would I still have been in awe of them, the way I was? From the way my mother taught me to appreciate beauty, I think I would have. The sun was high in the sky, and radiated down, its fingers of light settling on beds of flowers, making the pinks bright fuchsia, and the oranges almost red. The property was alive with color, vivid and bold and inviting. I had no time to gaze at the scene before me. I raced up to the cottage, and tumbled through the door.

I called out for Clay, just like I'd done yesterday, but there was that same stillness. Only patches of muted sun shining in spots on the floorboards. No noise, no shower scent, nothing out of place in his organized home.

It was hard not to let anger bubble through me. I'd explained and surely that was enough? I hadn't actually done anything, except have a ten-minute mind battle with myself. Arms crossed, I walked to the bedroom. The bedside tables sat solemnly bereft of the journals. And no paintings rested against the grainy wood.

I jogged outside to the barn, and hefted the door open. There was only a dot of oil, a small spill, where his truck would have been. I swung between fury and sadness. How could he walk out when we had so much to do?

I slammed the barn door shut and went to the porch, flopping down in the love swing. It smelled of him. I pushed the tips of my feet on the deck, and swayed gently, thinking of Mom, and Clay, and what would happen next.

My cell phone rang, and I hastily scrambled for it in my pocket.

"Lucy, my darling, I've got—"

"Mom… I made a huge mistake."

The rustle of bed linen greeted me, as I guessed she tried to pull herself into a sitting position.

"Baby, mistakes are a part of life. It means you're trying. I'm sure it's not that bad."

I grimaced at the thought of telling her. "It is. It is bad, and now Clay's gone. And the festival is tomorrow. I'm supposed to leave for Paris soon when all I want is to come home to you."

"What happened with Clay?" She easily sidestepped my wish to be back in Detroit.

"Long story short, it's that he thinks I was going to sell some valuable paintings of his, and leave. And I did consider it. But only so I could help us, get you a home of your own. He doesn't believe me." Mom wouldn't have the energy to listen to the whole saga nutted out.

"If he knows you well enough, he'll know you just aren't like that."

"He's gone. I'm at the farm and he's not here."

"Do you love him?"

"More than anything." It was like being winded, admitting it to her. I loved a guy who didn't trust me and never would.

"Well, then, you find him, and you make things right."

"What about you, Mom? I can't leave you there."

"You made me a promise, baby. And you're gonna stick to it and also—"

I interrupted, trying to convince her I should come home. "Sometimes I think why fight fate? You know? Maybe painting isn't for me. Paris is so far away... You and me, we're just everyday people. I'm not a fashionista, or a foodie. I probably won't fit in there. And all for the sake of an art course that takes me away from you. For what? On the off chance one day someone sees something in my work? I'd rather do double shifts all day long, and be with you." It was hard to keep my voice from shaking. I'd never felt so far away than at that moment. That urge to be with my mother almost took over.

"You're only thinking maudlin like that because of Clay. You've got such a bright future in front of you, baby, you just have to trust me. You have to trust *yourself*. You can work yourself to the bone in the diner, sure, but why waste that God-given talent you have? Do you know how many people are still wondering where their passion lies? Or what they want to do with their life? But you know… The world is open to you, Lucy. Can't you see? All you gotta do is take the opportunities in front of you and learn from them. You're just as good as anyone else is. Who cares if you're not into fashion or food—you're into art, and Paris is going to be a whole new world of discovery for you."

I bit my lip.

"Now go on and find that man of yours. The love god. And make things right. The reason I called is… Aunt Margot is here."

"She is?"

"There's a new place that's opened up near them, in New Hampshire. A facility like this, but more nurses and less patients, sorry, *residents*, I'm supposed to call us." She laughed and it sounded like sunshine. "So I've agreed to move there, to be closer to Aunt Margot, and… it's only three hours away from Connecticut…" She let the words flow over me so I caught their meaning. It'd be a leisurely drive from Ashford. "But, Mom are you sure? What's changed Aunt Margot's mind all of a sudden?" It was too neat, Aunt Margot walking back into our lives and wanting to make it better. What could we repay her with? What was she expecting from us?

"I'll put her on," Mom said over the rustle of bed linen, as she passed the phone.

"Hello, darling. No doubt you're asking why the swift change of direction from me?" Her silky voice was more relaxed than usual.

"I have to say I am, Aunt Margot. You go from not talking to us for years, and now this? I know all about the promise Mom made to you. How could you have wanted to take her daughter from her? I'm all she's got." Who would do that to a person?

"Yes," she said, a slight bitterness creeping in. "You know, Lucy, I loved you from the very moment I laid eyes on you. I was seething with envy, absolutely seething. Here was your mother, without a care in the world, without a proper home, not even a car, doing odd jobs and then having a baby. And then there was me, the perfect home, perfect marriage, so much love to give, yet unable to fall pregnant."

The maples in the distance looked enchanting with their russet-colored leaves, waving in the slight summer wind like they were encouraging me to speak openly. "That doesn't mean you try to take your sister's child."

She sighed. "I know, and really, I didn't want to take you purely for the fact I couldn't conceive. I honestly felt like you weren't safe, living the way she chose to do. What if she ran out of money, which she often did—then what? I didn't think you could have that lifestyle with a child in tow."

"But you were wrong, Aunt Margot. I had the *best* childhood."

One of Mom's friends was sputtering in the background, the sounds of various TV channels muffling down the line. "I see that now, I do. I came up to visit Crystal and saw how much care she needs and how's she living and I was just so disgusted with myself. I've let this silly fight fester for years over my pride, when she's needed me more than ever. I should have been there to help you when things got really hard, instead of offering my help when you were a child, when it wasn't needed."

I let out a long breath. What a waste of so much time between sisters. The things they'd missed in each other's lives was crushing. But there was still the future to look forward to. I'd make Clay see, too, that I didn't want to have a fight with him that spanned my entire life. It would poison me bit by bit if I didn't make amends, but he had to understand too.

"So what now?" I asked, feeling roiling emotions, and hoping Aunt Margot meant what she said.

"Crystal moves closer to me, and I can spend my days with my sister, catching up on all the things we've missed out on because we were pigheaded. And it's not going to be all sunshine and lollipops, I'm sure we'll argue just as much as we did before, but this time, I won't let it split us apart. She needs me, and I need her. I'm here from now on."

My chest expanded with love for them both. I was proud they'd managed to make up and admit their mistakes. No doubt there'd be fireworks, because there always had been when they bumped heads, but that was siblings for you.

"I'm so glad to hear it, Aunt Margot. I was thinking I'd come back once I'm done here with the Sugaring-Off Festival…"

"Oh, no, no, you won't. I've got things covered. I'll put your mom back on."

"There you have it, honey. So will this help you move on, and enjoy the rest of your vacation?"

Would it? I'd always worry, but I felt a damn sight better knowing Mom had family with her. "Yes, Mom, I guess so." Maybe the world wouldn't stop spinning if I spent more time away from Mom. While her voice was weak her will wasn't.

"Now go and find the love god, and sort things out. I see a wedding on the cards for my baby."

I scoffed. "That would be a miracle, Mom. I love you, and I'll call you soon."

Things had come full circle, and I couldn't quite believe it. The fact Mom would have someone to visit her every day was a gift, and even better that it was her sister and they could be themselves.

I had to find Clay, and the piece of my heart that was missing.

***

Two hours later, back in Ashford, even the sight of customers milling in Walt's store, running their hands over the smooth furniture, couldn't produce a smile from me. Though I was happy for Mom and Aunt Margot, I still couldn't find Clay. Would he even come back? Or was he waiting for me to leave?

The doorbell jangled a little too cheerily as I pushed open the door of the Gingerbread Café.

Seeing my hangdog expression, CeeCee clucked her tongue and said, "Still no word?"

I shook my head. "Lil told you?"

She gave me a sad smile. "She told me Clay'd left, but we knew the rest, anyways. You see, Jessup wasn't such an enigma for all o' us. There were a select few who knew his secret, and me and Lil were two of them. But we'd surely never tell another soul. Man's gotta have friends, right?"

"You knew who he was all that time?"

I sat heavily on the sofa, rolling into the dip in the middle. Cee sat opposite and put her feet on the footstool. "We knew for the last six or seven years. We helped him make maple syrup, and that's how it all started. When the end was near, he confided in us, made peace with it all, and then went to join her, and that's all he ever wanted."

My head throbbed with the sheer amount of information I was being told today. Life was so complex. "I'm so glad he had some real friends," I said and meant it. To think the old man did have someone traipsing around the maples with him made me smile in spite of it all.

"So, where do you think Clay is, then?"

"I don't know, Cee. But I've got a feeling he'll just wait for me to leave."

"Ain't nothing you can do but wait, cherry blossom. Clay's the type o' man who's gotta do things his way. He's probably holed up somewhere trying to make sense o' it all. After all, it's a big deal, those paintings."

She sat on the sofa opposite and knitted her fingers together. I reached for my cell phone to call him again, only to discover I'd left it at the farm.

Trying to mask the anguish in my voice, I said, "I'm leaving in a few days, Cee. What if he's not back by then?" The thought of not saying goodbye, not resolving it all, brought tears to my eyes. It would be like losing a part of me.

"Mark my words, he'll be back. That boy loves you; any fool can see that."

"Sometimes I think I should stay, but what kind of person gives up their dreams as quick as that?" I'd toyed with the idea of staying. I loved Clay, and Ashford had become a home for me, but worry edged into my mind— what if I later regretted it? The desire to paint, and learn from masters, couldn't be extinguished no matter what I was leaving. "He might never come back though, if I do."

"True love, Lucy, will always find a way. You go off and have your adventures. Ashford will still be here when you get back."

I wiped my eyes with the sleeve of my sweater. "Will the rest of the world dim, in comparison to here?"

CeeCee kicked her shoes off and put her feet back on the stool. "You listen up: you one o' us now, Lucy. We always be here for you. No matter where you go, you'll be in our hearts. No one can take that away from you. This place won't change much, it never does, but you will. Folk round here will say, 'Remember Lucy? I wonder where she be now? I bet she's doing real great in Paris. She be back soon, we just know it.' No matter where you are you be right here." She tapped her chest. "Forever."

CHAPTER TWENTY-THREE

The Sugaring-Off Festival day arrived with a flurry of nerves. There was still no sign of Clay. High-pitched voices rang out in the Gingerbread Café. Everyone was talking atop each other, raising their pitch to be heard. I'd lost count of the amount of times Lil's mom, Sue, had bumped into me, making me clutch whatever dish I was holding, my eyes wide with fright.

"Oh, golly, sorry, Lucy," Sue said. "I'm such a klutz!"

Lil strode from the back of the café, her arms full of boxes, her big blues eyes peeping above. "What is she doing here?" she said with a heave.

"Now, don't be like that!" Sue said. "You shouldn't be carrying boxes in your condition!"

"They're just napkins and such," Lil said. "Why are you here, Mom? I thought Dad was driving you to the farm so you could stay out of trouble?"

I stifled a giggle, remembering Lil's horror stories about her mom in the kitchen. I had no idea that Lil didn't know she was helping—to use the word loosely—today.

Lil's mom sighed, and waved her away, ignoring the question.

"What has she demolished? Be honest!" Lil stared hard at me, her hands on her hips.

"Erm…" I squirmed. "A few bottles of maple syrup, and a handful of plates, one or two casserole dishes, but they were empty," I hastily added.

"Out!" Lil pointed to the front door. "You're supposed to be helping Sarah and Becca at the farm!"

Sue rolled her eyes and faced me. "She's so dramatic, sometimes. I've got my checklist here, and I'm crossing things off as I go. Sarah and Becca have things well under control, so all that's left is the food." Sue took a pen and slashed lines through her list.

"Are they really all set up there?" Lil asked me.

I nodded. "Yep, I made a start last night, after I left here." I didn't say I'd slept on the sofa in the cottage, hoping Clay would come home. Lil and I'd baked up a storm the night before, and I'd been too keyed up to sleep, so had trudged the long lonely road out of town, and wound up at the farm under the cover of moonlight.

"The girls are hanging the decorations, and all we have to do is finish baking and cart it over there." Tension mounted—in a few hours' time we'd be serving people gourmet dishes, and swaying along to a jazz band while people celebrated the art of making maple syrup. Still no sign of Clay, and the thought of him missing out hurt, but there was nothing else I could do except throw myself into making the festival a success.

Lil dragged me back to the present by admonishing her mom. "Well you know you're banned from the kitchen. God help us if you started another fire. Why don't you mosey on over to the farm and see to the tablecloths, and the cutlery. We'll bring the crockery over ourselves." She gave her a pointed stare.

I tried not to laugh. Sue's face was the picture of innocence, as though she thought Lil was over-reacting to her previous disasters. "Tablecloths, cutlery, right. I'll cross them off, and see you girls over there."

"She's a list person," Lil said, watching her mother retreat.

"She is," I said. "She asked me what I was doing so she could have the satisfaction of writing it on her pad and then running a line through it. I'm exactly the same."

Lil smirked. "You weren't born with the clumsy gene though."

I nodded, and then feeling slightly overwhelmed, said, "You girls have done so much work, I don't know how I can ever say thanks enough." There was a group of at least ten people scurrying around, setting up at the farm, and there'd been people helping out in the lead-up to it, all for a thank you, and a handshake. It still stunned me, the way Ashford locals banded together for the common good.

"No… It's helping us out, Lucy, more than you know." Lil donned her apron, and placed her hands on my shoulders. "Things have been quiet here, despite the glorious weather, so we can never rest on our laurels. This is a big boost for us, and hopefully for Clay."

I went back to the bench to peel a tower of fresh pears that were so big, I didn't think we'd ever get to the bottom of the pile.

CeeCee barreled into the café, her brown cheeks rosy from exertion. "Sorry, I know we got a ton to do. See, I was just at Walt's and he not only walked outta that house o' his, he darn near strutted."

"Where's he going?" Lil asked, taking the position beside me, and grabbing another peeler.

"To the Maple Syrup Farm. He and Clay have been talking for the last few weeks without us bein' none the wiser. And that phone o' his was blaring not two minutes ago. Seems Clay's been held up only God knows where, and he asked Walt to pick up the bain-marie, and a few other bit an' bobs, because he's running late."

"Clay called Walt?" My mind boggled. I tried not to let the hurt settle over me. He called Walt?

CeeCee clapped her hands. "That boy gone and proved himself time and time again. He might come across as a bit reserved, but he ain't. Walt says Clay's been phoning to ask a bunch o' technical questions about makin' furniture, and they've become friends."

"Clay asked technical questions?" Lil asked, her brow furrowed. "But he made the most amazing pieces before, without any help."

CeeCee clucked her tongue. "Well o' course he did. It was just a ruse to get Walt talkin', get him excited about making furniture again. What that boy's done for Walt makes my heart sing."

"Wow," I said, stunned. "So he's held up, but we don't know where?"

She shrugged. "Walt didn't know... but said Clay'll be there as soon as he can and to pass on his apologies."

I tried to mask the anguish on my face, but failed miserably. CeeCee gave me one of her great big launch hugs. "Don't you fret. Things gonna be just fine, you'll see."

I gave her a shaky smile but let it drop. There was no point harping on about the fact Clay wasn't speaking to me. The girls knew.

"Where we at?" She put her hands on her hips, and surveyed the bench.

Lil said, "The maple and cardamom spiced pears with pecans, and a few more sweets, and we're done."

"I ain't never seen so many pears," CeeCee said, her voice booming around the café.

"We got word, from the next town over, that their social club are coming. That's another fifty people,"

I said, my belly flip-flopping at the thought. "What if we run out of food? Or drinks? Or something happens?" I'd expected it to be a busy day, but the numbers were steadily growing.

CeeCee hemmed and hawed. "Not a chance o' that happening. Damon's gone to the farm with the rotisserie... roasted, maple-glazed beef, you can almost smell it from here! People are gonna be lining up, eager to get their mitts around a burger bun filled with that slow-cooked meat, that's for sure."

***

I'd dressed hastily in a floral patterned dress, slipped on some ballet flats, and tidied my unkempt hair by pinning it back with a red clip. I shoved my jeans and T-shirt into my backpack, and stashed it in Clay's cupboard. It was odd using his cottage as a dressing room when he wasn't there.

Lil and CeeCee were out front greeting people, who arrived in droves. Car doors slammed, and feet crunched up the graveled driveway.

There was a quick rap on the door, and Becca popped her head in. "Ready?" she asked, her voice plaintive.

"I guess," I said, spritzing on perfume. "I thought he'd be back by now."

She leaned her head against the door, and played with a tendril of hair. "You know he loves you," she eventually said.

"He's never said so."

A warm smile spread across her face. "He does, but I'll let him tell you. Are you OK?"

I gave a hollow little laugh. "I've had so much to think about, Becca. I don't know how I'm supposed to feel anything other than exhaustion. I just want to see Clay and sort it out. He called Walt, to tell him he's running late, and not me. I'm glad for Walt, that he's got a friend, but it makes it pretty obvious to me that Clay's giving me the silent treatment."

Becca crossed her arms over her cobalt-blue dress. "Will you still leave?"

I looked away. "Yes. I'm booked."

She nodded her brown eyes, sad. "Maybe you can come back after?"

I moved to hug her, inhaling her vanilla-scented perfume. "Maybe." If I couldn't be with Clay it would be too painful to come back.

She hugged me hard, and then clutched my hand, and pulled me into the bright sunlight.

***

The jazz band members stood under the shade of a maple tree, clutching steins of cider. CeeCee motioned her head to a microphone. I coughed, clearing my throat as nerves made my hands sweat. I tried to surreptitiously wipe them on my dress, before heading to the small wooden stage that had been set up for the day.

Public speaking. Could it get any worse? "Welcome, everyone." My voice shook so I tried to mask it with a wide grin. "Thank you all for attending the Sugaring-Off Festival today. It's a tradition among maple syrup farms, and one we hope to replicate each year. After all, who doesn't love a good party?" The crowd cheered and clapped and I gave a thank you nod.

"Thanks to the girls from the Gingerbread Café, and to Damon from The Shoppe, we have a smorgasbord of dishes, each made with maple syrup. As you can see—"

I pointed to the bain-marie behind me "—there's plenty to choose from. We also have a range of sweets that we'll be serving once the main course is over. I had a speech prepared—" the page fluttered in my hand "—but I can see you're all ready to get started, so I'll wrap up with this: the man who once owned this farm believed maple syrup could cure all ills, that it was a magical potion in the right hands. He believed you had to wait for a full moon to tap, and that you had to talk to the trees, become friends with them. I think it's his legacy, the work he did here, that makes our maple syrup the very best it can be. Thank you to everyone who helped make today possible and to all of you for coming." I stepped down from the uneven stage, and walked to CeeCee, my heartbeat erratic.

"That was beautiful," she said. "Truly beautiful. Jessup would've been proud."

With a hand to my chest, I caught my breath. "That was terrifying with so many pairs of eyes on me."

CeeCee laughed. "It's over now. Let's serve these fine folks some food." She glanced at her watch, and then over her shoulder.

I pursed my lips. "Maybe he's not coming back because of me."

She gave me a playful push. "What kinda talk's that? He's on his way." How did everyone know he was on his way? Was he calling everyone bar me? My guilt was slowly being replaced by disappointment in him. I didn't deserve to be ostracized.

I motioned for the jazz band to begin. They raised their glasses, before chugging back the last of their drinks.

Behind the bain-marie, Becca, Sarah, and Lil stood, helping dish up for a long queue that had formed already. I hurried over to help, Henry stopping me midway. "Hey there, wanderer, you all set for next week?"

He gave me a lopsided smile.

"As ready as I can be, I guess," I said weakly.

"You don't have that same sparkle in your eye. Are you nervous about flying?"

If only it were that simple. "No, it's just… it's Clay. It's leaving Ashford. I never expected to find a home when I set off on this so-called adventure, and now I have to leave it."

"It gets under your skin, this place. You've selected your tickets, Lucy. The final one brings you straight back to the good US of A." His ruddy face lit up, and he gave me a pat on the shoulder. "When you go away, everything changes, and nothing stays the same, except one thing," he said, his voice serious. "Home. It'll always be where your heart is, and you'll know because you'll feel it call you back."

"Thanks, Henry, I think I already know where that place is." The maple leaves swished in the breeze above, a comforting sound.

People were clinking glasses, cheering each course of food. I gave Henry a hug, and hurried over to help the girls serve. As soon as I approached them Lil broke away and picked up the microphone, standing pretty on the stage in her yellow polka-dot dress, her round belly prominent now.

"Sorry to interrupt, folks. But as most of you know, Lucy is leaving us soon to head over to Paris." There were murmurs of awe. "I know, I know, it's always sad saying goodbye. But she'll be back. CeeCee says it's true, so it must be." Laughter rang out over CeeCee's alleged visions. "Lucy," Lil turned to me. "We all chipped in, for a thank-you present to help you on your travels. Getting to know you has been a highlight over these last few months, and me and the rest of the gang are going to miss you." She jumped down from the stage, and presented me with a proper leather suitcase and matching art portfolio.

I held in a gasp of surprise, unable to talk, touched by their generosity. People milled around hugging me, and wishing me well on my travels. I shook hands, and thanked everyone profusely, trying my best to see through a blur of tears. Balloons popped in the distance as children ran around clutching forks, and bursting them. Their parents chased after them, wrenching cutlery back, and giving the giggling kids a stern talking-to.

"Go mingle," Lil said, when I went back for the third time to help serve. "We've got this covered." She was giving me the chance to say goodbye properly.

I smiled, crossing my arms and walking away, taking in the sights around me, soaking it up so I could remember it later. The joy on their faces, tables laden with food, the spilled drinks, a crimson splash across white tablecloths. The scent of maple syrup, hanging above like a cloud of sugar. Children playing kiss chasey, their squeals punctuating the day. Women, in clusters, heads bent over their wine glasses, gossiping. Couples flirting, one girl fluttering fake lashes like a movie star. I committed it all to memory, every single thing, the pulse of fairy lights above like stars in the daytime. I would paint this scene, so it would last forever. I'd paint Clay in the picture too. I knew every plane and groove on his face, the feel and fire of his lips, the flecks in his eyes. And the way he made me feel like no one ever had.

The party kicked on, well into the late afternoon. The stage was filled with people dancing, languidly as the heat and the wine made them sleepy. Streamers were scattered over the grass like ribbons.

It had been a successful day, and I was proud of it. I bent to pick up balloon carcasses, and napkins that had flown away in the wind. There were still stragglers, people who didn't want the day to end. I thanked them all for coming, and sold them bottles of maple syrup, shocked to see how many we'd sold throughout the course of the day. Clay wouldn't have any more to sell until the following year.

***

Once the pandemonium was over, I took a deep breath and wondered where on earth to start cleaning first. The last few couples strode back down the driveway, hand in hand. Moving to the tables, I picked up plates, and put the cutlery on top.

Balancing dishes in my hands, I ferried them into the kitchen in the cottage. Washing up would be a monumental task, with blackened cookie sheets, and sticky saucepans galore, but I'd convinced the girls I'd do it alone later. They'd protested, but I was resolute. They'd worked so hard these last few weeks, they needed a break. It had been exhilarating pulling off the festival for such a huge amount of people, with only a few accidents, like a speaker blowing up, and a smashed plate or two, that needed fixing throughout the day.

Outside, CeeCee and Lil sat nursing iced tea, spent, after a busy day.

I joined them, falling into a sun lounger, and shading my eyes.

"Walt's clearing the chairs over yonder," CeeCee said. "Man won't listen when I said we'd do it."

I followed her gaze, to see Walt's stooped figure slowly nesting the white plastic chairs. "He's waiting for Clay too," I said.

Lil and CeeCee averted their eyes, while Becca and Sarah chatted over a table by the stage, eating a plate of food that had probably gone cold by now. Poor girls had been run off their feet all day and hadn't once stopped to catch their breath. My own stomach rumbled but I was too keyed up to contemplate eating.

"He surely is," CeeCee said.

I didn't think it would end like this. My stay in Ashford. I mustered a fake smile, and said, "I'm going for a quick walk, and then I better get things packed up."

"Want some company?" Lil asked.

"It's OK," I said, pointing to her glass. "You enjoy your drink, I won't be long."

The partygoers had left with full bellies, and big smiles after the festivities. The laughter and music had been replaced with quiet—the sudden halt of music and chatter—that somehow gave me a headache.

I wanted one last wander through the maples, while the light was still good.

Once I got to the clearing between the trees, I craned my neck up to the bright blue above. The sky was awash with maple leaves. Shades of red and orange, daubs of yellow. The leaves fluttered in the wind, like they were waving. I slowly inched around the maples, touching each trunk like I'd done before when I warned them about the tapping season. Now though, I said their names and whispered goodbye. The marks from the spiles were healing. It would take time, but they'd be forever changed. Like childbirth, the indelible scars, the wounds, amounting to something special, a marker that you were now greater than yourself. That's what the maples had.

I thought of Jessup. And the two lives he led, beautiful in their own poignant way. He'd had the kind of love that some people only dream about. And while it ended too soon, she remained in his heart for the rest of his days. He felt her presence, her soul close by, helping him heal, urging him to live on without her.

I'd come so far in the time I'd been here. I'd learned to relax, and laugh. I'd learned what a mother's love is capable of. And I had also learned what true, once-in-a-lifetime love felt like, even though I'd lost it. It wouldn't fade—I was now certain—that grip he had on my heart.

The lake glistened under the sunlight, making me squint. I crouched down and ran my fingers through the cool water, as though it was holy, and would heal me.

The sound of a car rumbled in the distance. The front gate creaked open. It didn't sound like Clay's truck crunching down the graveled driveway but I stood quickly, drying my hands on the swell of my skirt.

A cloud of dust rose up around the car as it made its way to us. A small silver sedan, with an unfamiliar license plate. The car crawled to a stop, and out jumped Clay, dwarfing the car with his big solid frame.

He walked straight to Walt and shook his hand, mumbling a few words. I stood frozen to the spot, not knowing what to do.

The girls exchanged glances, and then made a show of looking the other way, as Clay made his way to me.

We stood inches apart. I wanted to reach out and touch him, but I couldn't gauge his mood. "I'm so sorry, Lucy," he said, causing my heart to skip a beat. "I had to go."

I gave him the ghost of a smile. "I know."

He nodded. "I should've let you explain properly. It was almost like déjà vu—I thought it was happening all over again."

Reaching for my hands, he entwined his fingers through mine. "But that didn't give me the right to leave you like that. Especially with the festival. I went to my mom's house, in a fit of pique, to find out the truth. And then my return flight was delayed, so I had to hire a car to get back. A disaster, really. I've been trying to call your cell phone all day."

I'd forgotten about my cell! It lay on the porch, cast aside. "What did your mom say?"

He took a deep steadying breath. "That Jessup never got over losing his wife, Claire. Nothing mattered to him after that. And I can understand him in a way I couldn't before."

"Why now? Because of the paintings?" I asked.

"No, Lucy. Not because of them. Because of you. The thought of you leaving rips me up inside, and even more now that I know you've struggled with your life, that things haven't been easy for you. How am I supposed to live without you? You've changed my whole life, Lucy, and without you, I'll be lost."

I closed my eyes, and let his words sink in.

"I love you, Lucy."

My eyes flicked open. It was everything and more than I'd hoped for. "I love you too," I said quietly. He turned and led me back to the maples, only stopping when we got to our usual spot. "Do you have to leave?" he asked. "I want you to stay."

I ran a finger along his jawline, over the soft flesh of his lips. Thinking how lucky I was to have someone like Clay love me. "I have to go... I found out this morning I was accepted into the institute." In the hubbub, I'd merely tossed the letter aside, and planned to obsess over it later.

"So you're really leaving?" He cast his eyes downward.

I swallowed a lump in my throat, at the thought of being away from him even for just one day. Not being able to caress his bare chest when we lay in bed, the warmth of his body pressed up against mine. The flush of pleasure as he called out my name, gripping my hands above my head. And the long nights, under the stars, where we just held each other. How could I go on without that?

"I'm really leaving," I said, while my mind screamed no.

He let out a guttural moan, and bent to kiss me, desire flooding me. When we broke apart, his eyes glittered.

"Why don't you come with me, Clay? We've just about sold out of syrup, and the next tapping season is six months away. Come away with me." My voice had a pleading note to it I couldn't disguise.

"Leave the farm?" Clay's face broke into a wide, sexy grin. "I thought you'd never ask. Meet me under the Eiffel Tower on Tuesday?"

I laughed. "Why Tuesday?"

"I've got to go pick up my truck, and work out what to do with the paintings."

I looped my hands around his waist. "Hide them," I said, solemnly. "Jessup didn't want the world to have those pictures. They were private. His secret. They were an old man's love story. One of the greatest love stories of all time."

"Hide them?" Clay repeated. "But the money, I was going to…"

"Shh," I said, putting a finger to his lips. "I don't want the money, and I don't need it."

"I never thought I'd find real love, Lucy. I was so opposed to letting anyone in ever again, and then you walked up that driveway in the middle of winter, that determined glint in your eye, and I knew it, the moment I laid eyes on you, that my life was going to change." He smiled almost shyly. "I didn't know love could feel like this."

I blushed hearing the words. "My whole life has been one big race against time, Clay. And I want it to slow right down, so we can enjoy every moment we have together. I can't wait to explore Paris with you by my side." I wouldn't lose Clay—another person wouldn't walk out of my life. Instead this time they'd walk right beside me. "I wasn't expecting to find love under the maples."

"I'm glad you did."

"Me too."

He bit down on his lip, a gesture that made me want to ravish him. "Me and you, in Paris for Christmas?" he asked.

"Me and you forever," I said, and stood up on tiptoes to kiss him properly.

If you loved *Secrets at Maple Syrup Farm* then turn the
page for an extract from the first book in
The Little Paris Collection:
The Little Bookshop on the Seine

CHAPTER ONE

October

With a heavy heart I placed the sign in the display window.

All books 50% off.

If things didn't pick up soon, it would read *Closing down sale*. The thought alone was enough to make me shiver. The autumnal sky was awash with purples and smudges of orange, as I stepped outside to survey the display window from the sidewalk.

Star-shaped leaves crunched underfoot. I forced a smile. A sale wouldn't hurt, and maybe it'd take the bookshop figures from the red into the black—which I so desperately needed. My rent had been hiked up. The owner of the building, a sharp-featured, silver-tongued, forty-something man, had put the pressure on me lately—to pay more, to declutter the shop, claiming the haphazard stacks of books were a fire risk. The additional rent stretched the budget to breaking level. Something had to change.

The phone shrilled, and a grin split my face. It could only be Ridge at this time of the morning. Even after being together almost a year his name still provoked a giggle. It suited him though, the veritable man mountain he was. I'd since met his mom, a sweet, well-spoken lady, who claimed in dulcet tones, that she chose his name *well* before his famous namesake in *The Bold and the Beautiful.* In fact, she was adamant about it, and said the TV character Ridge was no match for her son. I had to agree. Sure, they both had chiseled movie star cheekbones, and an intense gaze that made many a woman swoon, but my guy was more than just the sum of his parts—I loved him for his mind, as much as his clichéd six pack, and broody hotness. And even better, he loved me for me.

He was the hero in my own *real-life* love story, and due back from Canada the next day. It'd had been weeks since I'd seen him, and I ached for him in a way that made me blush.

I dashed inside, and answered the phone, breathlessly. "The Bookshop on the Corner."

"That's the voice I know and love," he said in his rich, husky tone. My heart fluttered, picturing him at the end of the line, his jet-black hair and flirty blue eyes. He simply had to flick me a look loaded with suggestion, and I'd be jelly-legged and love-struck.

"What are you wearing?" he said.

"Wouldn't you like to know?" I held back a laugh, eager to drag it out. So far our relationship had been more long distance than anticipated, as he flew around the world reporting on location. The stints apart left an ache in my heart, a numbness to my days. Luckily I had my books, and a sweeping romance or two helped keep the loneliness at bay.

"Tell me or I'll be forced to Skype you and see for myself."

Glancing down at my outfit, I grimaced: black tights, a black pencil skirt, and a pilled blue knit sweater, all as old as the hills of Ashford. Not exactly the type of answer Ridge was waiting for, or the way I wanted him to picture me, after so many weeks apart. "Those stockings you like, and…"

His voice returned with a growl. "*Those* stockings? With the little suspenders?"

I sat back into the chair behind the counter, fussing with my bangs. "The very same."

He groaned. "You're *killing* me. Take a photo…"

"There's no need. If you're good, I'll wear the red ones tomorrow night." I grinned wickedly. Our reunions were always passionate affairs; he was a hands-on type of guy. Lucky for him, because it took a certain type of man to drag me from the pages of my books. When he was home we didn't surface until one of us had to go to work. Loving Ridge had been a revelation, especially in the bedroom, where he took things achingly slow, drawing out every second. I flushed with desire for him.

There was a muffled voice and the low buzz of phones ringing. Ridge mumbled to someone before saying, "About tomorrow…" He petered out, regret in each syllable.

I closed my eyes. "You're not coming, are you?" I tried not to sigh, but it spilled out regardless. The lure of a bigger, better story was too much for him to resist, and lately the gaps between our visits grew wider. I understood his work was important, but I wanted him all to myself. A permanent fixture in the small town I lived in.

He tutted. "I'm sorry, baby. There's a story breaking in Indonesia, and I have to go. It'll only be for a week or two, and then I'll take some time off."

Outside, leaves fluttered slowly from the oak tree, swaying softly, until they fell to the ground. I wasn't the nagging girlfriend sort—times like this though, I was tempted to be. Ridge had said the very same thing the last three times he'd canceled a visit. But invariably someone would call and ask Ridge to head to the next location; any time off would be cut short.

"I understand," I said, trying to keep my voice bright. Sometimes I felt like I played a never-ending waiting game. Would it always be like this? "Just so you know, I have a very hot date this afternoon."

He gasped. "You better be talking about a fictional date." His tone was playful, but underneath there was a touch of jealousy to it. Maybe it was just as hard on him, being apart.

"One *very* hot book boyfriend… though not as delectable as my real boyfriend—but a stand-in, until he returns."

"Well, he better not keep you up half the night, or he'll have me to answer to," he faux threatened, and then said more seriously, "Things will slow down, Sarah. I want to be with you so much my soul hurts. But right now, while I'm freelance, I have to take whatever comes my way."

"I know. I just feel a bit lost sometimes. Like someone's hit pause, and I'm frozen on the spot." I bit my lip, trying to work out how to explain it. "It's not just missing you—I do understand about your job—it's… everything. The bookshop sales dwindling, the rent jacked up, everyone going on about their business, while I'm still the same old Sarah."

I'd been at this very crossroad when I'd met Ridge, and he'd swept me off my feet, like the ultimate romance hero. For a while that had been enough. After all, wasn't love always the answer? Romance aside, life was a little stagnant, and I knew it was because of my fear of change. It wasn't so much that I had to step from behind the covers of my books, rather plunge, perhaps. Take life by the scruff of the neck and shake it. But how?

"You've had a rough few weeks. That's all. I'll be back soon, and I'm sure there's something I can do to make you forget everything…"

My belly flip-flopped at the thought. He *would* make me forget everything that was outside that bedroom door, but then he'd leave and it would all tumble back.

What exactly was I searching for? My friends were getting married and having babies. Buying houses and redecorating. Starting businesses. My life had stalled. I was an introvert, happiest hiding in the shadows of my shop, reading romances to laze the day away, between serving the odd customer or two—yet, it wasn't enough. In small-town Connecticut, there wasn't a lot to do. And life here— calm, peaceful—was fine, but that's just it, *fine* wasn't enough any more. I had this fear that life was passing me by because I was too timid to take the reins.

It was too hazy a notion of what I was trying to say, even to me. Instead of lumping Ridge with it, I changed tack. "I hope you know, you're not leaving the house when you get home. Phones will be switched to silent, computers forgotten, and the only time we're leaving the comfort of bed is when I need sustenance." A good romp around the bedroom would suffice until I could pinpoint what it was that I wanted.

"How about I sort out the sustenance?" he said, his voice heavy with desire. "And then we'll never have to leave."

"Promises, promises," I said, my breath hitching. I hoped this flash of longing would never wane, the sweet torture of anticipation.

"I have to go, baby. I'll call you tonight if it's not too late once I'm in."

"Definitely call tonight! Otherwise, I can't guarantee the book boyfriend won't steal your girlfriend. He's pretty hot, I'll have you know."

"Why am I jealous of a fictional character?" He laughed, a low, sexy sound. "OK, tonight. Love you."

"Love you, too."

He hung up, leaving me dazed, and a touch lonely knowing that I wouldn't see him the next day as planned.

I tried to shake the image of Ridge from my mind. If anyone walked in, they'd see the warm blush of my cheeks, and know exactly what I was thinking. Damn the man for being so attractive, and so effortlessly sexy.

Shortly, the sleepy town of Ashford would wake under the gauzy light of October skies. Signs would be flipped to open, stoops swept, locals would amble down the road. Some would step into the bookshop and out of the cold, and spend their morning with hands wrapped around a mug of steaming hot tea, and reading in any one of the cozy nooks around the labyrinth-like shop.

I loved having a place for customers to languish. Comfort was key, and if you had a good book and a hot drink, what else could you possibly need to make your day any brighter? Throw rugs and cushions were littered around seating areas. Coats would be swiftly hung on hooks, a chair found, knitted blankets pulled across knees, and their next hour or two sorted, in the most relaxing of ways.

I wandered around the shop, feather duster in hand, tickling the covers, waking them from slumber. I'm sure as soon as my back was turned, the books wiggled and winked at one another, as if they were eager for the day to begin, for fingers of hazy sunlight to filter through and land on them like spotlights, as if saying, *here's the book for you.*

Imagine if I had to close up for good, like so many other shops had in recent times? It pained me to think people were missing out on the real-life bookshop experience. Wasn't it much better when you could step into a dimly lit space, and eke your way around searching for the right novel? You could run a fingertip along the spines, smell that glorious old-book scent, flick them open, and unbend a dog-eared page. Read someone else's notes in the margin, or a highlighted passage, and see why that sentence or metaphor had dazzled the previous owner.

Second-hand books had so much *life* in them. They'd lived, sometimes in many homes, or maybe just one. They'd been on airplanes, traveled to sunny beaches, or crowded into a backpack and taken high up a mountain where the air thinned.

Some had been held aloft tepid rose-scented baths, and thickened and warped with moisture. Others had child-like scrawls on the acknowledgement page, little fingers looking for a blank space to leave their mark. Then there were the pristine novels, ones that had been read carefully, bookmarks used, almost like their owner barely pried the pages open, so loath were they to damage their treasure.

I loved them all.

And I found it hard to part with them. Though years of book selling had steeled me. I had to let them go, and each time made a fervent wish they'd be read well, and often.

Missy, my best friend, said I was completely cuckoo, and that I spent too much time alone in my shadowy shop, because I believed my books communicated with me. A soft sigh here, as they stretched their bindings when dawn broke, or a hum, as they anticipated a customer hovering close who might run a hand along their cover, tempting them to flutter their pages hello. Books were fussy when it came to their owners, and gave off a type of sound, an almost imperceptible whirr, when the right person was near. Most people weren't aware that books chose us, at the time when we needed them most.

Outside the breeze picked up, gathering the leaves in a swirl and blowing them down the street in waves. Rubbing my hands for warmth, I trundled into the reading room, and added some wood to the fire. Each day, the weather grew cooler, and the crackle and spit of the glowing embers were a nice soundtrack to the shop, comforting, like a hug.

The double-stacked books in the reading room weren't for sale, but could be thumbed and enjoyed by anyone who wished. They were my favorites, the ones I couldn't part with. I'd been gifted a huge range from a man whose wife had passed on, a woman who was so like me with her bookish foibles, that it was almost like she was still here. Her collection—an essential part of her life—lived on, long after she'd gone. I'd treasure them always.

Wandering back to the front of the shop, the street was coming alive. Owners milled in front of shops, chatting to early-bird customers, or lugging out A-frame signs, advertising their wares. Lil, my friend from the Gingerbread Café, waved over at me. Her heavily pregnant belly made me smile. I pulled open the front door, a gust of wind blowing my hair back, and fluttering the pages of the books.

"You take it easy!" I shouted. Lil was due any day now, but insisted on working. Times were tough for all of us, so Lil had to work, but claimed instead she wanted to spruce things up before she left. Nesting, her best friend and only employee CeeCee called it.

Lil tossed her long blonde curls back from her face. "If I take it any easier, I'll be asleep! Besides, how are you going to survive without your chocolate fix?" The wind carried her words to me in a happy jumble.

"True," I agreed. "I'll be there as soon as my tummy rumbles." It was torture, working across the road from the café, the scent of tempered chocolate or the yeasty smell of freshly baked bread wafting its way to my shop. I'd find myself crossing the street and demanding to be fed, flopping lazily on their sofa, while they flitted around making all my food dreams come true. The girls from the café were great friends, and often gave me a metaphorical shove in the back when they thought I should step from the comfort of my shop and try something new, like love, for example.

They'd set me up with Ridge, knowing I wouldn't take the leap myself. When I'd first met him, I couldn't understand why a big-shot reporter from New York would be interested in a girl from smallsville. It wasn't that I didn't think I was good enough, it was more that our lives were a million miles apart, and the likes of him were a rarity in Ashford.

My girlfriends hadn't seen it that way, and *literally* pushed me into his arms, at a dinner party the night of the infamous man-crease fiasco. I wouldn't say that's when I fell in love with Ridge, my face pressed up against his nether regions after a "fall" on the uneven deck, but it was pretty damn close. My so-called friends had orchestrated the night, including the "whoops" shove in the back from Lil, so I toppled ungraciously towards Ridge, landing on my knees at his hip level. My breathing had been uneven, as his sweater rode high, and jeans had slung low, giving me ample opportunity to scrutinize the deep V presented to me. My lips a mere inch away from his tanned flesh, until he scooped me up, before I almost licked his skin to see what it tasted like. I had this strange burning desire to see what flavor he'd be. That's what reading too many romances does to a girl.

Recalling the evening still provoked a blush, because it was so unlike me. I mean, imagine if I *had* flicked my tongue against his exposed skin? He would have been running for the hills before the entrée was served. But that's the effect he had over me, he made my mind blank, and my body act of its own volition, including a thousand scenarios I'd never have entertained with any other guy. Dumbstruck by love was a real thing, I'd come to learn.

Lil's boisterous laughter brought me back to the moment. "See you soon. I'll have a chocolate soufflé with your name on it."

"You'd tempt the devil himself!" I joked and gave her a wave before stepping back into the warmth of the bookshop.

My email pinged and I dashed over to see who it was from. That's how exciting my life was *sans* Ridge, an email was enough to make me almost run, and that was saying a lot. I only ran if chocolate was involved, and even then it was more a fast walk.

Sales@littlebookshop.fr

Sophie, a dear Parisian friend. She owned Once Upon a Time, a famous bookshop by the bank of the Seine. We'd become confidantes since connecting on my book blog a while back, and shared our joys and sorrows about bookshop life. She was charming and sweet, and adored books as much as me, believing them to be portable magic, and a balm for souls.

I clicked open the email and read.

Ma Chérie,

I cannot stay one more day in Paris. You see, Manu has not so much broken my heart, rather pulled it out of my chest and stomped on it. The days are interminable and I can't catch my breath. He walks past the bookshop, as though nothing is amiss. I have a proposal for you. Please call me as soon as you can.

Love,

Sophie

Poor Sophie. I'd heard all about her grand love affair with a dashing twenty-something man, who frequented her bookshop, and quoted famous poets. It'd been a whirlwind romance, but she often worried he cast an appraising eye over other women. Even when she clutched his hand, and walked along the cobbled streets of Paris, he'd dart an admiring glance at any woman swishing past.

I shot off a quick reply, telling her to Skype me now, if she was able. Within seconds my computer flashed with an incoming call.

Her face appeared on the screen, her chestnut-colored hair in an elegant chignon, her lips dusted rosy pink.

If she was in the throes of heartache, you'd never know it by looking at her. The French had a way of always looking poised and together, no matter what was happening in their complex lives.

"Darling," she said, giving me a nod. "He's a lothario, a Casanova, a…" She grappled for another moniker as her voice broke. "He's dating the girl who owns the shop next door!" Her eyes smoldered, but her face remained stoic.

I gasped, "Which girl? The one from the florist?"

Sophie shook her head. "The other side, the girl from the *fromagerie*." She grimaced. I'd heard so much about the people in or around Sophie's life that it was easy to call her neighbors to mind. "Giselle?" I said, incredulous. "Wasn't she engaged—I thought the wedding was any day now?"

Sophie's eyes widened. "She's broken off her engagement, and has announced it to the world that *my* Manu has proposed and now they are about to set up house and to try immediately for children—"

My hand flew to my mouth. "Children! He wouldn't do that, surely!" Sophie was late-forties, and had gently broached the subject of having a baby with Manu, but he'd said simply: absolutely not, he didn't want children.

The doorbell of her shop pinged, Sophie's face pinched and she leaned closer to the screen, lowering her voice. "A customer…" She forced a bright smile, turned her head and spoke in rapid-fire French to whoever stood just off-screen. "So," she continued quietly. "The entire neighborhood are whispering behind their hands about the love triangle, and unfortunately for me, I'm the laughing stock. The older woman, who was deceived by a younger man."

I wished I could lean through the monitor and hug her. While she was an expert at keeping her features neutral, she couldn't stop the glassiness of her eyes when tears threatened. My heart broke that Manu would treat her so callously. She'd trusted him, and loved him unreservedly. "No one is laughing at you, I promise," I said. "They'll be talking about Manu, if anyone, and saying how he's made a huge mistake."

"No, no." A bitter laugh escaped her. "I look like a fool. I simply cannot handle when he cavorts through the streets with her, darting glances in my bookshop, like they hope I'll see them. It's too cruel." Sophie held up a hand, and turned to a voice. She said *au revoir* to the customer and spun to face me, but within a second or two, the bell sounded again. "I have a proposal for you, and I want you to *really* consider it." She raised her eyebrows. "Or at least hear me out before you say no." Her gaze burned into mine as I racked my brain with what it could be, and came up short. Sophie waved to customers, and pivoted her screen further away.

"Well?" I said with a nervous giggle. "What exactly are you proposing?"

She blew out a breath, and then smiled. "A bookshop exchange. You come and run Once Upon a Time, and I'll take over the Bookshop on the Corner."

I gasped, my jaw dropping.

Sophie continued, her calm belied by the slight quake in her hand as she gesticulated. "You've always said how much you yearned to visit the city of love—here's your chance, my dear friend. After our language lessons, you're more than capable of speaking enough French to get by." Sophie's words spilled out in a desperate rush, her earlier calm vanishing. "You'd save me so much heartache. I want to be in a place where no one knows me, and there's no chance for love, *ever* again."

I tried to hide my smile at that remark. I'd told Sophie in the past how bereft of single men Ashford was, and how my love life had been almost non-existent until Ridge strolled into town.

"Sophie, I want to help you, but I'm barely hanging on to the bookshop as is…" I stalled for time, running a hand through my hair, my bangs too long, shielding the tops of my eyebrows. How could it work? How would we run each other's businesses, the financial side, the logistics? I also had an online shop, and I sourced hard-to-find books—how would Sophie continue that?

My mind boggled with the details, not to mention the fact that leaving my books would be akin to leaving a child behind. I loved my bookshop as if it were a living thing, an unconditional best friend, who was always there for me. Besides, I'd never ventured too far from Ashford let alone boarded a plane—it just couldn't happen.

"*Please*," Sophie said, a real heartache in her tone. "Think about it. We can work out the finer details and I'll make it worth your while. Besides, you know I'm good with numbers, I can whip your sales into shape." Her eyes clouded with tears. "I have to leave, Sarah. You're my only chance. Christmas in Paris is on your bucket list…"

My bucket list. A hastily compiled scrappy piece of paper filled with things I thought I'd never do. Christmas in Paris—snow dusting the bare trees on the Left Bank, the sparkling fairy lights along the Boulevard Saint-Germain. Santa's village in the Latin Quarter. The many Christmas markets to stroll through, rugged up with thick scarves and gloves, Ridge by my side, as I hunted out treasures. I'd spent many a day curled up in my own shop, flicking through memoirs, or travel guides about Paris, dreaming about the impossible… *one day*.

Sophie continued: "If you knew how I suffered here, my darling. It's not only Manu, it's everything. All of a sudden, I can't do it all any more. It's like someone has pulled the plug, and I'm empty." Her eyes scrunched closed as she fought tears.

While Sophie's predicament was different to mine, she was in a funk, just like me. Perhaps a new outlook, a new place would mend both our lives. Her idea of whipping my sales into shape was laughable though, she had no real clue how tiny Ashford was.

"Exchange bookshops…" I said, the idea taking shape. Could I just up and leave? What about my friends, my life, my book babies? My fear of change? And Ridge, what would he have to say about it? But my life… it was missing something. Could this be the answer?

Paris. The city of love. Full of rich literary history.

A little bookshop on the bank of the Seine. Could there be anything sweeter?

With a thud, a book fell to the floor beside me, dust motes dancing above it like glitter. I craned my neck to see what it was.

Paris: A Literary Guide.

Was that a sign? Did my books want me to go?

"Yes," I said, without any more thought. "I'll do it."

The perfect wedding that never was...

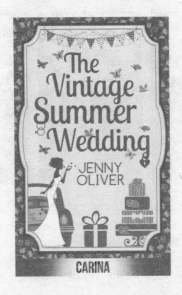

Years ago Anna Whitehall pirouetted out of her cosy home-town village in a whirl of ambition to fulfil her childhood dream of becoming a prima ballerina. Now she's back in Nettleton with fiancé Seb, their wedding and careers postponed indefinitely...

This one summer is showing Anna that your dreams have to grow up with you. And sometimes what you think you wanted is just the opposite of what makes you happy...

Don't miss the brilliant sequel to
The Parisian Christmas Bake Off

Out now in print

CARINA™

When your name is Lizzy Bennet and Mr Darcy
lives next door, romance is anything but simple…

A film crew has just arrived to shoot *Pride and Prejudice* at the
Darcy estate… next door to the Bennet sisters. And when Hugh
Darcy, the one who got away, arrives home after 8 years absence,
Lizzy can't help but think it's fate. Until, that is, he introduces her
to Holly – his fiancée…

What can Lizzy do but try not to feel too prejudiced against
Hugh's new woman – a city girl who knows nothing about
country life, and seems more concerned with her film star ex
than her current fiancé?

There's no denying that there's something suspicious about
Holly's interest in Hugh…and when he begins to have doubts
about his high-maintenance fiancée, it seems a break up is on the
cards. But is it too late for Lizzy to swallow her pride and get her
Austen ending after all?

Don't miss the all new Jane Austen Factor series from Katie Oliver!

Also from
CARINA

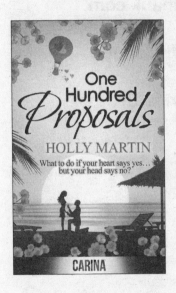

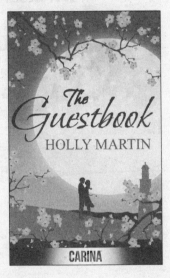

CARINA™

Visit Us Online

www.carinauk.com

 @UKCarina

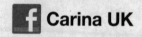 Carina UK

0216_CARINA_P_SM

What if the person who broke your heart, is the only one who can help you find your future?

Great friends. Amazing Apartment. An incredible job. Paige has ticked off every box on perfect New York life checklist... until disaster strikes. Her brother's best friend Jake might be the only person who can help her put her life back together. He also happens to be the boy she spent her teen years pining after, and Paige is determined not repeat her past mistakes. But the more time she spends with Jake, the more Paige realises the one thing that was missing from her world all along...

Bringing you the best voices in fiction
🐦 **@Mira_booksUK**

'Domestic Diva' Halle Best is world famous
as Queen of the Kitchen, and for making a
successful career in TV, despite having a
baby at sixteen.

Now 38 and happy with her success, Halle panics
when she discovers that her ex is writing a book
that could expose all of her secrets. In order to
stop him, she'll have to speak to him face to face,
which could also mean falling infuriatingly in
love with him all over again!

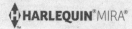

Bringing you the best voices in fiction
🐦 **@Mira_booksUK**

M443_SNTYB